THE
CLOCK
IN THE
WATER

C R I S S I   M C D O N A L D

THE
CLOCK
IN THE
WATER

CRISSI MCDONALD

Lilith House Press

Lilith House Press
Estes Park, Colorado

ISBN 978-1-7369673-9-3 (softcover)
ISBN 979-8-9858101-0-3 (eBook)
Library of Congress Control Number 2022911389

Cover and interior design: Jane Dixon-Smith/jdsmith-design.com
Editor: Susan Tasaki
Cover art: Carissa Sorensen
Author photograph: Lindsey A. Sutherland/http://www.lindseyasutherlandcreations.com

RETROSPECTION

I cover my bare neck with a shaking hand as Keet and I walk away from the Camas Island airport terminal. The buzz of a plane taking to the sky draws my eyes upward, but distracted by memories, I don't see it. In my mind, the past year unspools like an old movie: jittery and smooth, dark and light.

When my now ex-husband told me he'd fallen in love with a man named Carlos, we'd divorced. The anger I felt at his betrayal was the first genuine emotion I'd had in the two decades of our colorless marriage. The only reason I hesitated leaving Texas was my daughter. But after months of debate, I sold our family home and moved to an island in the Pacific Northwest. I'd adopted two dogs and made peace with my ability to know what an animal is experiencing by the feelings in my body—a long-denied skill I no longer care to suppress.

I remove my hand from my neck, recalling the whirlwind love that had grown between Keet and me. I hear the echoes of his deep voice telling me he was Keykwin, one of the last of a dying race of beings who could live as both human and orca. He called them Blackfish. After surrendering to my feelings about him, feelings I thought were long dead, Keet was captured as orca. Weeks after his escape and finding his way home, he left me, saying he couldn't be human anymore. He changed into orca and swam away. Still knifing through my heart is the intensity of heartbreak that the gray and solitary winter did nothing to soothe. I remind myself that I'd spent twenty years being alone with a husband. Being in the company of dogs is easier.

Yanking open the car door, I'm as far from giving in to the memories of Keet as the plane high overhead. I throw myself into the driver's seat, jam the key into the ignition, and rev my old Honda's engine. On the passenger side, Keet barely shuts his door before I hit the gas and turn the wheel toward my cabin in Osprey Bay.

ONE

Keet stares out the window as I tell him about the solitary orca I saw in the bay near our homes.

"Are you sure it was a female orca? Alone?"

"Positive. I hope she's still there when we get back." I take my foot off the accelerator as we approach the pothole that yawns ahead, threatening, as it has all winter, to swallow my Honda whole. Sunlight reaching its long fingers through the trees' new leaves casts spangles across the road's surface. In another month, the forest floor on either side will be covered by the brighter greens of ferns. The month of April is a hesitant walk between winter and spring here on Camas Island.

"Tell me again what you saw."

"Only her head, bobbing on the waves; she was spy hopping. Her eye-patch was thin and long. The strange thing is, she seemed to be looking at your house."

"That doesn't sound normal to me, either. Think she—or he—was sick?" He's holding on to the grab bar, steadying himself against the rackety ride.

"I got the feeling she was watching. Even with the binoculars, I couldn't see her saddle patch, but her dorsal fin was small and pointy, not rounded like yours. I believe we can assume she's a she."

"Huh." Keet releases the grab bar and runs his hand over the dark stubble that covers his head like velvet. There's more silver at his temples than I remember. Hell, I have gray in my hair, too.

"No saddle patch? No markings behind her dorsal fin at all?"

White-knuckling the steering wheel, I shake my head and swerve to miss another pothole. I loosen my grip as I breathe, hoping also to loosen the grip of my anxiety about Keet. The sound of his voice brings up memories, which I then shove down. He keeps talking, which makes it harder to shove.

"I was thinking she might be part of an offshore pod. But offshore orcas, as a rule, don't come in this far, and their saddle patches are visible. And it might be a coincidence, but I haven't seen the seal or the otter in several days. I wonder if she's been hanging around and they've found somewhere safer?"

"Or she ate them."

After checking to see that I have a smooth stretch of road, I throw him a look.

"Let's not talk about death right away, shall we?" I feel my hands tightening around the steering wheel again, and my breath is stuck somewhere in my chest. I clear my throat, hoping the anger that's whipping around me like a hurricane will thin out, at least long enough for him to get out of my car without me saying something I might regret.

Both his glance and his smile are quick and nervous. "Sorry. I didn't mean to sound heartless. But she doesn't sound like a Resident orca, and if she's not a Resident, that means she may eat other mammals."

I'm about to snap that I've already heard the spiel but swallow the words. The memory of my first whale watching trip on his sailboat flashes through my head, and the graceful arc of the black backs of the orcas through the waves we saw that day.

I clear my throat again. "They've kept me company. I don't like to think of them being eaten. Especially when they seem to feel safe in the cove." Keet's profile is familiar but his presence, not so much. I take some more deep breaths, but the flames of my rage are searing me from the inside. Hoping to extinguish them, I continue to describe the mysterious orca.

"Besides her exhale, which wasn't that loud, I couldn't hear a thing. Not a click or a chirp. And I didn't feel much either. She felt like a female to me, but other than that, it's like she's a ghost orca. No pictures in my head, none of the feelings I get when your pod is around."

We make the turn down the hill, curving back toward our houses. I park in front of the A-frame cabin that's been my home for a year. Not for much longer, though. I'm going to need to decide at some point: renew my lease or find somewhere else to live.

When I thought Keet was gone for good, it was hard for me to decide my next step. Figuring out what to do now that he's back complicates things. That isn't the source of my anger, however. As I park the car and open the door, I realize that I resent Keet for coming back and acting as though nothing had happened. My anger has been simmering for months, and his return is the spark that's set it ablaze.

Above the clunk of the car doors, I hear Fae in the cabin, yipping with excitement. Wallace will be beside her, but in the two months I've had him, I have yet to hear him vocalize much. As I walk up the steps, I turn and see Keet still standing by the car.

"Wallace is leery of strangers. Don't try to pet him and he'll be okay."

Keet nods. He can't have missed the change in my tone of voice, and I notice he's gazing at his house. Opening the door, I ask both dogs to wait. They sit side by side, tails wagging, Fae clicking her teeth in excitement; she sounds like an agitated rattlesnake.

"That'll do, dogs."

Released, they burst from the house, nails scrabbling on the wooden deck before launching down the steps and into the cove in a flurry of white, red, cream, and tan. Almost as quickly, they emerge from the water and race down the crescent-shaped cove's rocky beach.

Keet follows me inside, waiting as I set my backpack on the table and my keys on the hook. The glint of Keet's house key fills my vision, and I take it off the hook.

"Fae's not much bigger, is she?" he says.

I turn, and for the first time, notice that he looks lighter. His eyes are no longer murky—they're clear and untroubled. In the seconds it takes for a feeling of buoyancy to flash through me, I realize that he now feels the same as a human as he does when he's orca. This does nothing to douse my anger.

"Nolee?"

I give him his key. "Your other set of keys is on your kitchen table. I aired out the house and put sheets on the bed yesterday, but there isn't any food."

"Thank you for doing that. You didn't have to."

I shrug. "No problem. And you're right ... Fae isn't much bigger. Wallace makes up for it, though." I look out the window at the dogs, who are both paddling again in the shallow, sunlit waters of the cove. Wallace, twice Fae's size, will swim in almost any weather—sun or fog, smooth glassy water or turbulent waves. For the hundredth time, I think that Wallace is part seal; I can't keep him out of the water.

As though he's read my thoughts, Keet asks, "If his head were darker, he'd look like a seal. How did you end up with him?"

Turning, I walk outside to the rocky beach, and Keet follows me.

"I worked with him for a while at the shelter, and he was doing great. The volunteers could interact with him, and if they were quiet and didn't make sudden movements, he was okay. He met Fae, and they played well together. In February, we tried adopting him out to a nice older couple. I thought they would get along."

"Since he's here, I guess it didn't work out?"

"It didn't. He hardly left his crate for days. The couple called the shelter, and we agreed to take him back. When I went to pick him up, he left the crate and sat by my car. He's been mine since then." I smile at the memory and feel my shoulders loosen. Listening to the breeze through the pines, watching the undulations of the water and the dogs playing also helps.

"Do you think it's because he knows you can hear him? And he gets scared if that isn't happening?"

I glance at him, not wanting to look into his eyes. Not wanting to throw my anger at him just yet, though I know I'll have to tell him how I'm feeling at some point. "Maybe."

After a long silence, he seems to realize that I'm not going to offer any personal insights. "I'll go check on my house. Do you need anything from the market?"

I shake my head. "No, thanks."

"Cereal?"

Despite trying to keep a firm grip on any show of affection, I catch myself smiling. "I have plenty."

"Okay. Thanks for picking me up, Nolee."

"You're welcome."

He waves and walks toward his house, and I watch him walk inside, leaving his door open. That's the third thing I notice that's different. Shaved head, a light in his eyes, an open door … I feel as though I don't know him, and yet I do. I want to know more. And I don't want to get closer than I already am.

Climbing the steps up to his front door, Keet still feels warm from seeing Nolee again. He's surprised by her short hair, and how it shows the pale slope of her neck. He had to stop himself from reaching out and touching her, warned off by her double expression of nervousness and anger. Her light auburn hair, with its strands of silver—like pale silk caught in the bark of red cedar trees—is also curlier than he's ever seen it. He wants to tell her this, and to share everything that's happened to him, everything he felt and saw and everything he now knows. He wants to hear everything she's gone through. But mostly he just wants to hear her.

Keet thinks back to their hug at the airport; it was quick, her body stiff and unyielding. He knew he'd asked more questions than she was comfortable replying to on their trip back home. He wonders about the tension in her voice, certain this is how she used to sound when she was married to her first husband, Nate. His own nervousness had led to him blurting out the remark about the seal and otter being eaten. In his mind, in the milliseconds before thoughts became words, it was his practical observation; death and life are wedded, a marriage of absolutes.

Even after trying to draw her out, she's contained, a fury without sound. Keet realizes that a storm's coming, and he's prepared to face it head on; her anger doesn't scare him as much as her distance. He watches her join the dogs, then turns to enter his house for the first time since last year, when he was captured as an orca, while swimming with his family pod.

Pocketing the key, he looks around. He wonders if his house has always looked half-lived in, thinks about the years he spent here before Nolee moved in next door. Those memories are as vacant as the house feels. Opening windows, he moves through the kitchen, dining room, and then living room, shaking the curtains as he goes. He makes a mental note to give the local cleaning company a call and find out if they can stop by. He doesn't mind cleaning, but he also needs to run to town for groceries and stain for the neglected deck. He spent so long convincing himself that he'd have to give up being human that it had become a habit to ignore many things, including his house. Including himself.

Keet opens the bathroom windows, then goes into his bedroom, where he sees Nolee's drawn the curtains back to let in the warm afternoon light. The bed's made up with wrinkled sheets. Keet's heart sinks when he realizes Nolee chose the oldest set of sheets in his closet, instead of the newer sheets that he'd had on the bed when they spent their first night together. He shakes his head, refusing to be daunted by her choice of bedding.

Walking back to the living area, he looks through the doorway. Keet enjoys letting in the sea and sky. He no longer needs to close the door, keeping himself a prisoner in his own life. He lays his spare key on the table, where it makes a soft click as the metal greets the wood. *This key belongs to Lia*, he thinks, calling her by the name he hears in his heart. Her parents may have given her the name Magnolia, and the world may know her as Nolee, but Lia is the name he hopes to say to her out loud again one day. He looks out the window as she hurls a bright tennis ball into the sea, with Wallace in hot pursuit. The dogs are having a blast. Nolee, it seems, isn't. Keet picks up his car keys, closes the door behind him, and gets into his car, smiling as he thinks about the ways he can inhabit his life once more.

Fae pants beside me as I throw the ball into the cove for Wallace. The rev of Keet's 4Runner and the loud beat of drums and bagpipes from his sound system follow him as he drives away. I focus on the dogs, throwing the wet ball my dripping-wet dog has brought back for me.

"Last one, Wallace, and then it's time for lunch." Whipping my arm back, I fling the ball as far as it will go, hoping my anger will follow it. No such luck. If anything, it seems to grow.

Wallace swims out to the orange ball, snaps at the water until he grabs it, then paddles in a long, slow arc back to shore. Fae makes her way closer to the water, looking first at Wallace and then back at me. As Fae's white paws dance across the rocks, Wallace shakes the water from his coat with a loud jingle of his tags. After rinsing the ball under the spigot, I grab a towel and dry off the dogs on the porch. They both shake now, spraying water on the windows I need to wash. The windows, made hazy by a film of sea salt, match my own feeling of not being able to see clearly. I wish washing off the anger stampeding inside me was as easy as sponging off those windows will be.

No time like the present, as the sages say. Filling up a bucket with warm water, dish soap, and vinegar, I watch the bubbles, an impatience I can't understand bubbling just as rapidly inside me. I haven't been this angry at anyone since Nate, my ex-husband, said he was leaving me for a new love. For months after Keet left, I got up each day and did my best to remember how to breathe. I remind myself that my mantra every day was that I didn't need a man who couldn't—or wouldn't—find a way to fight for himself, or for us.

I run my hand over the short ponytail at the nape of my neck. Earlier in the year, in a fit of grief, I had my long braid cut off. I'd wanted to shave my head, but my stylist—and my daughter Abbie—were the voices of sanity and suggested going short first.

Warm spring air and sunshine flood through the open door as I attack the windows on the ground floor. While scrubbing, it occurs to me that if I'm not careful, I could break the glass. Wringing out the rag, I step away, put my hands on my hips, and tilt my head to a sky I can't see through the scrim of my tears.

"Shit."

TWO

Once in Northsound, Keet stops at the hardware store, waving hello to the clerk before gathering what he needs to fix the deck.

"Looks like you've got plenty to do today," the clerk says, peering at Keet through his Buddy Holly-style glasses.

"I do. Staining the deck. It's a good day for it." He reaches for his wallet.

"Don't envy you, no sir. I enjoy a cool beer outside, but staining a deck? Back-breaking work."

Keet gives a short laugh. "I don't mind. My house needs some attention, and that's where I decided to start."

The clerk nods. "Need anything else before we make it final?"

"I think I do. Are those half-barrels with the flowers for sale?"

"Sure are. Let me find the code and I'll ring that up too. Just the one?"

"How many are there?"

"We have three left." He peers at Keet over the rim of his thick-framed glasses.

"I'll take them all."

"If you want more flowers, the garden center two blocks over has some nice arrangements. Might look good on that deck." He types the code into the computer, jabbing at the keys with the first finger of each hand.

"You know, Dave," Keet says, reading his nametag, "you may be right. Thanks."

"You bet. What's your name?"

Keet shakes Dave's hand. "Keet Noland. I have—"

"You're that whale-watch guy. Captain a boat called *The Salish See.*"

Keet's used to the big gossip of small towns, especially small island towns. "Yes. Have you been out on a tour?"

"I haven't, but my daughter has. Said it was the best one she'd ever taken. She might've had a little crush on you." Dave's blue eyes sparkle with mischief.

Keet laughs, then sees Dave looking at his left hand. He tucks it quickly into a pocket. "Tell her I'm glad she enjoyed it. I'd better get back home to my girlfriend—and my deck." Dave gives him a wink and a thumbs up.

"Need help loading those barrels?"

"No, I believe I can get them on my own."

Keet waves and walks out the door, the small bell tied to the handle jingling when it swings shut.

By the time he gets home, his 4Runner is packed from the passenger seat to the hatch. Not only does he have the tools for staining his deck and the barrels of flowers, but more flower boxes, eight bags of groceries, two bags from the local clothing store (where he stopped to pick up a few things that weren't black), a bag from the local bakery, and another from a gift shop that carries beeswax candles. On the passenger seat is a framed print of four killer whales drawn in a circle in black and red, swimming against a white background, painted in the Indigenous style by a woman from the Tlingit Nation. Keet smiles as he touches the black metal frame, thinking about where he'd like to hang it.

Once he's parked, Fae runs over to greet him, and Wallace approaches close enough to sniff the legs of his jeans. After petting Fae, Keet begins unloading the car; glancing up, he sees Nolee on the small balcony outside of her upstairs bedroom, cleaning the sliding glass door. She's going at it like she wants to destroy it. He decides that waiting for her to warm back up to him isn't going to happen if he sits around and waits. He'll need to break the ice that freezes her against his presence. He could wait until the sea froze over and she'd still be standing, anger in one fist and rage in the other. The goddess of lightning bolts, both aimed at him.

When Keet pulls in, I'm still on my balcony, watching the dogs as they sniff with stiff-tailed intensity at something on the ground. Hearing the car door slam, they both look up, and Fae bounds over to Keet, Wallace following at a cautious distance.

Keet kneels to pet Fae, but Wallace's tension is visible; as he sniffs Keet's legs, his nose is pointed forward but the rest of his body leans back, ready for a quick escape. As I'd asked him to do, Keet ignores Wallace and keeps petting Fae. Then, standing, he opens the SUV's hatch and I see that it's loaded with half barrels of colorful flowers, what looks like paint cans, bags of groceries and other bags I can't identify. Before he catches me looking at him, I go back to cleaning the glass door. He's wearing blue jeans that define his long legs, but I don't want to notice. The attraction that runs down my spine is not something I want to feel—or that I'm ready to feel.

The dogs trot back onto the porch below me, then take loud, slobbery drinks from their water bowl. Finished with the door, I pick up the bucket and go back downstairs. Time for spring cleaning inside.

By late afternoon, the windows are washed inside and out, the rugs hang on the porch rail, the hearth is swept, the ashes are removed, and the wood and kindling are replenished. Wiping a grimy wrist across my brow, I feel more orderly now that my house is too. Taking a glass of sweet tea out to my favorite log, I smile at the sight of the dogs, lying on their sides sunbathing and panting after more surf-chasing.

Soaking in the heat of the beach rocks' deep warmth, I close my eyes and listen to the waves. A sound nearby startles me, and I see it's Keet, shutting his garage door. When I turn back to the sea view, my spine rigid, it occurs to me that over the past months, I've become used to being here with only the dogs for company. Life is quiet when it's just fog and sea. Life is orderly when it's only me, making my own meals, working at the animal shelter and Chena's pet store.

As I sit, my thoughts slowing with my heartbeat, I hope Keet doesn't decide to come over and join me. For the first time today, I feel settled. Leaning back again, I close my eyes, stretch out my legs, and allow my arms to relax at my side, a warm rock in each hand. That lasts until Fae comes over to lick my nose and whuffle in my face. Wallace follows, his large ears laid flat, his white grin and wagging tail making me smile too.

"Must be dinner time for doggies," I say, petting each of them. "Let's get off this beach and inside. Dinner time for me, too."

The next morning, I'm on the beach with the dogs when Keet joins me.

I motion at his house after throwing the ball. "Looks like you're fixing up your place a bit."

Keet's standing close enough that I can feel the heat of his body. I take a step back and see that he's also taking in his newly stained deck and the flowers that are brightening it up. He gives me a small smile.

"She was looking forlorn."

"Are houses like boats then, 'she' instead of 'it'?" I grab the wet tennis ball and chuck it into the cove. Fae, bedraggled and dripping, waits on the shore for Wallace to swim back with it.

"For me they are."

Smiling, I watch Wallace emerge from the water. Bounding to me, he drops the ball at my feet, and I throw it again, harder than I mean to. Wallace leaps into the water and makes a beeline for the ball. Turning to answer Keet, I see him sprint for the dock; his shirt is on the ground beside me. On the dock, he shimmies out of his shorts and dives headfirst into the cove, an arc of grace and balance, barely making a splash. I keep my eyes on the cove as fire and ice course through my veins, brought on by the sight of his naked body. Within minutes, a notched black dorsal fin cuts through the water, and the blast of an exhale follows before the big orca submerges. I find myself suffused with joy at the sight of Keet in his orca form.

Far out in the water—too far out—Wallace's white-and-tan head is just visible above the surface. He's circling, trying to find the ball. I can tell from his increasing slowness that he's used up his energy swimming out to it. When a loud splash and roiling water draw my attention away from him, I notice that the commotion isn't as distant as I'd like. Whatever's going on is headed straight for my distracted and tiring dog.

Keet's dorsal fin rises, then his head, and I hear him clicking, scanning for Wallace. Once he finds him, he swims to him with a speed I wouldn't have imagined him capable of. I have a breathless moment reminding myself that this is Keet, that he wouldn't harm my dog. By the time I've finished that thought, Keet's his head is under Wallace and he's pushing him back to shore.

Panicked, Wallace flails, his body and legs rigid. I run into the water up to my waist, reaching for Wallace as he splashes to me. Wrapping my arms around his chest and hindquarters, I propel us both back to the beach. Once there, I watch Keet, still as orca, bending his shiny black and white body back and forth in the shallow water until he can float away and swim again. Taking a breath, he dives and heads out into the channel away from the cove, his notched dorsal fin finally sinking under the water.

The next time he comes up for air, a triangular dorsal fin is in front of him. The area behind this dorsal fin is solid black. Before I can think about grabbing my binoculars, the water churns again, and splashes and squeals carry on the still air. Birds circle above the activity, their cries mixing with the male orca's rising whistles.

I hear nothing from the smaller orca. I feel nothing except Wallace's terror reverberating through my body. A stream of pictures begins in my head; I close my eyes, as though that will make them stop. It's the female, and despite Keet's open mouth with his teeth on full display, she doesn't retaliate. Rather, she twirls like a ballerina.

Through the water's murky lens, I feel no anger from Keet, but do feel his confusion. Then another feeling overrides it: his intense desire to protect us. This registers somewhere in the far reaches of my heart and I open my eyes rather than dive deeper into it.

The smaller orca turns out of the bay and heads west, then exhales in an explosion of water droplets and dives, showing the white flash of the underside of her tail. Wallace is still shivering against my legs as I stand on my toes, trying to follow the two dorsal fins racing through the water. For every time the female blows and dives, Keet breathes twice, and he's soon outdistanced. Finally, I see his black bulk come to rest on the surface, then turn back toward Osprey Bay.

He dives as orca near one of the buoys that marks the bay from the cove and rises again as a man, rivulets of seawater running from his face. I walk toward Keet's house as he swims to the floating dock. Reaching for it, he folds both arms over the edge, looking over his shoulder at the empty cove. I feel the gentle rocking of the dock as I walk to where he's resting. He looks up at me through sunlit brown eyes. A long red scratch starts in his hairline and runs down the side of his nose.

"Need a towel?"

He nods and takes in my dripping clothes. "Looks like we both do."

As I go inside his house and grab a towel from the bathroom, I remember my first time there. Then, I had been borderline hypothermic, and he had carried me, almost naked, to a warm bath. Shaking off the memory of how it felt to be lifted into his arms, I focus on getting back to the dock. Putting the towel within his reach, I realize I need to thank him some way for saving Wallace.

"You're welcome to join me for an early lunch if you'd like." I point at his face. "Are you okay?"

He touches his nose. "I guess Wallace got me with one of his nails. Can't say I blame him."

"I have some ointment if you want it."

He looks over his shoulder out at the channel beyond the bay. "I'll take care of it." He rubs his hand over his head and says, "Lunch sounds great."

Fae trots beside me as I go back to my cabin. Wallace is on the porch, tail wrapped tightly around his body, large ears flat against his head. Though I can hear the distant thump of Keet's footsteps as he walks along the dock, my focus is on my trembling dog. I close my eyes and concentrate on how the world feels to Wallace. His terror and confusion swirls in my stomach, and I have a dim sense of him being lifted off his feet and slammed to the ground when he was small. Opening my eyes, I let out the breath I hadn't realized I was holding.

Instead of going to him, I sit on the ground and wrap my arms around my legs to warm up. Fae lies down behind me, leaning against my back and licking her wet paws, sharing her body heat.

The sunlight flickers in and out of the limbs of the bright-green-budded trees and darker evergreens. I think about gathering spruce tips for tea. I think about a warm fire and the safety and quiet of our home. Then I hear the soft pad of paws crossing the porch. Fae stands, body curved and tail wagging, to greet Wallace with licks to his muzzle. Panting, he raises his head and swipes his tongue across my face. I scratch his chest.

"There you go, buddy. You're okay now."

Taking a frayed towel from the porch railing, I rub the worst of the wet off the dogs before we go inside. They take long, messy drinks from their water bowls as I slip off my shoes and peel off my seawater-sticky clothes, then take a quick bath. After drying off, I put on jeans and a sweatshirt and go into the kitchen.

Taking two plates from the cupboard, I begin making lunch for me and Keet. As I look out the window at the cove, quiet on outgoing tide, it hits me: I feel numb. Not angry. Not irritated. But also, not sure about Keet's presence. *Don't have a come apart, girl, not now. It's lunch, not a date.*

Keet's sitting at the picnic table running his hands through Fae's damp coat; Wallace is still on the porch, ears up, alert. Walking between them, I set the plates on the table.

"Veggie wraps. Dig in. What do you want to drink?"

Keet holds up his battered stainless-steel water bottle. "I'm good."

When I come back with a mug of tea, Keet is still petting Fae, but Wallace hasn't relaxed his stance. I notice that Keet hasn't started eating.

15

"You didn't have to wait—please, eat." The tone of my voice surprises me; I almost sound like myself. Maybe I'm not as numb as I thought. "Did you take care of that scratch?"

I see Keet's already two large bites into his meal before he looks at me. Some things don't change; Keet's appetite is one of them. I skitter away from memories of his other appetites. I'm glad he can't read me with sound the way he can when he's orca; he'd know my heart is racing, tugging against the reins of my will to keep myself detached.

"I did." He touches the scratch with a tentative finger. "It'll heal."

"What happened out there?"

"It's the female orca you told me about. You're right, she's not a Resident."

"Do you know why she's here?"

Sitting forward on the bench, he places what is left of his wrap on the plate.

"I could see the physical shape of her, but I couldn't feel her. Ambiguity isn't usual with orcas. What you see—or hear, in this case—is what you get. I don't know where she's from or if she eats mammals, and I wasn't willing to wait and see if Wallace was on the menu."

"Thank you for that, by the way." I take a bite, averting my eyes from his.

"I can dive and change faster from the dock than I can by wading out into deeper water from the shore, so that's why I ran for it. Once I was in the water, I blocked her from getting closer to Wallace, then let her know she wasn't welcome here. She looks like any other female to me."

"But?"

He hesitates again. "I feel as though I know her, even though I've never heard or seen her before in my life. I'm sure of that." He shakes his head like he's trying to get water out of his ears. "She felt like mist. We're open with each other, whether we're Residents or Bigg's or offshore orcas. There are no secrets in our societies because we don't need them."

I continue eating, taking my time, sipping my tea, letting him figure this out, and—*admit it, Nolee Burnett*—enjoying the sound of his voice.

"That's what she felt like: secretive." He takes a long drink from his water bottle. I catch myself watching his throat move, then look down at Fae before he sees me watching. Sees me thawing.

"Maybe her curiosity's satisfied, and she'll go back to her own pod."

"Maybe." The tone of his voice tells me he has his doubts. "She's lightning fast. Even I couldn't catch her. But maybe I'm old and not as fast as I think." He gives me a rueful smile and takes a plate in each hand.

We stand at the same time. "Let me," he says.

As Keet moves toward the porch, Wallace pops from sitting to standing. His tail drops, his body stiffens, and I hear a low growl coming from him. The hair on his neck and shoulders is standing up.

"Keet. Stop where you are."

He does.

At sixty-plus pounds, Wallace isn't a small dog, and fear makes him bigger. I take the plates from Keet's hands and walk onto the porch.

"Inside, Wallace. Fae, inside." Fae trots inside and curls up on her bed. Wallace gives a low "whuff" and stalks stiff-legged into the house.

"I'll be right back. Wait here a moment?"

When I've put the dishes in the sink, I grab a bar of sea-salt dark chocolate and go out to the table. I hold the bar out to him.

"You don't need to ask," he says as he breaks the bar in half and hands it back. "What's up with Wallace? Is he afraid of me?"

"Seems to be. He's also confused because he feels the same things from you as a human as he felt from the orca who pushed him to the shore. Even though you saved him, you also scared him. That's the first time I've heard him growl, so you must've made quite an impression."

Looking out to the cove, Keet crunches on the chocolate. When a bar of sunlight catches in the short hair on the back of his head, I realize I'm staring—again—and look down at my own chocolate bar, then break off a chunk and eat it.

"I didn't mean to frighten him."

"He'll come around. He always does."

"What about you?" he asks.

"What about me?" My stomach clenches around my lunch, and my mouth dries up. I put the rest of the chocolate on the table and take a drink of tea.

"Have I scared you?" He's leaning on the table, head tilted, relaxed.

A nervous laugh escapes before I can stop it. I shake my head, looking away from the depths of his eyes to the channel beyond the cove. This time of day, the water looks like a long, rippling stretch of blue-green road. "You're harmless, remember?"

He doesn't join my laughter. He also doesn't answer and refuses to break eye contact with me.

"Shit, Keet. No, you don't scare me."

"What's going on, then? I didn't expect us to pick up where we left off …"

"Especially since where we left off was you leaving, and I thought it was for good. You apparently thought the same since you saw fit to hire a lawyer to clean up your life. I didn't realize you'd consider me to be part of the mess you left behind."

"Is that it? Is that how you saw what we had? A mess?" He's not raised his voice, but I hear the anger that's not far underneath. I watch from outside myself as I stand up hard enough to make the mug judder across the table.

"What was I supposed to think? I thought you came back after being captured so I could help you get better, that we would be with each other. And then you tell me you have to leave, and I could have your house and …" Before I know it, I'm rage-crying. "Dammit!" I run my knuckles under my eyes, looking out at the horizon, trying to breathe, trying to regain the tenuous control I've maintained since Keet came back.

"Nolee, I didn't have a choice!"

My voice rises like a tornado whipping down from swirling clouds. "You don't get to excuse yourself that easily. We always have choices. You made yours, and it didn't matter a damn bit how I felt."

Now Keet stands, his arms rigid, and I flash on Wallace and the scared rigidity in his body. I realize that it's fear, not anger, that's making my voice tremble and my heart race, and I deflate like a balloon, sitting before I collapse completely. Hiding my fear behind my anger wasn't how I wanted our talk to go.

"Please sit. I didn't mean to yell."

He gives me a wary glance and resumes his seat, arms on the table.

I take two deep breaths and try again. "I don't think you and I were a mess." My voice shakes as I talk. "It just felt so damn messy after you left. I couldn't …" I pause, reluctant to let him know how low I had sunk after he left. Especially after vowing to never again let who I was or how I felt depend on a man.

I blow out another breath and run my hands over the table's rough wood. "I couldn't get my feet under me. And the weather didn't help. I felt like I was going to be gray and cold forever. I still don't know what you went through, or why you made the choice you did. All I know is that you left me, and I had to get on with my life. I was beginning to feel like I had myself together again when you called from Sitka."

I shift my gaze from my clasped hands up to Keet. His brow is furrowed, his black eyebrows drawn together.

"But I told you I loved you."

The air whooshes out of my lungs.

I inhale, then answer him. "In my world, it made no sense for you to say that and leave. In my world, your words and actions didn't match up. Love isn't abandoning someone."

He looks out into the cove, and even though I'm balanced on the edge of anger and hurt, I can't ignore the beauty of his profile: the firm line of his nose, the sharp diagonal slant of his cheekbones softened by his full lips. He still looks drawn, his light brown skin taught against the bones of his face. I notice again the silver at his temples, which stands out against the rest of his short black hair.

Keet reaches across the table and lightly strokes my clenched fists. I open my hands and the warmth of his touch douses my anger. But although I want to forgive him, and I want to trust him, I can't. Not yet.

"Do you know we've been apart more than we've been together?" My voice catches in my throat.

He looks down at his hand covering my fists.

"I'm sorry, Nolee." He touches my cheek. "I wanted to let you know what you meant to me before I went away, which I thought would be for the rest of my life. Those words were all I had."

Every other sound, every other sight fade when our eyes connect.

"After I escaped from the aquarium, it felt like I had only two choices: swim away as orca or drown in darkness as a human. I was ashamed for you to see me so out of control. Now, I've made my peace with who I am. But how I feel about you hasn't changed." His eyes hold mine, and in a soft voice he asks, "Has it changed for you?"

Our hands remain together on the picnic table. I don't have an answer for him. I don't have an answer for myself.

"We need to spend more time together, Keet. I need a chance to know you again. It seems like you've changed, and you've not changed, and it confuses me."

"I get it. Take your time. I'm not going anywhere."

I smile, hearing in his words the echo of what I'd said to him so many months ago.

"Can I make you dinner sometime? Would you like to go out in the double kayak? The water's perfect for it right now."

I hesitate, mentally running through my schedule.

A flash of uncertainty crosses Keet's face. "No pressure about either one. Dinner is just a meal together, with no expectations. Same if you'd like to kayak today."

I'm relieved to hear the "no expectations" part. "How about dinner tonight? I've got a shift at the shelter in an hour."

He leans closer to me. "Tell me about that."

"Let me get the dogs first. You okay having them back out with us?"

"Of course."

I open the door and watch the dogs trot past the picnic table back down to the beach. Wallace makes a large detour around the table, and Keet. I sit down across from him again.

"The board of directors at the shelter liked my work with the animals and the volunteers. In February, they asked if I'd like to work for them part time and I said yes. It's work I'm good at, and more satisfying than my former business in Texas."

"In what way?" He doesn't reach for my hand again, leaning toward me instead.

"I feel like I'm benefiting the lives of humans and animals. There's genuine change in the people who show up to volunteer. They're different ages and from different backgrounds, but they all love animals and want to learn. I think I have a knack for teaching, along with my kind of weird knack for communicating with animals."

"Even cats?" He smiles, knowing they aren't high on my list of companion pets.

"Well, maybe not them so much, but I'm getting better. I've been hanging around in that part of the shelter to see if I can understand them."

He smiles. "I've missed you, Nolee."

I give him a quick smile in return. "Count me in for dinner. Does seven tonight work?"

"Yes. Fresh-caught salmon if we're lucky."

The comment surprises me into laughter as I realize he means to hunt in his orca form to get dinner for us.

"I'll keep my fingers crossed. Catch us a good one, Keet."

THREE

When I get home after work, the air has a green tang of spring and the light is soft, outlining the islands to the north in pink and gold. The picnic table where Keet and I had lunch that afternoon, and our first real conversation since his return, is dark with moisture. It must've rained on this side of the island. I let the dogs out of the car, go inside, and see the light blinking on the answering machine.

"Hi, Nolee, it's Ava. Just checking to find out if you need the cabin for much longer, honey. Also, Chena wants to know if you could take care of the store tomorrow for the morning shift. She has a doctor's appointment and I'm going to be traveling most of the day, running to Seattle and back."

I pick up the bulky cordless phone and dial Ava's home number. She answers, out of breath.

"Hey, Ava, it's Nolee. Is now a good time to talk?"

"Oh sure, honey. I was just chopping some wood for next winter. Getting ahead of things—you know how it is."

"Better ahead than behind. I can work the morning shift at Chena's place. I'll text her. Also, could you give me sixty more days to figure out what I'm doing? I'm happy to pay you extra rent if you'd like."

"Don't worry about it. Stay until June or July, then let me know what you decide."

"Thanks, Ava."

"I heard Keet Noland is back in town?"

The island grapevine is alive and well, I thought. "He is. How'd you hear?"

"Chena's husband Mike mentioned talking to him at the market. Said he's back for good. He'd been up in Sitka helping his grandmother."

I don't know what Keet's been telling people and make a mental note to ask him when I go over for dinner.

"Mike said Keet seems happier. Well, honey, I just realized it's late and Pete will have dinner coming off the grill. He gets irritable if I don't show up while it's hot." We both laugh, then end the call.

I feed the dogs and check my appearance in the bathroom mirror, which reminds me that I need to change out of the frayed, dog-hair-covered hoodie I'm wearing and run a brush through my hair. Finally, I put on a gray sweater and pair of silver earrings and call it good.

Keet's door is open. I wait outside and call, "Hello?"

"C'mon in! I'll be right there."

As I walk in, my stomach in knots, I smell rosemary and garlic, see a loaf of bread on the table, as well as two Scotch glasses. The table's dark wood surface, no longer dusty, gleams under the overhead lights. I hear Keet's footsteps, then watch as he comes into the room. His jeans ride low on his hips, and his loose orange t-shirt has the word "Orca" in black capital letters and, in smaller letters underneath, "Center for Whale Research."

"Dinner smells amazing."

"I'm running a little behind—had to go farther for the salmon. They're sparse around here now for a lot of the year."

"How far did you go?"

"Toward Lummi. I know a spot where they hang out. I also met my family while I was out there; they stayed so they could get enough to eat to last them for a while."

"You must've set a speed record. Thanks for going so far."

"The salmon is worth it. This time of year, they're nice and juicy." He moves to the stove, switching a light on so he can check the fish, his feet bare and brown against the recently cleaned hardwood floor.

Curious, I ask him, "You must be famished after that big swim."

"Hungry, not famished. Before I came back, I caught and ate a few salmon. If I hadn't, I would've swallowed the one I caught for us, and then we wouldn't have had any dinner."

"Practical of you. How's your family?" We're talking about the six members of his orca pod, not his human family—his grandmother and uncle in Sitka. My gaze goes to the Scotch glasses. A drink right now would be a good idea; the conversation is bordering on fantastical.

"My family's good, although a little hungrier this spring. The salmon are smaller and harder to find. I caught as many as I could for them before I swam back."

"Now I feel extra grateful you brought one back for us. If the Scotch is handy, I'll pour."

"It's right here." Retrieving it from one of the cabinets, he hands me the unopened bottle. "I got Balvenie." Breaking the seal, I twist the cork and pull. The smoky waft of whisky fumes calms my nerves; its amber gold glints in the light as I hand him a glass.

Before I can toast, he says, "Sláinte. Is that right?"

"Yes, it is." I take a healthy swallow, letting the peat and cinnamon glide over my tongue and warm my belly. "That's better. Thanks for remembering my preferred drink."

"I was going to try for margaritas, but …"

We both smile, recalling the Mexican restaurant we visited early in our relationship.

"Scotch is perfect. I lose my head a little bit with margaritas."

"I remember." Pulling the baking sheet with a large fillet of rosemary-topped salmon out of the oven, he sets it on the stove, then opens the refrigerator to get the salad.

"Here, let me put that on the table." I hold out my hands for the bowl.

Our fingers touch when he hands it to me, and when I look up at him, we freeze. The kitchen disappears as vivid memories of our first dinners together pop into my mind. But rather than rush away, I stand my ground, willing my breathing to stay slow.

Releasing the bowl, he clears his throat and thanks me.

I hear the stove open a second time. This time, it's roasted potatoes—also sprinkled with rosemary—coming out, sizzling in olive oil. The potatoes go into another bowl, which I take from him, making sure our fingers don't meet this time. Finally, he transfers the salmon to a serving board, squeezes a lemon over it, and carries it to the table, his bare feet silent on the warm wood floor.

"Okay, we have the salmon, we have salad, potatoes, bread and butter … what else?"

"Salad dressing?"

"Give me a second, I'll whip it up. Please, have a seat and tell me about your shift."

The sip of Scotch warms in my hands; I've been clutching the glass like a lifeline. But I forget to be nervous as I tell Keet about the new litter of puppies we got in, and two new volunteers, a brother and sister, twins and still in high school.

"They'll fit in great. They're both very sweet and good with animals."

Keet brings the dressing to the table, shaking the cruet while keeping his eyes on me. When he sets it down, I don't see any trembling in his hands, and the haunted look is gone from his eyes. An earlier feeling washes through me again—a sense that his human self and orca self are now aligned.

"What are you thinking, Nolee?"

Startled, I set my glass down harder than intended. "Oh. I was thinking that you seem very much like you do when you're orca. I've never felt you this unburdened before, not as a human."

"I feel lighter. The time in Sitka was life-altering. My grandmother says she hopes to meet you one day."

"I'd like that too."

We avoid heavy topics while we eat, catching each other up on our day. Keet mentions that he checked on his boat, *The Salish See.*

"Oh yeah? How is she?"

"Alex kept her in much better shape than I did, and that's saying something. He had her name repainted, the bilge pump replaced, sails mended, and she has a new anchor. It impressed me." He stops to chew his last bite of salad. "I'm tempted to just let him have the business."

"You'd miss being out on the water, though, wouldn't you?"

"Maybe."

I push the last of my bread around the plate, mopping up the salad dressing.

"Besides," he continues. "I think I also remember promising you—" he pauses and looks down at his plate.

"What?"

"Perhaps that's a conversation for a different time."

"Keet. I'm not going to blow up again. Tell me." I'm smiling, and he grins at my nervous attempt at humor.

"I remember promising you a night on the boat."

"You did." I want to say something, but don't know what.

Keet solves my dilemma. "Let's get this cleaned up."

On my second trip to the sink, I'm finally able to look at him. "Are you going for a swim tonight?"

Steam from the dishwater rises around his face and over his head, reminding me of his breath in the cold air when he's orca. I miss seeing him that way. The excitement earlier today with Wallace happened so quickly that I'd had little time to appreciate his beauty the way I usually do. *Did,* I remind myself.

"No, I've had enough swimming for one day. I'd rather spend time with you."

I touch his bare arm, letting my hand rest on it, looking at the contrasting pale and dark tones. So many different feelings are swirling around inside me that I feel like a shaken snow globe. Whispering "That would be great," I turn away to get the rest of the dishes.

As I'm finishing another glass of scotch, I remember to ask what he's been telling the locals about his absence. "Ava called, and she mentioned a couple of things."

"What did she say?" Keet's leaning against the counter, his hands in his pockets.

"First, that I can go month-to-month on the cabin until July."

"That's good news."

I set the empty glass down, procrastinating. I see a ragged towel on the counter. "Looks like new towels for the kitchen would be a good idea."

He laughs. "Yeah, I had to put the others in the rag basket; they were stained beyond redemption. What else did Ava tell you?"

I smile, thinking to myself that his focus is sometimes a curse. "She said Mike saw you at the market. You said your grandmother was feeling better, and that you'd been in Sitka for a while."

He laughs again. "Which is mostly true. I was in Sitka with my grandmother, but when I left, she was healthy and back in town in my Uncle Jerry's apartment."

"What's this about your grandmother being in an apartment?"

"That's part of what I want to tell you. We have a family cabin on a beach. It's where I grew up. When I left here, I swam with my orca family up to Sitka, to my grandmother's cabin by the ocean. Grandmother was sitting on the beach, waiting for me. She said she had a dream I was swimming home. Once she decided to no longer swim as orca, she moved into an apartment in town with her Jerry. When I decided to come back here, to Camas, he picked us up at the cabin and dropped me off at the airport, then took Grandmother back to the apartment."

I stifle a yawn with the back of my hand, not yet ready to hear what happened while he was gone. For him, it's history. For me, it's a reopened wound.

"Nolee?"

I lean toward him, then stop myself. My guard is down, I've had too much whisky, and it would be easy to let this "just dinner" turn into "just staying the night." Not yet. I feel better about him being back, but not that much better.

"You've had a full day," he says. "We can talk another time about what happened in Sitka. Let me know if you'd like to take the kayak out tomorrow. The weather is supposed to be even more gorgeous than today. I'll take care of the dishes."

"I'll take you up on that. Thanks again for dinner."

I give him a wave, leave his house, and walk back to my cabin. I can't get there fast enough. Letting the dogs out for the last time before bed, I hear them snuffling as they investigate who and what's been near. As the silver glow on the western horizon shifts to black, I hear music that raises goosebumps on my bare skin.

"*Well, it's a marvelous night for a moon dance, with the stars up above in your eyes…*" Looking over at Keet's house, I smile to see him dancing by himself, moving back and forth past the still-open doorway, arms akimbo, at ease in his skin. *That makes one of us*, I think.

After calling the dogs inside, I climb the stairs to my room. Before I have time to second-guess myself, I text Keet: *Who, what, and when is that song?*

I'm not sure he's found his phone, or even remembered how to charge it. But then I see three floating dots and then, *Van Morrison, Moondance, 1970*. Then phone chimes. It's Keet. *Goodnight, Nolee*. I respond, add a snoring emoji, and set the phone to silent. Warm under my orca quilt, I look through the clean glass doors at the dark sea and realize that I'm smiling.

May has arrived, and with it, batches of puppies and kittens who need homes. The shelter is jumping with baby animals, and I work longer hours and meet more locals in two weeks than I have in a year.

Keet and I haven't done much more than greet each other from our porches and take quick walks on the beach with the dogs. He doesn't suggest another dinner or going out in the kayak together. It's as though he intuits that I need time to sort through the mix of my feelings. But watching him work on his house, I realize I'm becoming accustomed to seeing him there again.

I'm also wondering where I'm going to live next. I want to rent the A-Frame cabin for another year, and I can't figure out why I'm hesitating. Letting go of that worry, I decide to take another tiny step closer to Keet and see where it goes.

The next morning, I text him from the sun- and sea-bleached log outside my cabin. *I have the day off. Are you free to go kayaking?* Just after hitting send, I hear Fae bark. She and Wallace are chasing small whitecaps washing over the wavy and uneven line of marine detritus at the high-tide line.

Out in the cove, I see the otter, flipping her tail as she dives for breakfast. No orcas in the area, then. I think about that odd female orca and wonder where she is. I hope she's okay; it's rare—at least, in my experience—to see orcas by themselves. It would be a lonely existence for an animal who normally lives within touching distance of their family.

When my phone chimes. I snatch it off the log and see that it's Abbie. *Whatcha up to, moms?*

I smile. My educated daughter loves to play with spelling and language. I respond in kind.

Nuthin much. Sipping tea, watching the ocean. You missed you're chance with 'to'; spell it too *next time. :) Howzit with you?*

Just got out of class. Aced my calc test.

Calculus. Her favorite subject. I text back. *That's great honey! You're brilliant. I'll call later, I may be going kayaking with Keet.*

The next time my phone chimes, it's Keet. *Lost track of time in the bubble bath. Meet me on the beach in 10?* I send him a thumbs-up emoji. As good as his word, he steps out of his house within minutes, dressed in tan shorts and a blue t-shirt and moving with feline grace. *Whoever came up with that phrase never watched orcas in the water*, I think to myself.

Another chime announces Abbie's response. *Is that the same Keet who left last winter? He's back?*

I sigh. And type. In my peripheral vision, I see Keet checking both kayaks.

It is the same Keet, and he is back. Talk tonight? xo

I wait for her reply, and smile when I see it.

Oh hell yes! I want all the deets!

Back in the cabin, I jam my hair under a baseball cap, brush my teeth, and roll up my jeans. After slipping on my water shoes, I toss the dogs a couple of treats and head out the door, willing my heart to stop racing.

I walk over to where Keet is standing, paddle in hand.

"Good morning."

His smile goes all the way into his eyes. "Good morning, Nolee." He leans forward as though he wants to get closer, but I don't move. Instead, I ask, "Do you want to take out both kayaks, or just the double?"

I have wonderful memories of that double kayak, all of them involving Keet. A riptide of images swirls together: Keet and orcas and sun and jellyfish and the green Salish Sea. My heart is going wild again, and I distract myself by looking out at Sucia Island in the hazy distance.

"I think the double. What about you?"

"Sounds good." I take hold of the short rope at the stern, and he grabs the one at the bow. We lift at the same time and carry the kayak into the cold, shallow water.

After we're both settled and paddling out toward the Point that's west of Osprey Bay, I relax into the kayak's rhythm and soft sway. Then we both stop paddling and revel in the silence, the only sound the soft lap of waves against the kayak.

"How deep is the water here, Keet?"

"I've never measured it as a human . . . but I'd say more than 150 feet once you're closer to the channel. I can easily dive and jump and not come close to the bottom. It gets shallower closer to shore; there's a gradual slope along most of the coast of Camas. There are also great little outcroppings, like underwater mesas. I wish I could show them to you."

"Speaking of, I have a question for you." I begin to paddle again, the silken glide of the kayak settling my nerves.

"Sure."

"Is it still difficult to change back and forth, between man and orca?"

Our paddles and the splash of gulls as they settle into the water are the only sounds I hear for a long moment. I'm used to the unhurried pace of conversations with Keet. The closer a question hits, the longer he takes to answer it ... as though he's interpreting what his heart knows into words.

"I'd like to tell you about my time with my grandmother in Sitka, Nolee. That will take longer than we'll be out here. The short answer to your question, though, is no, it's not difficult anymore. It's as easy as changing clothes."

"I remember you describing it that way when you were learning to change as a child. And that it got more complicated as you got older."

"That's right."

I hear a splash and look out into the channel, hoping it's Keet's orca family. I haven't seen them since the day he called to tell me he was coming back. But it's the seal, her dark, shiny head and watery eyes peering at us above the waves. She melts back into the water, and we don't see her again.

"That answers one question: the seal is okay." I feel a rush of gratitude. "And I saw the otter earlier this morning. I guess I can be less nervous about that female orca."

Our paddling synchronizes as we glide past a beach strewn with logs of all sizes. They look like larger versions of the pick-up sticks I used to play with as a child. I look the other way, seeing sailboats in the channel and the bobbing black bodies of cormorants huddled in messy circles.

"I'll feel better when I know why she's here," Keet says.

We've paddled past the Point and are turning back toward home before he speaks again.

"You can't think of anything, any clue she gave you?"

I shake my head. "Nothing. I felt what you did and saw both of you like I was underwater, too, but I couldn't get anything from her that would tell us what she's doing here."

Keet grunts, sounding displeased. "I hope she gets back together with her pod, wherever they are. The farther away she is from us, the better."

"Why is that?"

"One, because I don't want her harassing you and your dogs. Two, because a female orca by herself isn't usual. It isn't even rare. It doesn't happen."

I don't answer, focusing instead on the kayak and the V it creates as the prow pushes through the water. After sliding up into the shallows, we carry the kayak from the beach closer to his house. "Want some lunch, Nolee?" After setting down my end of the kayak, I turn to him. He runs a hand along his head and without thinking about it, I smile.

"What? Is it weird my hair is so short?"

"Not weird. I like it." I reach over and give him a playful shove. "Lunch would be great. I'll go let the dogs out and be right over."

FOUR

Back at Keet's house, Fae bounds onto the deck and sniffs around, while Wallace stays beside me. On a round wooden table in front of the chimney's rockwork are two glasses of water.

Keet comes around the corner holding two plates. "Tuna sandwiches okay with you?"

"Sure. Thanks." I pull out one of the matching chairs and sit, looking out at the shoreline where Wallace is now wading in the quiet afternoon waves. Fae lies down with a thump between Keet and me.

"I haven't seen this table before. Did you just get it?"

"Nope. Pulled it out of the garage and cleaned it. Next on the clean up list is my hammock."

"I'll help with that if I can also borrow it sometimes. Reading in a hammock is my ideal way to spend a summer afternoon."

"You're welcome to it, whether or not you help." He smiles and takes another gigantic bite of his sandwich.

We eat for a few minutes, and I find I'm enjoying myself—the warmth of the day, the food, and the sounds of the island waking up after a long and dark winter. The waves are quiet, and I hear the hum of passing boats and the whine of an airplane as it takes off. The birds are out, both in the trees and on the sea, and across the water, I hear kayakers laugh as they glide past us, paddles flashing in the sun.

"Is now a good time to tell me what happened up in Sitka?"

Keet looks up, folding his napkin before placing it on his empty plate. He nods.

"When I left here, I thought being orca the rest of my life would let me leave behind the torment of being human. But after swimming north with my family for about a week, I didn't feel better. They were patient with me, and I helped hunt and feed us, but for the first time, the darkness I felt as a man followed me into being orca."

He pauses, pushing the plate to the middle of the table and resting his folded arms on its wooden surface.

"When we got near Sitka, they forced me to choose between life or death."

"How did they do that?"

He gives me a quick smile, shaking his head. "They tried to drown me."

"What?!"

"Six against one, even when one of the six is a baby, was no match. I would get a quick breath before they were on top of me again, forcing me down. The last straw for me was when Nana took my tail in her teeth and tried to drag me deeper. I got angry, broke away, and changed back to a man. I wasn't even aware that I'd made that choice; it was pure survival. They let me swim to the surface and swam with me to shore. This was near the beach where my grandmother's cabin is."

"Does that mean you chose life?"

"It does, but I didn't realize that. They knew that if I kept living in the in-between, not alive but also not dead, I would put our whole pod at risk."

"How's that?"

"By being a less involved and effective hunter. By being a shadow in the pod instead of fully myself. For any kind of marine mammal, living in a state of disconnection isn't an option. Not if you want to survive. People live this way all the time, but in nature, there are consequences for that lack of presence."

Laying my napkin on my plate, I think about what he's saying.

"Can I get you a cup of tea, Nolee?"

"That would be great."

When Keet returns with two steaming mugs, I take the one he hands me and sip, closing my eyes as its sweetness hits my tongue; he's added just the right amount of honey. Elbows on the table, I wrap my hands around the familiar pottery mug, absorbing its warmth.

"Thanks. What are you having?"

"Hot chocolate." He smiles and takes a sip. "Might've put in enough chocolate for two cups."

"Living on the edge?"

He laughs. "I am. Edges are more interesting."

The question I was going to ask is erased. I can feel myself teetering on my own edge of a choice point, an edge between being friends with Keet, or resuming our relationship as lovers. I push back further into my chair and recover the question, using it as a shield against my discomfort.

"So, your family let you surface after changing to a man, and they swam with you to shore?"

"They did. My grandmother was there, waiting like she knew I was coming. Turns out, she had a dream while she was still at the apartment in town. The morning after that dream, she packed up and insisted that my uncle drive her out there and leave her. I guess she almost had to shove him back into his car."

It's my turn to laugh. "She sounds like a strong grandmother."

"Oh, that she is." He takes a large drink and sets down his mug. "We've learned in my family to not cross her. Out of respect, but also because she's tough. And smart."

He's quiet for a moment, then continues. "It had surprised me when I changed back to a man again, especially because I hadn't planned on doing it. I hoped that if I was orca long enough, I would get back to my old self … that I'd lose the memory of being human."

Leaning back in my chair, I look through the tea's amber surface. This isn't a simple conversation for either of us, but the sadness of his words hits me like icy rain. I look up at him, hoping that the lump in my throat and the ache in my chest will stop freezing me from the inside out.

"My grandmother and I sat by the fire, and I told her about my life, about you, about my capture while I was with my pod, my escape as a man, and how you tried to help me. I realized that even though my body had come back, I was still in the tank back in San Bolsa. I was still imprisoned at OceanMagic."

My breath catches in my chest, but I don't move. I don't want to do anything to distract Keet from saying what he needs to say. My eyes are unable to look anywhere except him.

"My grandmother and I talked into the night. We had dinner and went to sleep. That night, Nolee …" He switches his gaze to the bright water. But I can tell from his expression that he's not seeing it—he's watching whatever image is playing in his head. "I still don't know if I went back into the ocean or not. It was like I was hallucinating, but I knew I wasn't. I saw myself as both orca and man. And at the end, I saw you sleeping next to me, here, in my bedroom. When I reached out for you, I must have touched the stove because when I woke up, I was still in the cabin, and still a man."

He takes a long drink from the mug he's gripping with both hands.

"After that, I swam every day with my pod before they began their trip south, back here. I thought about returning with them, but I wanted time with my grandmother. She and I had long talks, also many hours of silence. She told me …" I can hear the catch in his voice. He gives me a look, jutting out his chin as though gathering strength for what he has to say.

"Grandmother told me I was wearing a cloak that wasn't mine to wear. That it was given to me by mistake. She told me it was the cloak of choice, that I had to either be orca or be human but couldn't be both. My grandmother had taken that cloak from her mother, as I took it from my mother. But it wasn't ours to take or give."

He places the mug on the table.

"When my pod forced me to choose life or death, that was the actual choice. It doesn't matter to them whether I'm human or orca, or both. Just like it doesn't matter to you."

I give him a small smile and nod, then reach across the table. He takes my hand and squeezes it.

"My grandmother reminded me of something I had forgotten."

"What's that?"

"It doesn't matter what form I choose because I'm always the same inside. My spirit is unchanging, and the body I choose doesn't matter."

"That's a powerful lesson to absorb," I say, squeezing his hand. I can feel the edge of the chair along the backs of my thighs, my stomach pressed against the edge of the table.

"It is. The truth has a way of cutting through doubt."

"And now here you are."

"Here I am. Here we are."

"Thank you for telling me, Keet." We sit for a moment before I ask, "Want to take a walk on the beach with me and the dogs?"

"Absolutely."

We take our plates into the kitchen and wash up, then head for the beach, where we hold hands and watch the dogs chase the ball. I'm looking out into the bay, idly wondering about our mystery female orca, when Keet says, "I hope our mystery female is long gone. Let's sit down for a moment."

Standing with his hand in mine, watching the sun on his lined face, I'm wonder again about his knack for reading my thoughts.

"How about right there?" I point to a large log that the sea had pushed up onto the beach the previous winter when a storm engulfed the island.

We sit side by side, the log at our backs, the length of his leg next to mine, shoulders touching. For the first time since his return, I feel at ease in his presence. Resting my head on his shoulder, I close my eyes, enjoying the warm rocks and the heat coming from his body. I feel him move, then the weight of his arm across my shoulders as he gathers me to himself.

He didn't know what he was expecting, though if he were honest, he hoped she'd let him get closer to her. He feels her face against his shoulder, her body turning toward him, her arm around his waist. One of her legs slides over his, and he can feel the soft roundness of her breasts against his ribcage. He closes his eyes, breathing the scent of her, letting his head rest against the log. He doesn't fall asleep, but he can feel the moment she does, her breathing becoming deep and even.

At her other side, the dogs stretch out on the sand, panting, eyes half-closed. No more planes are flying overhead, and the boats are far enough away that he can't hear them. She makes a quiet sound in her sleep; when he looks at her, he sees a slight smile on her face. He smiles too and gathers her closer, leaning his head back again and taking in the wide blue spring sky.

He feels her switch positions and comes out of his reverie.

"Did you sleep too, Keet?"

"No. How was your nap?"

She gives him a quick squeeze, then untangles herself and sits up, stretching her arms over her head. Not for the first time, he remembers seeing her naked form bathed in a full moon's silver light—like a goddess rising from the dark night.

"Good. I needed it. I guess I'd better head to the market, though." She pauses, pulling at the t-shirt twisted around her torso. She looks at him, her green eyes bright. "Want to come with me?"

The car bumps down the road, and he watches her as she concentrates on avoiding the potholes. Resting his hand on her thigh earns him a quick smile. "What would you think about getting takeout from Casa Mariachi?"

She slows to a stop, looking both ways before turning onto the paved road. "Sure. You know I'm always up for someone else fixing a meal."

"We can eat out on the deck again. I'll call it in, and we can pick it up after we shop." He holds the cell phone up. "I even programmed their number into this thing."

Her eyebrows shoot up, and her laugh makes him laugh too. "Look at you, mastering technology! I'll have a chimichanga, lots of sour cream."

"Margarita to go with that?"

"Are you trying to get me tipsy again, Keet Noland?" She gives him a slow smile, her nose crinkling.

"Not at all. I remember how much you enjoyed them last time."

"I'm good with anything except a margarita tonight. I need to back off on the booze." He almost asks why but lets the question rest between them. He doesn't want to spoil this familiar intimacy, and so he chooses to enjoy her, as though the possibility of them being together again is not a product of his constant hope. As though she could forgive him.

At the market, they each grab a cart. He notices that she's buying real food instead of filling her cart with the snacks he used to hear her talk about. Then he sees four different chocolate bars and five fresh cheeses, and smiles. Nolee notices him checking her cart as she stops to grab a pint of ice cream, saying, "Between us, we have a whole pantry full of food." He's saved from blurting out, right there in the middle of the frozen aisle, that he would love to not only share a pantry, but a house, by a young mother pushing her cart down the aisle toward them. One wailing child is in the cart and the other is holding her hand and chanting "icecreamice-creamicecream…" Keet moves behind Nolee to make room, and his gaze drops to her hips. He yanks his eyes up, looking opposite the freezer at the rows of drinks, adding a couple of bottles of sparkling water to his cart.

Back at his house, they eat in the day's waning light, then clear the remains of their meal off the table. Nolee drains the last of the sparkling water from her glass. "That was halfway decent. Maybe we could add some fruit juice to it next time."

Keet smiles. "At the restaurant, I thought you might cave and order a margarita to go."

She laughs. "Not this time. I've got a big day tomorrow and I need to have a clear head."

"What's going on?"

"Training day at the shelter. Wallace and Fae will be helping me show the volunteers how to work with dogs who have different temperaments."

"Hard to believe that Fae used to be so defensive. She's a lap dog now." Hearing her name, Fae trots over to Keet, her tail brushing against his legs as she leans against him. He strokes her back, then scratches above her tail. Her amber eyes close as she points her nose to the sky.

"She'll follow you anywhere if you keep doing that."

Keet stands up, looking at Wallace who is laying at Nolee's feet.

Catching his glance, Nolee scratches Wallace's head. "It's Fae's job to help me tomorrow. I'm not sure how ready Wallace is. He's still cautious around people he doesn't know."

"It's good to keep exposing him though, right?"

"It is," she nods.

"Was he hurt by a man or a woman?"

"A man."

"Maybe he has two things he's trying to sort out: that I'm a man and that I'm also orca."

"Maybe," she says. But doesn't sound convinced. "He warms up to some of the male volunteers at the shelter. When I had him at Chena's shop, he'd let little boys and some of the old guys touch him."

"Are you saying I should take his fear of me personally?" He didn't mean the question to come out with barbs, but even he can hear its sharp points. Nolee looks at him, then at Wallace, then at him again.

"No, dogs don't operate like that. I don't think he knows what to think about you, so he's staying away until he does. The process of him feeling safe takes time."

Keet sighs. "You're saying the best thing for me to do is be patient."

She smiles. "Yes."

Spring is in full-throated celebration on Camas Island, and Keet and I have been seeing each other with increasing regularity. He guides a few tours a week, I work part time at the shelter, and we often share dinner. Seeing him each evening has become part of my life's background music.

He's the same man I met and became infatuated with a year ago, and different. I'm different, too. Not only do I accept him being part of a race of people who can change into orca, but I'm meeting him on firmer ground. Now—the divorce from Nathan two years in my rearview and surviving the crucible of losing Keet last winter—I feel as though I've found my own rhythm, one that is not laid claim to by a partner, or a parent, or a child. As though I've reclaimed the Nolee Burnett who's more than a mother, daughter, friend, or lover. It may have taken me half my life to accept myself, but I'm becoming the kind of woman I like.

I'm as close to choosing Keet again as I've been since he's been back. The promise of the bright June days shines inside me, warming my conviction that I could be in a relationship with him without losing myself.

We throw our packs in the back of Keet's 4Runner, then move so the dogs can jump in.

"That hike never gets old," he says.

I turn and look back at the trail, the long shadows of tree trunks stretching across it like crooked rungs on a ladder.

"Mt. Pelorus doesn't disappoint." I pat Wallace and Fae, close the door, then slide into the front seat. After leaving the parking lot and beginning our journey down the winding road back to Osprey Bay, Keet lays his hand on my thigh. I take it in my own and feel my insides quiver.

The SUV dips into a pothole. Glancing away from the window toward Keet, I expect to see him watching where he's going. Instead, he's smiling at me. "Thoughts?"

"Many." I squeeze his hand.

"It's been amazing being with you again, Nolee. Thank you."

"Is that some Keykwin ability?"

He glances at me, then back to the road, steering to avoid another pothole.

"What's that?"

"Bringing up something I'm thinking about, like you can hear my thoughts."

He shrugs, puts both hands on the steering wheel, and pulls himself forward, shifting in his seat.

"I can't hear you, so your thoughts are safe."

"But?"

"Maybe we're on the same wavelength. We've always been close that way, don't you think?"

"True." I look out at the valley below us, dotted with sheep drifting along like fuzzy white bushes against a green backdrop. The memory of being carried to shore last year by Keet in his male orca form surfaces.

"Is that how you knew I had my kayak accident last year? When you put me on your back and saved me? Is that 'wavelength' amplified when you're orca?"

I feel Keet's thigh relax under my hand as he eases up on the gas pedal. "Yes. I heard and felt you flailing around. Why's this coming up now?"

"A lot happened for us after that. I had so many questions once I found out who you are, and that particular question went to the back of the line."

We coast through the trees, sunlight flashing on Keet's face, moving from shadow to light. It reminds me of the thin clouds that passed over the sun when I took out the kayak … the day I ended up being rescued by Keet while he was orca.

"I forgot to ask about something else, Keet."

He smiles at me. "The kayak?"

"You're doing it again. I never thanked you for saving me. So, thank you. Now tell me how you brought the kayak back."

"I was worried that you'd get out of the bath too soon and see me out there, swimming with it to shore. I was amazed that you didn't even ask about it."

"That's what a waterlogged brain and a crush will do. Did you change into orca to get it?"

"I couldn't risk that, not with you in my house. I swam out to get it. When I got back inside, I took a quick shower in the guest bathroom. I even had time to dry my hair and sit down with a book before you got out of the tub."

We get to the sharp bend in the dirt road. Keet steers through it, then looks at me with a glint in his eye. "Tell me more about this crush."

I laugh and thump his thigh. "You knew I liked you, Keet Noland."

"I did. But I think I liked you more. What else were you thinking about?"

"I was thinking how good I feel, like I'm becoming the person I'd like to be. And how much I enjoy spending time with you." I put my hand on his thigh again, noticing the way his muscles shift as he changes from the gas to the brake. We roll to a stop at the edge of the dirt road.

When our eyes meet this time, I see that the sparkle has changed to something else. Something I feel mirrored in my own. In one motion, I release the seat belt and lean toward him. He puts his hands on each side of my face as we kiss.

We've been kissing a lot, but for the first time since his return, this kiss has heat behind it. All the thoughts I've had disappear in a furnace-blast of desire. His hands move under my shirt; his thumbs push under my bra, his fingers unclasping it from behind. I gasp. He looks at me, an unasked question, and I kiss him again. Flickering at the edge of this heat is a dim recognition of movement. I open my eyes and see that the car is rolling toward a tree at the edge of the road.

"Keet, put your foot on the brake!" I lean away from him, pulling down my shirt and reclasping my bra as he looks at me, eyes cloudy. Then his eyes clear and he smiles. I intend to give him a quick kiss, but once his lips are on mine, it turns into a long one. He moves his mouth to my cheek, then my neck, and says, "Kissing you is worth denting my car, Nolee."

I settle into my seat, running my hands over my face. Taking his hand in mine, I lean my head back, close my eyes, and smile.

After we share a quick dinner, Keet holds my hand as we walk through the twilight back to my cabin. The dogs trot ahead of us and wait on the porch; I let them inside, then turn back to Keet, his face soft and shadowed in the gray dimness.

He touches my face. "I'm taking a couple out to Patos so they can go camping. I'll be back in a couple of days."

"Sounds like a fun trip."

"I'd let Alex go, but the customers are regulars of mine."

"Will you be seeing your orca family?"

There's a pause, long enough that I wonder if he's going to answer me. When he does, his voice is soft; if I weren't standing close to him, I'd miss his answer.

"I hope so. I know they're north of here, but so are the Biggs." He takes a step closer to me, his hand tightening around mine. I was going to ask him why his family of fish-eating orcas and the mammal-eating Transients being in proximity was an issue, but instead, I move into the length and warmth of his body and touch his face. All the words evaporate when our lips meet.

After a kiss that was both too long and too short, I close the door, feeling my body tremble as I lean against it. The dogs watch me from their beds. "Big day tomorrow, dogs. Let's get some sleep."

After a long, hot bath and chamomile tea, I scoot into bed, nesting into the pillows and cracking open my latest novel. I know I won't finish it before I fall asleep. As my eyes begin to close, my phone pings with a text from Keet.

Still thinking of you. I'll text when I get back. Goodnight, Lia.

A flush of heat moves through my body as I text back.

I look forward to more of those kisses when you come home. Goodnight. Xo

It's past midnight when Keet sees the couple he'd sailed out to Patos crawl into their tent, freeing him to go back to his boat. After doublechecking the line to the mooring ball, Keet descends into the dark cabin, undresses, and goes back on deck. His skin bursts into goosebumps, but he doesn't shiver; the cold is a relief, a break from the sultry heat. Swinging a leg over the side, he lowers himself into the water and swims a dozen strokes beyond the inlet before diving, spinning, and changing to orca.

Rising through a tickling cascade of bubbles, he takes a rushed breath before diving deep enough to hear more clearly. The ocean is quieter at night, less disturbed by the artificial interference of human activity.

Keet feels the echo of a distant whale song vibrate in his head, but lets it fade, concentrating instead on the indistinct clicks and short whistling bursts north of him. He's found the mammal-eating pod he thinks the female comes from, but until he can get closer, he can't be sure. Even though they're the same species, the Transients' dialect and ways of thinking are foreign to him. He can get a picture of who they are from their heartbeats and shared experiences, but their signals are weaker than he's used to. Acclimating to a mammal-hunter's way of being is new to Keet, and—though he wonders why he's never tried it before—he knows the risk he's taking by swimming into their home territory.

A loud underwater bang interrupts his thoughts, followed by the head-jarring thrum of a container ship passing in the channel. Disoriented, Keet dives deeper, then surfaces, takes a breath, and raises his head above the water, waiting for the ship to leave the area before continuing his search. Circling the islands, he catches bits of Transient squeals, then feels them moving away, whether in pursuit of prey or to avoid meeting him, he can't tell.

Keet sounds, then clicks and whistles to announce his presence. Hearing only the distant bass rumble of the sea washing over the land, he catches and eats salmon under a night sky laced with moonlit streamer clouds and filled with the brightness of stars.

The sky is fading from black to gray when he returns to his anchored boat. He knows no more about the strange female and where she's from than he did before he went out. Casting a wary eye toward his clients' tent, he dives, spins, and is human once more. Swimming with sure strokes toward his boat, he wishes he was more convinced that the mysterious female orca was gone.

FIVE

It's the end of the afternoon before the deck of *The Salish See* is cleaned and her sails secured. Keet leaves the marina and drives home. He turns off the CD player, the sounds of the Spanish guitar not soothing him as he hoped they would. He thinks of Nolee—the press of her mouth against his, her body under his hands.

Turning onto the dirt road that leads him home, Keet realizes that in his rush to see her, he's forgotten to text. Making sure no one is behind him, he pulls over and stops.

Almost back. Would be great to see you if you want to come over.

He waits, watching for the three dots. After a few minutes, he pulls back onto the road, not willing to wait for a text when he could see Nolee that much sooner. Parking in his driveway, he switches off the motor, slams the door shut, and hears his phone chime. *I see you now. Be right over.*

He turns and sees Nolee coming toward him, her eyes locked on his, her hair lifting in the breeze, her breasts bouncing under her t-shirt. He only has time to take two steps before she reaches him.

We rush toward each other, closing the distance. He spins me around so that my back is against his car. He grips me against his chest, kissing me. I inhale his smell, his taste, his sounds. A new yet familiar yearning rises as his hand moves under my shirt.

"I need you in my bed," he says, his voice gravelly and low. This close to him, I can see the earth brown of his eyes, and his pupils, large and dark.

I know mine are the same, black pools outlined with small rings of green. I whisper "Yes," and he lifts me off my feet, carrying me across the deck, through the living room, and into his bedroom.

Our clothes disappear in a flurry, and he's kissing my belly. I sink my hands into his hair, not so gently pulling him up, but he resists. He goes lower, his mouth on my inner thighs, and then on me.

"Come here," I say after breathless moments, and he comes to me like a spring rain, mild at first, then pelting my skin with pleasure—like dawn's first light, gentle and soft, illuminating dark corners. His body is a wave crashing on the shore of my skin. Our limbs tangle together, our chests slick with sweat and tears. I touch his face and he touches mine—wiping away the tears, wiping away the past, wiping away the hurt. In its place is this communion of bodies, this melding of souls.

He rolls on his back, and I sit astride him, my hands braced on his ribs, my knees holding him in place as I once held a horse at a gallop. I lie against his chest, and our mouths meet once more, our rhythm synchronized, our hearts racing, our eyes open as we see each other anew.

The trees' shadows are long when I return to my cabin to let the dogs out. They bound down the beach, then, noses to the ground, investigate a new crop of smells. Propping open the cabin door, I walk back to Keet's house and return to his bed, where I'm lulled into semi-somnolence by his slow heartbeat against my ear.

The reverberation of his voice wakes me up.

"I have a question for you, Lia."

"Mmm?"

"When we first met, why didn't you get any impressions of me?"

"Of all the questions I was expecting, that wasn't one of them." I say.

"Give me a question you were expecting." He rolls onto me, and I sink into the bed in boneless surrender.

"What's for dinner?"

"You thought I'd ask about dinner after our first time together since I've come home?" His deep voice, so close to my ear, makes me squirm.

I struggle half-heartedly, and he leans down, kissing my neck and under my jaw as I gasp for breath, laughing.

"Or, 'when are you going to stop wearing my shirts?'" I laugh as he nibbles along my collarbone.

"Or, 'how are the dogs doing?'"

He stops kissing my shoulder and looks at me, his eyes bright and his cheeks flushed. "The dogs are the last thing on my mind." He leans in closer, his mouth warm and soft, stopping my laughter.

When we move apart, he props his head on one hand, the other on my belly. I feel suddenly exposed by his gaze, even more naked than I am.

"Go on now, Keet Noland."

"Go on where? I'm exactly where I want to be."

I pull the sheet up around my shoulders, mirroring his position, avoiding his eyes for as long as I can.

"What was your question again?"

He gives me a soft smile. "This is only pillow talk, Nolee. You don't have to answer me."

The tightness in my chest releases and I realize that, despite my acceptance of Keet back into my life, a small space inside me remains armored against the feelings I thought were safely chained but now clatter to be set free.

"Pillow talk." Lying down beside him, I rest my forehead against his shoulder. "I never thought we'd be here again."

He slides his arm underneath the pillow we share, wrapping it around my shoulders, embracing me as I twine my legs with his.

"I'd hoped we would be here again," he whispers, as though saying the words too loud would shatter us.

He rests his chin against the top of my head, and more memories of past times wash over me as I nuzzle into his neck.

"Ask me again, Keet."

"You get clear impressions of the dogs you meet. When you and I met, why didn't you know about me also being an orca? I thought for sure you'd figure it out after your kayak accident."

"I knew about you. But the knowledge came to me in dreams, remember?" He nods. "Besides, when we met, I was still ashamed of what I felt. I was hiding it." I move away so I can look at Keet, his shorn hair now longer, his brown eyes inviting.

"I guess that goes for both of us. I was ashamed of what I was, and I was hiding, too."

"I'm glad we don't need to hide anymore, Keet." Even as the words leave my mouth, I feel like a traitor for saying them, for justifying the armor to myself as protection.

He kisses me, brushing his fingers across my cheek. I hear a bark outside and break away. He smiles. "Go check on your dogs. I'll get up and throw something together for dinner."

I wiggle into my jeans and grab my shirt from the floor. "Be right back." When I turn, he's reaching for his clothes, and I leave his room smiling.

After feeding Wallace and Fae, they trot beside me back to Keet's house. He's on the deck, setting the table.

We talk over a dinner of vegetable minestrone, bread, and salad. Keet rests his foot against mine. As I gather our empty bowls and plates, he reaches up and touches my cheek. I lean down and kiss him, as natural as the tide that always returns to the land.

"What's your schedule like next week, Nolee?"

She looks up from her book, the hammock she's in swaying in the breeze. Feeling for her bookmark, she pats its faded striped material. Keet smiles, hearing her cursing under her breath. Seeing the missing book-mark on the ground, he picks it up and hands it to her. As he captures her hand and kisses it, he notices the store name, *Macdonald Book Shop*, and asks, "Where did you get that?"

"Colorado, when I was moving away from Texas. I made a detour after I'd heard about this cool bookstore, so I stopped to check it out."

"Everything you'd hoped?"

"And more," she smiles. "As far as next week, what are you thinking?"

"I'd like to show you something, but we need to sail out to an island to see it. At night."

"You sail at night?"

"Not usually, but it will take a day to get there."

"You're being mysterious." She smiles and moves to one side, patting the space next to her. He joins her, glad he'd had the foresight to get an extra-large hammock. "It's worth the wait, Lia." He rests his cheek against the top of her head. "Alex is out of town, and I don't have any tours sched-uled for the next week. I thought it would be a great time to introduce you to the surprise. What I'm going to show you only happens between now and September."

"Something that happens from July until September? I'm intrigued."

"Here's another clue: It's best when there've been a lot of sunny days."

"You're not going to tell me, are you?"

"What kind of surprise would it be if I did? Besides, we'll be sleeping together on my boat."

"In that case, let me check my schedule at the shelter." Sitting up, then positioning herself so she's straddling his thighs, she pulls out her cell phone and composes a text. Keet puts his hands on her hips and closes his eyes, relishing the warm air, the sway of the hammock, the weight of Nolee anchoring him between land and air.

"Done. Andi says she's blocked off Monday through Thursday next week. I'll work this weekend…" She trails off, looking at the dogs lying in the shade.

"Do we take the dogs?"

"We can. I'd planned to be on the water, but we can rework the schedule."

"Wallace hasn't been on your boat yet. And Fae just that once, last year."

"I'm going to leave that decision up to you. We would need to prep the boat on Monday and sail out Tuesday morning."

Nolee, phone still in hand, starts tapping her thumbs against the screen again.

"A big trip like that is probably not the best way to introduce the dogs to sailing. I'll ask Andi if she can stay with them."

"Good idea." Keet traces her body's curves, running his hands along her hips and around her back.

"You keep doing that and I won't ever finish this text," she says. She leans down, takes his lower lip between her teeth, then releases it and kisses him. He forgets to breathe until she sits up again, her skin flushed pink. Her phone pings and she looks at it, smiling.

"Andi can stay Monday night through Thursday morning."

Keet looks up at her, squinting in the dappled sunlight that reaches through the pines. "In that case, let's stay the night at the marina on *The Salish See*, and head out early on Tuesday."

As he pushes himself into sitting position, the hammock teeters, then tips and dumps them on the ground in a heap of laughter and tangled limbs. Fae joins them, licking faces and hands, and Wallace stands watching, his tail low but the tip wagging. Pushing Fae away, Keet holds out a hand toward him, low to the ground and open palm up, as Nolee told him. Wallace's nose twitches, then he turns and walks away, glancing back with narrowed eyes.

"I swear, the final two hours before a vacation lasts two years!" It's a quiet Sunday afternoon, the volunteers having left before lunch.

Andi looks up from her computer screen, smiling. "You and Keet getting along, Nolee?" She winks.

Heat suffuses my face and I'm unable to come up with a snappy reply.

Andi grins. "I'm happy for you, and happy to watch Wallace and Fae."

Wallace thumps his tail against the cabinets by Andi's chair.

"Really, I'm about ten kinds of amazed at how well Keet and I are doing. In some ways, I wish this had been the way we started."

She nods. "I get that. Maybe you both had to go through everything you did to get where you are now."

"True." Although I've shared most of what happened between Keet and me, I've left out the elephant in the room: Keet's orca identity. Keet and I have never discussed his comfort level with others knowing this, and I like being the only one who knows. The weight of this secret wraps me into itself, comforting rather than stifling. Who he is, and who we are together, is precious to me. Perhaps, the intimacy of that secret has been transformed from an unbearable weight to a welcome knowledge. Perhaps, in the first flush of falling for him again, everything is technicolor. Perhaps, once the alchemy we currently share wears off, the gold of our relationship will revert to lead.

I brush off my worries about how Keet and I will—or won't—grow together, then tell Andi that I'm going to take Wallace and Fae out into the yard with me while I clean it one more time.

She nods. "When you're done, let's go over their schedules again."

The hours pass in slow motion. I move around the shelter greeting dogs, playing with kittens, cleaning litter boxes. When I allow myself to glance at the clock, I'm relieved to see that I've whittled down the time to fifteen minutes. After doublechecking my dog-care notes, I give them to Andi. Fae and Wallace walk beside me to the car, then jump in and sit by its open windows, panting. Returning to the office, I bounce to the time clock to punch out, then turn to Andi, who's standing by her desk, purse slung over one shoulder.

"Thank you, Andi. You're a lifesaver."

She hugs me. "It's no trouble. Though I'm glad Wallace and I get along. Otherwise, it might've gotten tricky."

"He remembers you—plus, he likes the way you smell."

She laughs. "I suppose, coming from a dog, that's a compliment."

When our conversation stalls, she gives me a good-natured push and says, "I'll see you tomorrow, Nolee. Go home and start planning the trip with that man of yours."

Monday passes in a flurry of errands. They shop for groceries, prepare and pack the boat, run back to the cabin for Nolee's cell phone charger, then grab take-out from a local restaurant. Keet pulls a large duffel from the back of his 4Runner and hands it to Nolee.

"It's strange to be without my dogs. I feel like I'm forgetting something."

He picks up two smaller duffel bags—his is black, hers red—and follows her down the dock. "Does it feel the same as when you first moved here, before Fae found you?"

She sets the duffel at the stern and steps in the boat. "It does. A little stranger, though, because by the time I'd moved here, Luna had been gone for more than six months. I was in such a bad way by that time, it felt like just one more horrible thing I had to get through. The most horrible."

He steps into the boat and holds her close until she steps away. "Didn't you say you need to give Trish the trip details?" He nods, then leans down to give her a lingering kiss. He hears her sigh, feels her fingers in his hair. When he straightens, she still has her eyes closed.

"Why don't you take care of that, and I'll get the bed made and put away the food." She looks at him, her eyes bright.

After talking to Trish, he goes back to his boat, where he sees Nolee coming up from below.

"All set?" she says.

"We are. I just realized you and Trish have already met each other."

"I don't think we're each other's biggest fans." She folds a paper bag, crushing it against her chest. "She seems protective of you, like she's your mom, and I'm the unacceptable girlfriend, stealing you away." Her smile is a hard line across her usually soft face.

"It was just her and me for a lot of years. She's always kept a steady hand on the business side of things."

"I get that. And really, I don't need to be her friend."

Keet, though uneducated in the complexities of female friendships, has a sense of what Nolee means when she says that Trish acts like an overprotective mother. Perhaps he's been indulging Trish, treating her more like a mother than an employee? He shuffles that concern to the back of his mind as he runs his thumb across the stainless-steel rail in front of him. When he looks up, he smiles at Nolee. "You're right. And now, it's time for me to treat you to your first dinner on a sailboat."

I watch as Keet bags up our trash and sets it on the stairs leading up to the deck. He turns, folds himself into the seat on the other side of the small table, and takes my hand.

"So far, so good?" he asks.

"So far, so great!" I look around the cabin: the two-burner cooktop, the small door that leads to a smaller bathroom (the head, Keet says), and the open door behind us where I'd made the bed with new blue sheets and a comforter covered with a matching plush cotton duvet. A sudden blast of fatigue hits me.

"I think I'll need to get to sleep soon, Keet. Are we done for the night?"

He stands and raises me up, wrapping his arms around me. I lay my head against his chest, enveloping myself in his heartbeat and the warmth of his body. Above us, I hear a faint knocking. "What's that sound?" I ask.

"That's the halyard hitting against the mast."

The whisper and hiss of the waves against the boat nudge me toward sleep even as I'm standing.

"Let's get to bed, Lia. It's been a busy day, and I'd like to get an early start tomorrow."

Drifting up from sleep, I feel the boat's gentle rock and sway. Squinting, I look through the small round window and see that the night is beginning to lighten around the rim of the sky; morning is on its way. I close my eyes, turn toward Keet, and drift back to sleep.

When I open my eyes again, the light has changed, outlining every shape in pale hues. Keet leans over me, kissing me awake.

"Time to wake up, Lia," he murmurs.

I bring him closer. Our kiss deepens, and I feel his touch on my breast, my face. Then he rubs his nose against mine, kisses me again, and pulls away. "We'll continue this once we get where we're going."

"Promise?"

With a low laugh, he kisses my breast. "Promise."

SIX

An early morning breeze pushes *The Salish See* through the channel. Keet glances at a laminated chart, then puts both hands back on the helm.

"I think Patos might be too busy for us to find a mooring buoy," he says. Nolee, sitting next to him, watches as he steers where the tide guides him.

She gives his thigh a nudge. "The big surprise doesn't depend on the island?"

He shakes his head. "Not so much. We'll chart our course to Matia; it has a private cove. We also have a stern anchor, just in case."

"One anchor isn't enough?"

Keet corrects their course starboard, and the shudder in the helm diminishes as the boat finds her place in the current.

"One anchor is usually enough, but a stern anchor is useful when the wind and the swell don't line up. A stern anchor will hold the bow to rollers. That's what we want if we plan on a good night's sleep."

"That means …"

"We want to keep the front of the boat in the current, so the side-to-side motion is minimized. The bay I'm thinking of for us is small enough that there shouldn't be too much change in the current."

"That makes sense. We don't want to get bucked off our bed. Especially not tonight."

Keet watches Nolee as she leans closer to him, her pupils dilated and her breathing shallow. He pauses, his lips millimeters from hers, the warmth of her face blending with his. Laying his hand on her thigh, he feels his own breath catch. Their lips meet as the boat rises on a large swell.

I watch Keet check the stern anchor line.

"Why's your anchor line tied in two places, Keet?"

"My grandfather taught me that you always tie off the bitter end."

When I laugh, Keet looks at me, puzzled.

"Do you mean 'tie off *to* the bitter end'?"

It's Keet's turn to laugh. "The bitter end is the end of the line. You don't want to see that disappear into the water."

"Why's that?"

"Because it means you've lost your anchor."

I'm sure there's a metaphor in there somewhere, something about being cast adrift. I'm so dazzled by our trip that I can't dredge anything up.

Keet tests the line's tension before turning around and sitting next to me. I open the cooler and take out the sandwiches we made for lunch.

"The bitter end—or as it was called by sailors, the *bitt* end—is the end of the anchor line fixed to the ship's deck. They used to mark it with colored rags."

"You're talking in the early days of sailing."

"It has a lengthy history. Want to know more?" He leans over and kisses me on the cheek. When he speaks again, his voice is low against my ear.

"When the sailors lowering the anchor saw the rags on the bitter end, they knew there was no line left; the water was too deep to set anchor. To tie off the bitter end requires going to the last few yards of the anchor line."

As this information registers somewhere deep my brain, I turn my head and lean toward Keet. When our mouths meet, I almost drop the sandwiches I'm holding. He feels the shock too, catching my hands in his, laughing as he draws away.

"We could call this an early dinner," he says.

"And go to bed after?"

He pulls me toward him as he nods, meeting my mouth with his.

Once below deck, Keet turns to Lia and begins undressing her, until her skin, still warm from the sun, presses against the length of his body. He moves his hands from her face to her breasts, running his thumb over her nipples, following with his mouth. As he kisses the soft roundness of her belly, tracing the cesarean scar with his tongue, he hooks her panties around his fingers and draws them down. The boat rocks on the current. In the distance, he hears the loud chatter of people camped close by.

They make their way toward the bed as Nolee pulls his t-shirt off and unbuttons his shorts. Keet feels the edge of the bed against the back of his thighs. He sits and in the same motion, Nolee straddles his lap. Their voices echo down into the hull until Keet feels himself as only sound, dropping through the water, anchoring them to one another.

Keet wraps his arms around her shoulders, feels the strength of her thighs as she crosses her legs behind his back. She pulls him closer and as he moves, a million starbursts flash behind his eyes, a sky filled with diamonds. A universe that contains only her.

As they doze together, he feels her move behind him, cradling him as the boat cradles them both. The air is still, and the light is dim as he rolls over to face her, then takes his time kissing her.

"Why didn't you tell me sailboat sex was so amazing?" she asks as she pulls the sheet over them.

"It's something you have to discover for yourself, Lia." He feels her settling into him, one leg draped over his, their hands woven together.

"You may regret showing me." Her voice is muffled against his shoulder.

He squeezes her hand. "Never."

Outside, the sounds of the campers near their anchorage—laughter from the adults, squeals from children playing on the small beach—come to them on the evening breeze.

"When does the surprise happen?"

"After sunset. But not tonight."

"Why is that?"

"Too many people."

"Is the surprise shy?"

Keet smiles, runs his fingers across Nolee's belly, and feels her shiver. "Not at all."

"Is the surprise secretive?"

"Maybe. Locals know, but we don't talk about it much."

"I give up," she laughs. "It'll be tomorrow night before my curiosity is satisfied?"

"Correct. Tonight, we stay in the cabin, cook some dinner, and hang out. Tomorrow, we can kayak to the island. There's a great trail through the woods if you want to hike?"

"I'd like that." She's quiet for so long Keet thinks she's dozed off again. He's drifting toward sleep when his stomach growls; seeing that he's still awake, Nolee asks, "Can you show me how to take a shower on this thing?"

"Only if I can join you," Keet says.

After their shower, they dine on salad and lasagna. As they wash the dishes, they hear a piercing scream. Nolee walks toward the stairs, but Keet reaches out, wrapping his hand around her upper arm, stopping her.

"Don't you want to make sure that whoever screamed like bloody murder is all right?" Concern wrinkles her brow, and she leans away from him, still meaning to go up on deck.

"They're fine. Just having fun. I'll check and make sure."

"I'll go with you."

He wraps her in a hug. "Then the surprise won't be a surprise anymore."

He feels the tension leave her shoulders. She steps away and nods. "Make sure someone didn't just come close to drowning near our boat."

He jogs up the stairs, looking port side. Two teenagers in a double kayak are splashing their paddles in the water. Back into the cabin, he reports to Nolee. "All's well. Just two kids in a kayak."

"Why were they shrieking like that?"

"Having fun, I would guess. You're the one who raised a teenager. Didn't Abbie ever shriek?"

Nolee's face softens. "She did. I guess it makes sense. It's summer and they don't have to go to bed or do homework." She yawns, covering her mouth with her hand. "I, however, *do* need to go to bed."

"Go ahead. I'll finish cleaning up."

The next morning, they eat their breakfast on deck. Keet looks around, seeing boats passing by the mouth of the cove.

"If no one else comes in, I think I can show you your surprise tonight."

Nolee wipes her mouth with her napkin. "I hope so. Otherwise, I'll think you got me on your boat under false pretenses." He reaches over and brushes a crumb away from the corner of her mouth.

"Is that such a bad thing?"

"No. I don't care what pretenses you used. This has been amazing, Keet."

"You're amazing, Nolee. Sailing is better with you here."

"I think we need to spend more time sailing together, then." She looks up at him, touches his face, smiles.

"Are you ready to kayak and take a small hike?"

"Let's go! We're burnin' daylight, as my father used to say."

They start gathering the dishes, then Keet says, "Let's do these when we get back."

"Anything to help the time pass. I feel like a kid waiting for the Fourth of July fireworks!"

Keet wonders if she's guessed her surprise, but she seems unaware of what she had just said.

After pulling their kayak up onto the beach, they walk along the trail, and Keet feels the silence filter through the trees like sunlight. He motions left when Nolee looks back at him, and they walk at a steady pace, not talking. He admires the sturdy set of her shoulders, the way the dappled sunlight catches the silver in her hair, her clear voice as she sings the parts of songs she knows.

As they walk around a curve in the trail, Keet sees the dock, which now has a boat tied to it; he hopes the owners leave before nightfall. Otherwise, the mooring buoys are empty, the picnic tables are vacant, and only the sounds of moving water can be heard.

"Looks like we might have the island to ourselves tonight, Keet."

"That's what I'm hoping for, too." He jogs up behind her. She turns at the last minute, laughing as he sweeps her off the ground, twirling her in a circle.

The sunset sky is streaked with gold, orange, and fuchsia when the boat Keet saw earlier speeds past the cove. Nolee, sitting between his outstretched legs, leans back and sighs.

"Ready for dinner, Lia?"

"You mind reader. I was just thinking about that. How much longer until surprise time?"

He turns his head, checking the sun. "It'll be best in a couple of hours."

"Let's have a leisurely dinner, then. And maybe a nap. This sailboat life is so relaxing—I feel like I could sleep forever!"

Kissing the top of her head, he squeezes her close to him, then stands. Adjusting to the rocking of the boat, he takes her hand and helps her up. She says, "Come here, you," and bringing his mouth to hers, kisses him.

After they eat, he cleans up the remains of their dinner as she washes their plates and silverware, drying them and putting them back in their places.

"I could get used to this kind of minimalist existence, Keet."

"Why's that?"

"It shows me how little we actually need, and how much stuff we hold on to."

"That's why I enjoy staying aboard a sailboat from time to time. Life gets simpler."

"I miss the dogs, though."

"Nothing saying we couldn't bring them along."

She smiles. "It would be something to work toward."

He nods, dries his hands. "I'm going to lie down for a bit. Want to join me?"

"Lead the way."

He closes the curtains on the small window and lies down, patting the bed next to him. After she's made herself comfortable beside him, he closes his eyes and sinks into sleep.

It seems only seconds later that he hears his name. When he opens his eyes, the cabin is dark. The water laps at the hull and outside, there's silence.

"Keet, wake up. I've waited long enough!" She nudges his shoulder.

"I'm awake." He runs a hand over his face. "Ground rules. Change into your wetsuit in here. After that, your eyes stay closed. I'll lead you to the back of the boat, and you sit at the stern. Okay so far?"

"Yes, sweetheart. Then what?"

"Then I'll dive in. When you hear me surface and take a breath as orca, you can open your eyes."

"The surprise is you?"

"Much better." As he pushes her out of bed, she laughs, then turns around and takes both of his hands, hauling him out with her.

"Get a move on, mister. I've been patient enough."

After leading Nolee to the back of the boat, Keet dives into the cold sea and feels its eager fingers embrace him. Kicking deeper, he uses his momentum to spin, feeling the familiar sensation of being pulled in two directions. The next moment, he sends out a series of clicks and a picture of the sea floor appears behind his eyes—rocky crevices and stretches of smooth sand. The anchor is lodged against a large barnacle-encrusted rock. He flips, his flukes and tail acting in synchrony to bring him to the surface, where he feels Lia waiting. As his rostrum rises from the water, he can see her, hands over her eyes. Floating to the surface, he feels the cool water clear his blow hole and exhales. Taking another deep breath, he waits.

I'm sitting at the stern, hands over my eyes and legs dangling when I hear the splash as Keet dives, then an explosion of air when he surfaces. This is my cue. When I take my hands away from my eyes, I see the shimmering length of his body outlined in electric blue and undulating green. He dives, doubles back toward the boat, then surfaces again. With each flick of his pectorals and tail, he splashes a cerulean stream through the black water. He dives deeper the next time, and I see the outline of his form begin to fade before he flips his belly to the sky and drifts upward. When he arcs out of the sea, blue water like blown glass sprays from his body. I sit, enchanted, watching this psychedelic orca acrobatic show that contains flashing blue sparks, like water made into fire. I'd read about bioluminescence, but had no idea I'd ever get to see it. Yet here I am, sitting on Keet's sailboat on a summer night, getting ready to swim in water that looks like deep space.

Taking a deep breath, I pull on my mask and snorkel, bracing myself for water that Keet told me would be at its warmest: fifty-three degrees. I slip into the water, holding my breath until I clear the snorkel. I swim toward Keet as orca, watching my hands. It's as though I'm finger painting in blazes of azure across a black canvas.

Kicking closer to Keet, I reach for his dorsal fin, gasping as he does a quick turn and speeds out of the cove. The water curls away from us, flashing like fireworks in shades of ultramarine, sapphire, and indigo. His body becomes a mesmerizing light show, and I watch our passage through my mask, losing track of where we are. The islands disappear. The moonless sky and its millions of points of light are mirrored in the water that sparkles around us. My attention shrinks to the distant sensations of my cold body and the feel of Keet's warm dorsal fin. I lift my mask and snorkel and look at the world around me. We're swimming in liquid light, clear and cold as space, warm and alive as the orca who swims through an oceanic galaxy of stars.

Returning home the next day, Nolee points out to Keet that June's green forest undergrowth has yellowed in the late-July heat. Nolee kisses him before they're surrounded by Fae and Wallace's wriggling bodies, Fae whining and panting.

"You'd think we'd been gone for years, instead of days," Keet says.

"They're pack animals. They like it when everyone is together." Nolee asks the dogs to sit before she gives his arm a squeeze. "I'm going to unpack. See you later?"

"Absolutely."

Through the window, Keet watches Nolee talking on her phone as she throws a ball for the dogs. He's startled from his reverie by the trilling of his cell phone. When he looks at the screen, he sees it's his grandmother and answers with a smile that quickly fades. He listens, answering when he's supposed to, but in the back of his mind, he's churning through options for the situation his grandmother is describing.

"Let me think about this, Grandmother. I'll call you back in a couple of days." Ending the call, he hears Nolee's footsteps on the porch but can't stop staring at the cell phone in his hand.

"Everything okay?" she asks, standing in front of him in her cropped jeans, a t-shirt with a dirty paw print, and dried dog slobber on one leg. "What's going on?"

"My grandmother just called."

"Is she alright?"

"Yes."

In the long silence that follows, Nolee tries to wait him out. Eventually, she gives up.

"And?" she says.

"And she wants to move here, to be close to me. My uncle got a job in Juneau, and she doesn't want to go with him."

"So, what's the problem?"

He gives her a sharp glance. "You don't know her."

"I don't, but I'd like to. Do you not want her living with you?"

"I have plenty of room, but that's part of it, yes."

"Does she need a lot of care?"

He gives a sudden but humorless laugh. "No…"

"What is it, then?"

Keet leans against the counter, his arms crossed.

"Uh-oh," Nolee says. "This must be serious. I rarely see you with your guard up."

He gives her another squinty-eyed glance, thinking about what he wants to say.

"Let's just say my grandmother is formidable."

"I guessed that from what you've told me about your time with her."

He uncrosses his arms. "She's in her eighties. Being older has mellowed her a little. She tends to…" He rubs his hand across his jaw. "She's an Elder, Lia, and I have a duty to respect her point of view."

"Does that mean you have to do everything she says?"

"Not exactly, but it means I have to listen to everything she says, and she has a lot to say. Some conversations take days."

"Well, at eighty-something years old, I suspect she's seen a lot. It would take days just to hear it all."

"It's not that she talks a lot. Everything has a point—she doesn't waste or mince words. But sometimes she … what is it you say? Takes the long way around the barn?"

Nolee laughs and nods.

He shoves his hands into his pockets. "Her views are from her own life, as well as from the lives of her mother and grandmother, and the lives of a long line of women before that. She's a walking encyclopedia. Speaks Keykwin, Tlingit, and English; knows Alaskan geography inside and out; and makes a mean halibut stew."

"She sounds amazing. It's understandable that you'd feel intimidated by her."

He looks at her in surprise, his dark brows raising.

"I'm not intimidated by my own grandmother!"

Nolee smiles and pats his arm. "Okay."

"I'm not … much." He laughs. "Though I feel about twelve years old when she's around."

"I think that's a common experience when we're around our parents or grandparents."

"You've never said much about your family, aside from the Scottish farrier who was your great-grandmother's lover; your two brothers, Frank and Maney; and your sister Lily, who got the best middle name."

"Okay, Mr. Deflection, we'll talk about my family. I'm impressed you remember all that."

He smiles and gives her a brief kiss. "Do you want tea? A walk with the dogs?"

"The dogs! Oh my god, I forgot!" Turning, she trots out to the beach, and he follows. They're still running through the water, chasing a tree branch too big for them to bring to shore.

"How about tea and a walk? That way I can keep an eye on the dogs. It's been a while since we've seen the female orca, but I don't want to leave them unsupervised."

Nolee and Keet walk on the beach, sipping tea, backs to the midday sun.

"So where are your mom and dad now, Lia?"

"Mom died five years ago of a heart attack, and my father's in an Alzheimer's care facility in Odessa. My brothers and sister see him a lot, but he's confined to bed these days. We didn't get along when I was a child. My siblings thought he hung the moon, but then, they took over the ranch. That's the life they prefer, and more power to them. I've never had much in common with any of them, except my mom."

Keet stops and pulls her against him. She takes a deep breath and looks up, giving him a wavering smile.

"I was close with her. She and I were a lot alike. We both were voracious readers and preferred our own company, or the company of animals."

"Do you look like her, or your dad?"

Her smile is stronger this time. "My hair and eyes are from her side. But the rest is my dad. He's tall, but I'm short like my mom. My brothers and sister got their height from my dad's side."

They resume walking, dodging a pile of tangled kelp. Keet says, "I think you're the perfect height."

"I've made my peace with it. I wanted to be a ballerina. I didn't have the long legs."

He stops, sets down his mug, and motions for her to do the same. Then he lifts her as though she didn't weigh more than the mug he was carrying. She wraps her legs around his torso, her head thrown back in laughter.

"Your legs are perfect, too." He kisses her, the sounds of the sea in their ears and the sun shining on their heads.

When he puts her back on the ground, they pick up their mugs and turn to go to the house.

The dogs run to them, the ball dripping with water and drool. Fae flings it at Nolee's feet, but Keet picks it up. "Can I try?"

"Sure."

Wallace and Fae back away as Keet aims the ball down the beach, then take off like twin bullets after it.

"Wallace doesn't seem to be as worried about me," Keet says, watching the dogs race away in a spray of rocks and wet sand.

"He'll figure you out. Maybe if you spent more time at my place? Or I could bring him to your house more often. That might help."

Keet stops in his tracks as an idea takes shape. Nolee walks a couple of paces in front of him, head turned, watching the waves.

"I think I saw the seal again ..." She stops, notices that Keet isn't beside her, and turns around. "What is it?"

"Nolee, I have an idea. Before you give me an answer, I want you to know there's no pressure."

"Okay. No pressure. What's your idea?" She glances at the wet ball at her feet, two sets of eyes darting between her and it. She looks at the dogs and says, "Wait." Fae drops into the rocks, tucking a dainty, wet paw under her chest. Wallace sits in slow motion.

"What if you moved in with me?"

Two opposing feelings fight in the ring of my heart. One is fear, the other, elation. Keet's "what if" question has sent me into a tailspin the likes of which I haven't felt since finding out about Nathan's affair. He must see this, because he stays where he is, even when Wallace makes his cautious way over to him, dropping the ball not quite at his feet, but within easy reach.

"You don't have to answer right now." I see the nervousness run across Keet's face, as though he'd like to swallow the question he just asked. But the light in his eyes is stronger.

I clear my throat. "Throw that ball for the dogs, would you?" Turning toward the sea, I hear them scrabbling through the rocks, a sound that gradually fades away. Keet must have thrown it as hard as he could. Good thing it didn't go in the water; even Wallace might not swim that far.

Keet stands beside me. We're not touching, but I can feel the warmth of his body. I take a breath, thinking, *What if, Nolee? Hell, you're almost living together now. This past month, you've barely been in your own cabin. It's a place to store your stuff.* Here's another edge, I realize, another chance to free fall instead of trying to keep life clenched in my fists.

"I still haven't seen all of your house," I look over my shoulder at him, seeing his gaze soften.

"Why don't we go back, and I'll show you around?"

I nod. "No promises on an answer. I might need to sleep on it. Can I ask why you're thinking about this?" I look up at him, squinting into the sun. He moves to block the glare, then reaches out a hand to hold mine. I feel trembling, but I don't know if it's me or him.

"Your lease is up at the end of July, right?" I nod. He continues, "That's next week, by the way."

"I've lost track of time. I thought we were still in the middle of July."

"If you move in with me—which I've been thinking about for a while, Nolee, but it seems like the right time to ask—" he pauses again, and I focus on taking slow breaths. "If you move in with me, we could move my grandmother into the cabin."

"Wait." My hand tightens around his. "You want to move your grandmother here, and my cabin is up for grabs?"

"No, that's not what I said …"

I let go of his hand and grab the ball. "That's it dogs, we're done." Throwing me disappointed looks, they trot to the cabin. "What *are* you saying?"

"I'm telling you—badly, it seems—that I've been thinking about asking you to move in since we got together last year." I interrupt him, but he raises a hand. "Just a sec, Nolee. I need to say this."

I nod, quick and curt. Behind my anger, or maybe within it, I feel the beginning of something like hope. What is it that Emily Dickinson said? *Hope is the thing with feathers that perches in the soul.* The words wrap around me, banking down the burn of my anger.

Keet waits.

"Please, keep talking," I say.

"I didn't ask you last year because of everything that happened. At one point, it was too early in our relationship. By the time I felt I could ask, I had been captured. We know what happened after that."

In the silence between us, the warm breeze and cool waves comfort me; they would be here long after Keet and I were gone. To nature, Keet's terrifying offer is a nanosecond, its scale as small as a water droplet to the thundercloud that holds it. I look out into the cove. The water is flat, no dorsal fins or shiny seal heads. No otter flipping her watery tail as she dives.

Keet's next words tumble out in a rush. "I'm asking now because I'd like to share a life with you. Which we're already doing, I don't deny that. We could have two homes if you want—I'm not saying move in with me or we're over." He steps closer to me. "I'm in love with you, Lia, and I'd like it if the house I live in could be home for both of us."

"Keet …" I blow out a breath, speechless. When I look up at him, I see that his gaze is focused on the channel, and the boats speeding across it. I wait for him to bring his gaze back to me. When he does, the words come out: "I'm in love with you, too." I realize that I've whispered them, as though my voice would scare this fledging emotion away.

His smile shifts from nervous to gentle as he takes my hand in his. He leans down to kiss me and my heart unfurls its wings, the feathers catching an updraft that lifts me away from rage to a sunlit world waiting to be explored.

SEVEN

"I still need to sleep on it," I say, once we move apart.

"Of course. Nothing changes between us, whatever your decision is."

We walk back to his house, Keet holding the two empty mugs in one hand and my hand in the other. I'll sleep on the idea, but I'm already thinking about how my stuff will fit with his. I smile.

"Something funny?" He asks.

"I'm happy right now, sweetheart. Just happy."

His own happiness shows in the tilt of his head and the light in his smile.

Once inside, I stand in the living room, turning, looking out the picture windows on either side of the fireplace. I hear him set the mugs in the sink.

"Want to see the rest of the house? Or," he pauses, "did you look around while I was gone?"

I turn back to him, my attention drawn to the tightness in his voice.

"I wouldn't look around while you were gone, Keet, much less poke around. Even my nosiness has limits."

"Let me show you then."

We pass spaces I'm already familiar with: living room on the right, dining room and kitchen on the left. He stops at a distressed wooden farm door just past the living room and slides it open.

"Laundry and pantry."

Windows on the far side light the room, with its bare but clean shelves; vacuum, mop, and broom; and a pile of black clothes in front of a washer/dryer combo. The opposite wall is broken by a wooden door.

"Where does that go?"

"Outside. I thought …"

"You thought what?"

"No pressure. I'll tell you another time."

"How about you tell me now? Otherwise, I'll be awake half the night obsessing over the mystery of that door."

He laughs. "I thought that if you moved in, we could fence in part of the yard on the other side of this door for the dogs. We could also use this space as kind of a mud room to clean them up." He casts a quick glance at me, his face relaxing when he sees I'm smiling.

"That's a good thought."

We walk out of the utility room and down the hall. "You know about the bedroom," he points to his right.

"I like the bedroom."

"And the bathroom." I nod.

He turns to his left and slides open another farm door, then reaches for a light switch.

When the light comes on, I stop in the hallway beside him, leaning in to see an empty, pale-yellow room. Dusty floral curtains frame the large window that faces the forest at the back of the house. Spider webs adorn the corners.

"I thought this could be whatever you wanted."

"What did this room used to be? Those curtains are as out of place as a snake in a snowdrift."

He laughs. "Sascha picked them out after we were first engaged. I haven't taken them down because I never come in here. They need to be thrown away."

"Agreed. Where does that door go?" I point at the door next to the empty room.

"That's a second bathroom. It's between another room there, just down the hall."

"Could that be an office?" I ask.

"Sure."

"I've sometimes wondered why you live in such a big house."

"Well," he says, running his hand through his hair, "life gets away from us sometimes, doesn't it? Some things change, and other things don't. Or they change too much, and then you're wandering around a big space alone, wondering how you got there. Life was one whiplash after another. Until I met you."

I take his hand, holding it between both of mine. "I can't say there won't be whiplashes now and again. But I *can* say that I'll always be honest with you. And right now, honestly, I want to say yes to moving in together—"

Before I can finish, he sweeps me off my feet and twirls me around. By the time he sets me down, we're both laughing.

"Are you sure? One hundred percent? Because I mean it when I say take your time. We'll find another option for my grandmother."

"Keet, we're both in our fifties. Unless you tell me that Keykwin are immortal, neither of us is getting younger. I might've played coy ten years ago, but we don't have the luxury of time anymore. I want all the happiness I can give ... and get. If that means we move in together tomorrow, then I'm all for it.

"I'm not one hundred percent sure of anything, but I *am* sure of you, and of us. Besides, you had me at 'backyard for the dogs.'"

He laughs and kisses my shoulder. "I'm not immortal, or bullet proof."

I step away. "Good. I'd fret if I knew you'd go on living, and I couldn't. Besides, where else am I going to be able to swim with not just one orca, but a whole pod?"

He kisses my temple, then my earlobe and along my jaw.

He strokes my face with his finger, looking into my eyes. "You're good for me."

"What makes you say that?"

"Because you remind me of something I used to feel about being Keykwin. You remind me of the joy of it. I spent so long feeling tortured that I forgot what a gift it can be."

Hearing a distant bark, I pat my back pockets and realize I must've left my cell phone on my kitchen table. "What time is it?"

"It's almost five o'clock."

"Which means it's almost dinner time for Fae and Wallace. Oh! Keet, if we do this, you'll have dogs in your house."

He laughs, "And?"

"And that means slobber and dog bowls and dog food in your refrigerator and dog food in your pantry, and dog hair, and walking dogs—"

"Lia!" he interrupts me. "It's all okay. I wouldn't have asked you if I wasn't ready to welcome your dogs into my life. It's our home now, as much yours as mine."

Another thought occurs to me. "I have one rule about dogs in the house, Keet."

"What's that?"

"They don't sleep with us. They have cushy beds of their own."

"I agree. When we're in our bed, I want you all to myself."

"Same here, sweetheart. Besides, I can't abide a hairy bed."

As we head out the door, another thought occurs to me. "There's something I want to do tonight."

"What's that?"

"I want to sleep in the cabin one more time—I love that space. You're welcome to stay with me."

"I need to go check on my orca pod. I'll join you when I come back. Tell Wallace not to take my head off."

"Text me before you come over and I'll meet you at the door. I can't make any promises for Wallace."

"I won't be too late."

"Doesn't matter. Take your time."

Keet once again lifts me off my feet, this time with restraint, and holds me close. I close my eyes, breathing in his scent, calming my nerves. After lowering me to the ground, he asks, "Can I try feeding Wallace before I swim out?"

It's an evening when fog and sea melt together. The sky drops into the water, the sea reaches up into the clouds, and the orca pod swims in this numinous, liminal space, a panorama of gray and white. Islands and waves and sea birds float above the black dorsal fins.

Keet and his pod are on a long swim, breathing together before diving and sounding for salmon. His family's bellies are almost empty, and he can't hear any traces of the fish they need to survive. He turns east, singing his intentions to Nana, listening for her decision. In slow motion, she surfaces and hangs on the darkening waves, then turns her body east as well. The rest of the pod fans out behind her, clicking, listening, watching. Finally, they hear salmon, ahead and deep below. Keet stays with Nana and George, while his mother, Atma, and Poppy and Belle dive to herd the fish toward the surface. He hears his family's whistles and high calls as they turn as one, sending out clicks to find the fish.

The sound begins as a hum in the distance, then escalates to a low rumble that interrupts the pod's feeding. Their calls change as they try to make themselves heard above the din, try to stay connected. The rumble turns to thunder, and a high-pitched whine from the rotors of the intruding ship obliterates the orcas' sense of direction. Their cries become more strident, a continuous chain of sound, slowing only when they're able to swim away from the noise, away from the meal they were about to catch.

The ship's whine and rumble have rattled their inner ears, and they lift their heads above water to take a breath and ease the effects of the noise. They come together, rising and breathing, sinking and swimming, moving away. When they've gone far, the orca pod circles in place, touching each other; their sounds are softer, interspersed with a zipper of clicks as they resume the hunt for the salmon they need. The sharp twist of hunger grows more insistent as they circle and dive, sounding for the vanished fish.

It begins to rain, the drops hitting the water with a gentle hiss. In the distance, they hear the hum of another boat in the strait. There's no room for silence here, or for the orca and their needs for family and food.

The lowering clouds and pewter sea hold each other in a watery embrace, and the inky silhouettes of sea birds dive and fly within the fog. But of the black dorsal fins, there isn't a sign.

A volley of deep barks wakes me up from a sound sleep, and I hear Fae's whine and the sound of her paws as she trots back and forth.

"Nolee?" It's Keet, yelling outside the open front door.

Rubbing my eyes, I get out of bed and switch on the bedside lamp. It's almost three in the morning.

"Stay where you are, Keet. I'll be right there," I yell. Still half asleep, I go downstairs, holding on to the railing for balance, willing my eyes to open. When they do, I see Wallace standing in front of the open door, where Keet stands still, his eyes on me.

"Wallace?" His head snaps around but doesn't leave his position. I see Keet in the dim light that means sunrise isn't far away.

"Wallace," I say again, this time softer. He whines. "Here." He gives me a dubious glance but turns and trots to me. Fae, back on her bed, curls up and watches. I don't touch Wallace, but instead, breathe slowly and deeply until I hear him thump to the ground. When I look at him, his ears are up, but he's still watching Keet.

"Wait." I walk to Keet, take his hand, and lead him inside.

"Was that meant for me or the dogs?" he asks.

"All y'all. Stay where you are and don't look at either of them." He nods, and I call to the dogs,

"Outside, you heathens." They run out, joyful doggy smiles at an early-morning adventure.

"I texted, but you didn't answer. I'm sorry about the noise."

"You're later than you expected. Is everything all right?"

"It is. We had to swim farther to find salmon." He rests a hand on my hip.

The cool air ruffles around my legs, up my thighs, hitting my belly and breasts underneath the loose nightshirt I'm wearing. I turn to Keet, balance on my tiptoes, and whisper against his lips, "Come to bed with me?" He kisses me, his tongue light against my lips.

I open the door, whistle for the dogs, and close it behind them. Keet follows me up the stairs, and we tumble into bed.

EIGHT

The next morning, Keet and I are upstairs packing my clothes into bags and boxes when my phone pings with a text. "Ava wants to come over. Can we wait another half-hour before we go to town?"

"Sure." He grabs a box and carries it downstairs.

After sending her a thumbs-up emoji, I put the phone down and walk to the open sliding glass door, needing relief from the barrage of emotions that's assailing me like a hurricane. I'm still there when Ava's truck pulls up. Seeing me on the balcony, she waves, and I go downstairs to meet her at the front door. Keet comes up the steps behind her and she turns and greets him, then walks into the cabin, giving me a hug, rubbing my back.

"I have to keep reminding myself that you're not moving away, just next door." When she pulls away from me, there are tears in her eyes. "You've been good for this place, Nolee. And for me. I'm so happy for you and Keet."

"Ava, I couldn't have asked for a better place to land, or a better friend than you. Thank you for all you've done for me this past year."

We both laugh, realizing we sound as though it's goodbye rather than just an acknowledgment of how we feel.

"I can't stay long, honey, but I wanted to give you something. It's up in the bedroom."

Keet and I follow her up the stairs and watch as she takes the ocean quilt off the bed, folding it with care. She turns and holds it out to me.

"I made this years ago. Found it right before you moved in. Seemed like you'd had a hard time, and I wanted you to feel at home. I'd like you to have it."

I take the quilt, holding it to my chest.

"Ava—" Now tears are blurring my vision, and I wrap an arm around her shoulders. "Thank you. This means the world to me."

We're standing by Ava's truck when Keet asks her about the cabin. "Ava, my grandmother is thinking of moving here. Is the cabin available, or have you promised it to someone?"

"You caught me just in time. I haven't answered the six emails asking the same thing. I'm happy to let your grandmother have it. When would she move in?"

"Next month, around the middle of August. We're happy to pay you for the entire month, and any deposits you need."

She pats his arm. "Just the month's rent is fine. No deposits. I don't think either of you are going anywhere." She gives me a wink. "What's your grandmother's name?"

"Sylvie Vent. She's from Sitka."

"That's a long trip. I hope she has help."

"Her son, my Uncle Jerry, is moving her."

"Good, good. Let me know if I can do anything."

We hug, the thick cotton and raised outlines of the quilt pressing into my bare arms. It's a symbol of the life I've built, the life that seems poised to become different with Keet woven into it.

The next morning, they drive into Northsound to have breakfast and go to the hardware store. Nolee balances two cans of paint, brushes, drop cloths, and a hammer as she backs through the shop door. Keet nods at Dave, rebalancing the bags he's carrying. "Thanks for the help. See you next time"

Dave waves, then turns to the customers waiting to check out. Keet hears the nails rattle in their box as he follows Nolee out, a curtain rod, curtains, a new drill, and a stack of muslin towels under his arm.

Wiping her hands on her jeans, Nolee looks at the 4Runner packed with supplies to redecorate the guest room. The cans of paint are labeled Dove Gray, and Keet smiles, remembering her saying that it sounded like a gentle color.

"Happy thoughts?" she asks.

He stacks the bags in the back and, leaning down to kiss her, takes her hand in his. "Thrilled thoughts. I like the reason you chose the color you did for our guest room—that it sounds gentle."

She blushes, then laughs. "It's not a word we use much, is it? Gentle."

"It isn't." He strokes her still-flushed cheek with his fingertips. "Come on. One more stop and then we can tackle the guest room. Whip it into shape."

Her laugh goes through his ears and straight into his heart.

"How about we improve its appearance? Gently." Her eyes sparkle with mischief, and he's still laughing as she kisses him.

Pausing to drink some water, I notice the way the trees outside the guest-room window soften the afternoon light. We've been working for five days, taking time only to eat and sleep. I feel the weight of Keet's arm around my waist and lean into him. Seeing a smear of paint across his forehead, I reach up and wipe at it.

"More paint?" He touches his forehead.

I nod. "You're a very enthusiastic painter. As controlled as you are in the kitchen, it's funny that your painting is so messy. I'm glad we got these drop cloths."

"Control isn't fun all the time. You taught me that."

"What's life without a few surprises?" I look at the floor, covered by wrinkled cloth that's spattered with the light gray of the walls and the dark brown of the stain we used on the floor-to-ceiling bookshelves Keet built. When I look back at him, he's peeling dried paint from his hands.

"I think those jeans are ruined, Keet."

He shrugs. "I'll save them for other home-improvement projects."

"Not bad for almost a week's work." I look around, imagining the room once it's finished. My eyes linger on the empty bookshelves. Most of my books are still in Austin, in a storage unit near Abbie. Before I start planning how we'll get them, Keet says, "I thought we could make it a mixture of books and CDs."

"Oh?"

He nods. "I'd like you to see your books in the living room. Our books."

"I wonder how many we can fit in this house?"

"How many do you have?" He walks to the middle of the room and starts bundling up the drop cloths, uncovering the sanded and stained hardwood floor.

"I brought a couple of boxes with me, and back in the storage unit in Austin I have…" I pause so long that Keet stops what he's doing and looks at me.

"You've lost count?"

"Oh, no. I was trying to remember if it was fifty boxes or sixty."

"That should fill the shelves." He folds each sheet, placing one on top of the other and adjusting them so the edges line up.

"Yeah. Thanks, Joe. See you next week." Keet hangs up the phone and turns to see Nolee smiling at him. "He'll be out next week to build the dog yard." When she walks closer and hugs him, he feels her quivering with laughter. "Did I say something funny?"

She steps away from him. "Not at all. It just amuses me that you use the landline more than your cell phone. In the week I've been here, I've heard the landline ring way more often than your cell phone."

He smiles, and shrugs. "Old habits. I have something for you. A moving-in gift."

"A moving-in gift? That's funny, because I have one for you, too." Giving him a kiss, she goes outside. He hears the slam of a car door. When she comes back in, she's holding a long thin box wrapped in yellow-and-white paper. Placing it in his hands, she says, "I hope you like this."

He lifts off the paper and turns the white box so the label faces him, revealing what looks like Japanese characters in angular slashes of black. When he opens the box, he sees the shine of stainless-steel knives with burnished wood handles.

"These are amazing. I've never invested in knives like these because I didn't think I would be around."

"Now you will be," she says. "I haven't seen these in your—"

"Our," he says.

She smiles. "Our kitchen. I'm glad you like them."

He sets the box and paper on the kitchen table, then wraps his arms around her. "I like them very much, but not as much as I like having you here."

After a kiss that makes him dizzy, he leads her by the hand outside and to the garage.

"I couldn't wrap it, so I hid it."

He pushes up the garage door, revealing an aquamarine kayak with a giant red bow on it. Rushing to it, she runs her hands along the sides. "I love these colors." He watches as she admires the blending of blues and greens.

"I thought you'd like it. There's even a slot in front for your cell phone." She smiles at him, then picks up the paddle, testing its balance, admiring its bright green blades.

"Keet! It's perfect." She hugs him, pressing into his chest, and he kisses the top of her head.

"Shall we take it out for a spin tomorrow?"

"Absolutely!"

We drag the kayaks onto the beach after spending hours on the water. Keet's back is to the bay, but I'm looking out at it. Outside the buoys, I see an exhaled cloud and then a small, triangular dorsal fin.

"Keet?"

"Yes?"

"She's back."

He turns and takes a step toward the water just as she dives. I put my hand on his arm. "Let's see what she does."

"I thought I'd convinced her not to show up here again."

"Maybe she wants to tell us something. Let's go sit on the dock." Sitting on its edge, I hear Keet's bare feet on the boards, then the dock tilts as he sits beside me. Emptying my mind, I feel the sun's warmth on my left side, the dock bobbing in the current, and the weight of Keet's knee resting against mine. I look out at the buoys, scanning for an exhale or a dorsal fin.

Long minutes pass and I think she's gone, then see her exhale again. Reaching out to her, I close my eyes and replay the vision George had shared with me last summer. The details are more vivid: the emerald-green sea, black-and-white bodies moving in an underwater waltz, water filled with chirps, clicks, buzzing, whistles. I breathe into the vision, then wait.

Nothing.

Opening my eyes, I look at Keet. "Anything? Because I've got zip."

"I can't feel a thing. Other than irritated that I can't reach her."

"Do you want to change? See if you can get a read on her? Maybe this time no chasing; it's not like you're going to catch her." I smile at the warning flash in his eyes. He stands up, removes his shirt and shorts, and dives into the water. I shiver in sympathy.

Once he's submerged, Keet twists and spins, feeling his body stretch and broaden, human to orca. For a moment, he hangs silently in the water, then rises to take a breath and swims closer to the buoys. The picture of her resting at the surface plays in his head, and he senses the thrum of her heart and the remains of a meal in her stomach. When she dives, Keet sends a long series of clicks in her direction. Another picture forms in his head: she's pointing her rostrum east and swimming away.

Keet calls and clicks, somersaults, and spends the few next minutes trying to work out where she went before having to admit that he's lost her. Taking a long breath in, he points his head down, sounds, and waits. The only things he sees are the underwater topography and the faint outline of a distant sailboat's hull. He turns, the cool water a caress against his skin, and swims back to the dock. When he clicks and sees the ground sloping up, he dives, spins, and is human once more.

I watch Keet's dorsal fin cut through the water, headed toward the buoys and the female's bobbing dorsal fin. He stops, resting on the surface. If he's trying to communicate with her, I can't pick it up. I hear her inhale, then see her dive. Keet stays where he is, and now I hear him call to her, a quick burst of low-to-high whistles and clicks ending with a sound like a slamming door. For at least the hundredth time, I wish I could understand what is being communicated.

Keet inhales and dives, and when I next see his dorsal fin, he's heading east, submerging and surfacing in regular intervals. It looks like he's following her.

Stretching my legs out in front of me, I notice that I'm still wearing my water shoes. Removing them, I lean over and dunk them in the water, followed by my sandy, kelp-slick feet. As I scan the horizon for Keet, movement by a buoy surprises me. Then I see the face of a young woman, or rather, the top half of her face: light-brown skin; large, dark eyes; slicked-back black hair. She's gripping the buoy with long fingers, and we stare at each other for a moment before she drops from sight. I stand, shade my eyes, and call out. "Hello?"

The memory of the lone female orca and the face of the dark-haired woman coalesce. And I know: The woman and the orca are the same. She's Keykwin. As if in confirmation, I see the blast of her exhale and watch as her small dorsal fin arcs through the water and disappears. The next time I see her, she's far out in the channel, alone.

Keet surfaces by the dock, wiping water from his face. "Couldn't find her. I thought I heard her go east, but she wasn't there. I scanned everywhere."

"Everywhere but behind you."

He looks up at me, frowning.

"Did she show up again?"

"She did. I'll tell you over lunch." As I gather up Keet's clothes, he wades into the shallows, water sluicing over his skin, then shakes his dark hair like Fae and Wallace after they've been playing in the sea. We pad into the house in our bare feet, and I let the dogs in as Keet gets in the shower.

"That was the best idea, ever, creating a yard for Fae and Wallace," I call out to him.

The dogs trot in, panting and wagging their tails. As I clean their feet with an old towel, I hear the water shut off. "It was a stroke of brilliance. And it got you to move in with me. Win-win."

I laugh and look up to see him standing in the doorway with a towel wrapped around his narrow hips. As he passes, I smell the clean scent of soap and ocean. Lightheaded, I pause, lost in the moment. Fae whines, and my attention returns to the task at hand as Keet, now dressed, walks down the hall to the kitchen.

"Good dogs. Go see Keet for a snack." Fae tilts her head, and then darts off, her paws soft along the floor. I stroke Wallace's head; he no longer seems to be afraid of Keet, but it's going to take a lot of treats before they're anywhere close to friends. He walks by my side to the kitchen, where Keet stands at the stove, warming last night's dinner of seafood paella. My mouth starts to water.

"I'll heat those corn tortillas you made, Keet."

We eat in silence, both of us focused on filling our bellies. Keet, finishing first, asks, "So what did you see?"

I wipe my mouth, placing the cloth napkin back in my lap.

"When you swam to the east, I was watching you. You weren't hurrying, but it seemed like you had a purpose. I wondered if she darted out that way."

"I thought she did. I thought I heard her swimming that way. But once I got out deep enough and sounded, I couldn't see her. I couldn't even feel her. It was that same spooky sensation—like a ghost orca. I don't like it." He looks down at his plate, picking up the crumbs from the tortillas.

"I don't know how much you're going to like this, then." He raises his head and gives me a questioning glance.

"I saw movement out by the same buoy where we saw the female orca. It was a young woman with black hair, but I could only see the top half of her face. Then she disappeared. I kept looking, and the female orca reappeared, heading west. I know they're the same, Keet. She's got to be Keykwin."

"That can't be." His black brows pull together, his forehead wrinkled in thought.

"Whether it can or can't is beside the point. I'm convinced she's like you." I pause before I ask the next question. "Do you think she's one of yours? A daughter?"

The surprise that crosses his face is almost comical, and I would've laughed were it not for the alarm I saw in his eyes. Giving himself time to think, he cleans off the table and washes the dishes. Once he finishes, he sits down again.

"I guess it's possible, but it's just not probable."

"What does that mean?"

"It means that for hundreds of generations, maybe thousands of generations, my ancestors have passed down the knowledge that only Keykwin women can give birth to other Keykwin. If we, as men, had children, they would be human. If we, as orca, mated with a female orca and she had a baby, that baby would be an orca. I don't understand how this lone female could be related to me. What bothers me is that I can't track her. I can't hear her with my ears, and I can't even pick up her presence with any kind of felt sense."

"Felt sense?"

"It's like what you experience when you communicate with dogs, or my pod. It's a term used to describe the sensations going on in one's own body, but I think for you, it's expanded to include those around you. Empathy is your superpower."

"Superpower or not, I'm sure she's like you, Keet. And for whatever reason, she's curious about us."

NINE

The dirt-spattered moving van sways, pitching back and forth on the uneven road. Keet, watching for his grandmother's blue pickup, rocks from one foot to another, unconsciously mimicking the van's movement. He hopes she'll pull in before the late afternoon gets later.

The van pulls up in front of the cabin and the driver gets out. Keet looks back over his shoulder and sees Nolee ushering the dogs into the back yard; she runs her hands over the redwood gate he built, which makes him smile.

The driver pulls out a vape pen, closing his eyes and exhaling a dense cloud of smoke. It reminds Keet of the dragons in the books he read as a kid. The drivers asks, "Where would you like me to park this beast?"

Keet points to the cabin. "You can back it up there." He walks toward the cabin, intending to help, wanting to be sure that the things his grandmother found important enough to pack aren't damaged.

The van stops near the porch, and two men get out. The driver shakes Keet's hand. "Name's Dario. That's my cousin Art." He tosses the vape pen on the seat, then walks to the back and unlatches the roll-up door.

"She has a lot less than most people. She's traveling light."

"You met my grandmother?" Keet looks at Dario and Art.

"Sure," Dario says. "She made us come in and drink coffee with her. We also had some kick-ass fish stew. Almost made us late for the ferry."

Keet smiles as Art slides a box toward Dario. "She didn't want Art to drive her truck. She was behind us once we got off the ferry. Haven't seen her since."

"She doesn't let her own son drive that truck. I'm barely allowed to look at it." They laugh. "My uncle was supposed to be with her. Did you see him?"

79

"Big guy? Doesn't smile much?"

"That's him."

"Yeah, he was with her. Didn't look so happy about her driving." Dario says.

Nolee joins them, puts her hand on Keet's back, and smiles at Dario. "Have I missed anything?" she asks.

"No, you're just in time to help." Keet leans over and gives her a quick kiss. "Do you know if she made it onto the ferry in Anacortes?"

"She did. I saw her sitting in her truck at the back of the ferry. Tried to get her to come up on deck, but she wasn't having it."

Keet laughs. "She probably sent Jerry upstairs to get food and drinks, then made him eat sitting in the cafeteria."

Dario pulls out a ramp and lowers it to the ground, then jogs into the back of the van and gets busy pushing more boxes toward the opening. Keet and Nolee take a closer look inside.

"What's that?" Nolee points to a large rectangular shape shrouded by an old sheet. It's almost the size of a coffin.

"That, ma'am, is the heaviest sonofa—" Dario clears his throat. "Sorry. It's a chest. Felt like a whole tree when we carried it down the stairs from her apartment."

Nolee turns to Keet. "Do you know what it is?"

He shakes his head. "I've never seen it. Jerry and I helped her move into his apartment and she didn't have it then. I don't remember her having it when we lived in the cabin on the beach, either."

The four of them are silent, contemplating the mystery of the chest. Then Art breaks through their reverie.

"Better get the rest of these boxes in. We can move the chest last. With any luck, Mrs. Vent will be here soon and will tell us where it goes."

They hear the distant thunder and growl of an engine. The truck crawls into view, first its white top, then its powder-blue body. It weaves toward them, missing trees by inches as it swerves in slow motion around the potholes. A frowning man sits in the passenger seat, one large brown hand braced against the dashboard, the other against the top of the cab. The driver, her hair in a silver bun on top of her head and both hands on the steering wheel, peers over it. Art lets out a long whistle. Dario says, "1969 F-100, V8, 390, power steering and brakes. That's a sweet ride."

Keet breaks away from the huddle and squares his shoulders. He watches the truck crawl down the hill, then turn left onto the road that leads to the cabin. When the pickup comes to a stop, the man leaps out and slams the steel door with a solid bang. His grandmother glares at his uncle's turned back, cuts the engine, and opens her own door, hunching as she gets out.

"Are you okay, Grandmother?" Keet strides over to her and puts his hand on her shoulder.

"It was a long trip," she sighs, looking up at him. Her body may be tired, but her eyes have their familiar sparkle, which quiets his concern.

He turns to his uncle, and they shake hands.

"Jerry. Good to see you. Congratulations on your new job in Juneau."

Jerry turns and looks at the calm waters in the bay.

"The water isn't as wild here, is it?" he says.

"Not this time of year. It gets rowdy in the winter."

They see Sylvie walk over to the moving van, her gait a slow shuffle. When she reaches it, the men lean over to hear her, and she places her hands on their arms.

"Still the charmer, I see." Keet smiles at his uncle.

Jerry grunts. "The older she gets, the sweeter she gets—to everyone else."

Keet gives his uncle a quick glance, then motions him to follow. "Come over and meet my girlfriend. We'll finish up unloading that van, then eat dinner at our place. What time do you board the ferry?"

They walk, the silence stretching between them. Finally, Keet hears Jerry sigh "Six-thirty in the goddamned morning."

"I'll take you. And thanks again for making this trip, Jerry. I know it's a long one."

Jerry grunts again, then straightens as Nolee walks toward them.

"Jerry, it's a pleasure to meet you. Come on over to the house and we'll get you something to drink." Keet hears Nolee's accent slip back into a Texas twang. She must be nervous.

Jerry smiles for the first time, his hand enfolding hers as they shake.

"You got anything stronger than coffee?"

"We have wine, or my personal favorite, Scotch."

"I'll give some of that Scotch a try. Never could get into wine."

As Jerry and Nolee walk toward the house, she glances back at Keet, shrugging her shoulders. Then, Jerry says something to her and Nolee laughs. Keet turns back to the van and the cabin, walking up the steps, following the soft lilt of his grandmother's voice.

"Thank you, boys. You've done a lot of work."

Dario and Art shove the folded bills into their pockets. "Mrs. Vent, it's been a pleasure to do business with you."

Keet puts his hand on Art's shoulder. "Can you stay for dinner? There's plenty of food."

Art and Dario look at each other, then Dario answers. "Thanks, man, but we've got to get back to Bellingham tonight. Catching the ferry to Sitka tomorrow."

Keet nods, then looks around. He doesn't see any sign of the gigantic chest or the sheet covering it.

"Grandmother, where did you have them put that chest?"

She points to the staircase. "In the closet. In the bedroom."

"It fit?"

"We got it in there." Dario says, pride on his face.

They wave and leave. A thick cloud of vape smoke streams from the driver's window as the engine whines its way up the hill behind the cabin.

Jerry slouches at the head of the table, one leg crossed over the other, a glass with a sliver of amber Scotch in his hand. I give the pot of seafood gumbo a stir and put my grandmother's cast-iron skillet with jalapeño cornbread in the oven. When I look back at the table, Jerry's finishing his drink.

"Can I get you another drink, Jerry?"

He sits up straighter, holding out his glass. "Water would be good."

As I set a glass of water down in front of him, Keet and his grandmother come in.

"Sylvie, what can I get you?"

"Coffee. Milk and sugar, please."

"When she says 'milk,' she means half coffee, half milk." Keet leans in and kisses my cheek.

It suddenly strikes me that I have a kitchen full of Keykwin, though Keet's never spoken about his uncle. Adding that to my list of questions to ask when we're alone, I snap back to the conversation when I hear Keet say, "Right, Nolee?"

"What am I saying 'right' to?" I give the bubbling pot a stir.

"I was telling my grandmother that we'd be happy to help her unpack tomorrow."

"Yes, of course."

I wipe the counter again, the circular motions and wet surface calming the nervousness I feel about meeting Keet's family. Everything is in such a knot, and I'm not sure which threads are mine and which are someone else's.

Fae rises from her bed and greets everyone, wagging her tail as she goes from person to person. I look for Wallace and see that he's still lying watchfully on his bed. I make eye contact with him and slow my breathing, sending him feelings of calm and safety. He yawns and stays where he is. It dawns on me that some of the agitation isn't my own: It's coming from everyone.

When the timer dings, Keet gets up, stirs the gumbo, then takes the skillet out of the oven. Turning to the refrigerator, he brings out the coleslaw he'd made earlier.

"Let me help," Sylvie says, pushing herself upright. Using the oven mitts Keet hands her, she places the skillet on a trivet in the middle of the table. Removing the oven mitts, she runs a hand lovingly across the table's polished surface.

"Your husband made this, didn't he, Sylvie?"

She looks at me, her eyes bright. "It took Jack months. He knew how much I wanted a place we could eat at as a family." I cover her hand with mine, and our eyes meet. She gives my hand a squeeze, then sits down.

As Keet sets the table, Jerry finishes off his water and stands to put the empty glass on the counter. The glass, trembling in his hand, chatters as he sets it down.

"Everything all right, Jerry?" I ask, ignoring Keet's warning look.

"Sure. Can I get some more water?" After refilling his glass, I reach for the pot of gumbo. "I'll get that, Nolee," Jerry says. Ignoring the mitts I hold out to him, he lifts the pot from the stove and sets it on the table with a thump, then sits down again, hands in his lap.

"How about we eat?" Keet suggests, his face closed and tense. The moment of awkward silence is erased by the clicking of spoons in bowls. In my peripheral vision, I see Jerry pick up his spoon and stare at it as though he could force it to stop shaking.

The trembling worries me, and I flash on a conversation I'd once had with Keet when I noticed a similar trembling in his hands. He told me it was because he'd been human too long. But I don't know Jerry anywhere near well enough to ask whether he needs to swim or not. Or even if he ever has.

"Sylvie, we're happy to have you here. I think you'll like the cabin."

She wipes her mouth and nods. "I already do. Thank you for suggesting it."

"Grandmother, I've cleaned out the garage. If you'd like to park your pickup in it, there's room." I'm happy to see that some of the tension has left Keet. I put my hand on his thigh, and he looks at me and smiles.

"Thank you both for dinner," Sylvie says. "It's good to have a home-cooked meal after a long trip."

Conversation stops when Jerry shoves his chair back with a scrape. A sharp spike of anxiety rises in my chest, and under my hand, I feel Keet's leg tense. When Wallace rises to his feet as well, Fae walks to him, tail wagging, and sniffs his muzzle. I'm not sure if the racing heart I feel is mine or Wallace's. I'm still untangling the sensations when Jerry says, "I'm done eating."

I look from Wallace to Keet, then back to Wallace. Keet gets up.

"Do you want something else, Jerry?" I ask.

"No. I need to lie down." He stands. Keet stands. I feel the crackle of something in the air. Sylvie, hands gripping the edge of the table, leans toward her son and grandson.

"Son—" she begins.

"No, Mom. Not tonight." Jerry looks at Keet. "Where am I sleeping?"

"Jerry. Keet. Sit down." I don't see her stand, but there she is, bracing herself on the table, leaning toward the two men who are inches apart, eyes locked. "Son, you need to eat."

"I'm not hungry."

Getting up myself, I kneel next to Wallace and stroke the top of his head. Fae, still at his side, fixes her eyes on me. After a few seconds, I glance at the table and see that Jerry, Keet, and Sylvie are now sitting. I join them.

Although the meal is one of my favorites, I don't taste any of it. It's dry as sawdust and choked with unspoken emotions. We eat in silence.

Finally, Sylvie scoots her chair away from the table. "Nolee, thank you for the meal. I'm going to bed now. Jerry, Keet walk me back." Keet nods.

I smile at Sylvie. Jerry moves toward the door with no indication that he's aware of how much his hands are trembling against his sides.

Throwing the door open, he strides out, Keet and Sylvie in his wake. The door closes, and I lean back into my chair and exhale.

Nolee looks up when Keet and Jerry come in. She's pale, her body tense. He wants to be closer to her but that will have to wait until he settles his uncle. "I'll show Jerry where the guest bedroom and bathroom are. Be right back."

"I'm taking the dogs out," she says.

"I'll join you in a moment." He leads Jerry to the guest room, again admiring the work he and Nolee have put into it. The shelves hold books, rocks and shells, family photos, and a jar of white sand from the Gulf Coast of Texas, and the thick off-white curtains are rich against the light gray walls. Ava's ocean quilt covers the double bed.

"Bathroom is through that door. Let us know if you need anything, Jerry."

Jerry drops his bag where he stands and turns to Keet.

"I'm good."

Ignoring his uncle's dull eyes and shaking hands, Keet nods and closes his door.

When he goes outside, he doesn't see Nolee, but notices Wallace, his coat glowing in the light of the half moon. Following the glow, he spies Nolee, wrapped in his black sweatshirt, walking along the beach. Fae yips with excitement when she rejoins them.

Keet catches up to her and puts his arm around her waist. She's unyielding; it feels like the first time they hugged when he returned from Sitka. "You okay?"

She flashes him a smile. "I am. Glad to be outside. I wasn't prepared for the way this evening went. Jerry caught me off guard."

They stop walking and Keet puts his arms around her. "He caught me off guard, too. I've not seen him like that in a long time. I thought he was done with it."

"What does 'it' mean, Keet?"

From the tone of her voice, he knows she wants to understand his family better.

"Jerry fought in Vietnam. When he came back, he was almost catatonic.

He didn't speak for months, and he would have these bouts of shaking. I remember sitting at the table as a kid, watching Grandmother feed him."

"That can't have been easy on anyone."

They begin walking again. "It wasn't. Jerry's a proud man. Once he recovered enough to take care of himself, he left Sitka."

"Where did he go?"

"He said he went all over."

"Trying to outrun his memories?"

"More like hoping new ones would replace old ones."

"I thought for a moment…" Nolee trails off. She turns her head away from the starlit sky and gives him an unsure smile.

"What did you think, Lia?"

"When I saw his hands shaking, it reminded me of you when you needed to swim."

"You remember that?" Keet steps away, focusing on the glint of moonlight in her eyes.

"I do. Has Jerry ever been orca?"

Keet shakes his head. "Not that I know of."

Fae and Wallace bound up to them, Fae with a stick in her mouth. Nolee takes it and throws, and Wallace catches it before it has a chance to land on the silver-plated rocks.

"What branch of the military did he serve in?"

"The army, I think."

Nolee takes Keet's hand as the dogs walk back to them, tails wagging. "You think?"

"He doesn't talk about it. I was barely walking when he went to Vietnam, and still a child when he came back. He always scared me."

"Does he still scare you, Keet?"

He stops, pulling Nolee against him.

"He doesn't. But I feel like I don't know him very well. Does he scare you?"

"No."

The silence between them is charged with unsaid words. Nolee's voice breaks the barrier.

"At first, I thought he might use booze like I used to."

"You had trouble with alcohol? I didn't know that."

"This honesty thing…" She takes a deep breath, then her words come out in a rush. "I drank regularly during the last few years of my marriage to Nate."

"I haven't seen you drink like that."

"Are you mad I didn't tell you this sooner?"

"Why would I be mad? It's your business. Besides, to me, you're not that person anymore."

"I don't think I was that person before. But it became a way to numb the loneliness, especially when Abbie was older and had her own friends."

They walk again, and he reaches out for her hand.

"After the night I manipulated Nate into sleeping with me and he told me about his affair with Carlos, I was halfway through a six-pack of beer for breakfast when it occurred to me that I might have a problem. At that point, I had lots of problems. Most of them self-induced."

"You drank beer?!"

She laughs, the heaviness around her eyes lifting as she smiles at him.

"I drank anything. But I found an AA meeting, found a therapist, and that was my life until I moved here."

"But you still drink, Nolee. Isn't that a problem?"

She's quiet as they walk, leaning down to pet the dogs when they circle back around to them.

"My father drank. He was quiet, though, or fell asleep in a chair while he was watching television. When I think about my dad, part of me justifies my past drinking by insisting that at least I was never an absent mother, and that I drank alone most of the time. I was asleep before I could cause much of a ruckus."

They stop at an outcropping of rocks, tops visible above the high tide. In the distance, the lights of Vancouver are bright and clear. Keet stands with Nolee, hearing the call of the sea, feeling as immersed in it as if he were orca. Wrapping her in his arms, he feels the weight of her head on his chest. Her voice is muffled when she speaks again.

"The first time we had dinner, I had that glass of Scotch."

"You did. And you've made me a fan as well."

"That was my first drink in a year. I wanted to see how it felt. If I could control myself. Or not."

"And?"

She steps away from him, her face pale in the moonlight.

"I liked the taste and enjoyed sharing it with you. But I didn't go home and finish the bottle. I drank because it tasted good. Not because I needed it."

"That's a good thing, right?"

The ghost of a smile forms on her lips. "I think so…"

"But?"

"No buts. I've had it drilled it into me that alcoholics are great at self-deception. I sometimes worry that I'm deceiving myself when I only have one drink."

The breeze lifts her hair away from her face. He hears the dogs somewhere nearby, and glancing at the dark cabin, he hopes his grandmother is sleeping.

"I've realized I don't have my father's need for alcohol. I'm satisfied after one drink, and I don't count the days until my next one. I don't hide it, and I don't feel ashamed."

"Those are good things."

She nods. "They are. I got the help I needed and saw my drinking for what it was."

"Which was?"

Nolee puts her arm around his waist as they continue walking. "An escape from my life. I did a lot of things back then to distract myself from the situation I was in with Nathan. When I was married to him, I drank to become numb. With my life here, and you, I drink because it's a way of celebrating us."

He stops, turns her toward him, and kisses her. Breaking away, he still feels her breath on his lips. "I celebrate us too."

Keet is kissing her again when they both hear a volley of orca exhales. Turning, they look out to sea, as do Fae and Wallace, who are standing with their front feet in the lapping waves. A shadowy rise and fall of dorsal fins heads into the bay, and Keet feels their call echo in his chest. He looks at Nolee; she's smiling, and he squeezes her closer to him.

TEN

"They've been away for a while. It's good to have them back."

"It's no accident that it's on the same night my grandmother and Jerry show up." The thought causes him to pause, and he sees Nolee glance up.

"I thought you'd be jumping into the water by now."

"I'm not leaving you alone with my human family yet ..." He stops speaking. His grandmother in her long white nightgown walks out to the dock like a specter, her hair floating behind her.

Taking Nolee's hand, Keet turns, and they reach the dock as his grandmother lowers herself in slow motion to its bobbing surface.

The soft moonlight sparkles on the waves as a smaller head and dorsal fin breaks the surface. Keet sees the gleam of George's eye as he swims toward the dock. He leaps from the water with a high-pitched squeak, the white of his belly in glimmering relief. Swimming closer to Sylvie, he rolls on his side, eyeing her. She leans toward him, reaching out a hand. George flips and raises his head above the waves, his white eye patch glowing. Hanging between air and sea, he touches her outstretched hand with his rostrum. Keet hears his grandmother murmuring a prayer he last heard when he was a child.

"What's she saying?" Nolee asks.

"It's the Honoring of the Blackfish."

They're silent again, the susurration of his grandmother's words mixing with the breeze winding through the trees, mixing with the soft exhales of the orca pod in the bay. The dogs are lying on the beach, heads lowered, shiny eyes watchful. Keet feels as though they're thousands of years in the past, caught between an ancient prayer and the promise of a new future.

George disappears under the waves, breaking the spell the night has cast over them. His dorsal fin pops up beside his mother's and the pod spyhops, six blunt rostrums and bright eyepatches in synchrony, dancers on a watery stage. Then, submerging, they swim close together back out to sea. Keet's grandmother sits, rocking back and forth in time with the dock, before standing up, stretching her arms to the sky. She walks toward them.

"It will be the Salmon Moon soon." She lays a hand on Keet's arm, smiles at Nolee. The breeze is gone, and the old woman's white hair lies around her shoulders like cotton fluff.

Keet places a gentle hand on top of hers. "I haven't heard you speak that in a long time. It's good for my heart."

Nolee glances up at him, then back to his grandmother. "Sylvie, would you mind repeating what you were saying?"

Keet sees the joy in his grandmother's eyes, watches as she closes them, feels the warmth and strength in her hand as she takes first his, then Nolee's.

The Keykwin words flow around them, the soft murmurings blending together, broken by consonants that come from deep within her belly. Glancing at Nolee, Keet sees she's under the spell of the words. When his grandmother's done speaking in Keykwin, she pauses, then repeats the words in English.

The people of the sea
The blackfish people
Catch the salmon
They eat the salmon and
Share with their family.

They eat until they are full
Swim until they sleep
Rocking in the moon-time water
Breathing above the sea.

The blackfish people share their
Salmon with the people of the forest
Who eat until they are full.
Sit by the fire until they sleep
The breeze rocking their houses
They dream with the forest.

The blackfish and the people of the forest
Dream of each other
Watching the salmon moon rise
Behind waving branches of trees
And over waves of the nighttime sea.

Nolee leans toward Sylvie and gives her a light kiss on the cheek. "Thank you, Sylvie."

His grandmother squeezes his hand, then turns and walks back to her cabin, her footsteps slow but sure. Nolee leans against his shoulder, then asks, "Why were you frowning earlier, when you saw your grandmother on the dock?"

Keet looks at her. "Was I?"

"It's not that dark, Keet Noland."

"I was wondering if she agreed to move here because she's ready to take her Walk Into the Water."

I watch Sylvie move across the rocks, her hair and nightgown blending in the soft moonlight. She reaches the front door and goes inside. Behind me, Keet wraps his arms around me, my back absorbing his warmth. I leave his remark about his grandmother's intentions alone, choosing not to worry about if his grandmother was ready to give up her life as a human being, swimming as orca for the remainder of her days. I wait to hear what he says next.

"She must like you."

"Why's that?" I lean my head back and feel him rest his cheek against it.

"She doesn't share the prayers with just anyone."

This nascent sense of discovering Sylvie softens the events of the evening.

"That makes me happy. Do you need to swim?"

"I'm going to bed with you tonight. I can swim tomorrow." He lightly kisses the tip of my nose, and we walk hand-in-hand toward the house, the dogs behind us. I feel as though we're absorbing magic from the warm summer night.

While Keet brushes the sand off his feet, I open the door and see Jerry huddled on the sofa, his hands gripping the edge so hard the material is puckering. He's rocking forward and back, his head a heavy weight, and I hear his breath, shuddering in and out in rapid bursts. When I turn and ask the dogs to wait, Keet looks up and sees his uncle. His lips set in a hard, straight line, he goes to the sofa and kneels in front of Jerry. Startled, Jerry looks at Keet, then moves one shaking hand from the sofa to Keet's shoulder.

"Nephew. Leave me be."

"Let me help, Jerry."

"You can't help. No one can. Go away."

I'm out of my shoes and across the floor, standing beside Keet. "Meet me in the kitchen?"

At the door, I see the dogs, their heads cocked to the side, watching.

"Come in, dogs." They trot to us, then over to Jerry. Fae lays down on his feet, while Wallace settles into his bed with a sigh.

I put my hand on Keet's arm. "Remember when you came back the first time, after having been captured?"

His reply is just as tense as the muscle under my hand. "Yes."

"Your uncle is going through something similar. But he's been dealing with it for decades."

"What do you mean?"

"Keet, he's having a panic attack. You said he doesn't talk much about his time in Vietnam."

"Let's get him to bed," Keet says. His words, though whispered, are hard and clipped.

"It would be better if we took him for a walk. He probably won't sleep in the state he's in." I leave Keet in the kitchen and sit down at a distance from Jerry. He's stopped rocking, but his breathing is still labored, and I can see that his whole body is trembling.

"Didn't manage any sleep, did you Jerry?"

He shakes his head.

"Bad dream?" I ask.

He looks over at me, hair hanging in his face, jaw clenched.

"How did you know?"

"Just a feeling. Do you want to take a walk with me? Out on the beach?"

There's no sign that he's heard my question, but the dogs jump up and stand at the door, tails wagging. Jerry looks over at them.

"They know English or something?"

"They know the word 'walk.' They don't have to come with us if you don't want them to."

Jerry stands so suddenly that the dogs startle. "I'll go. But it won't help."

"Maybe not," I say, watching as Keet opens the door and steps outside with the dogs. "But it might be better than sitting still."

Once we're outside, I trail behind Jerry. Minutes go by as he stumbles and trips over the stones. Keet, beside him, reaches out but Jerry shrugs him off, moving away from him. After a few turns on the beach with the backdrop of the rising tide's growl against the shoreline, Jerry's walk steadies and he slows. When he stops, I stand in front of him.

"Jerry, do you see that line of trees over there?" He follows the direction of my hand to the forest, and the moon that hangs over all of us.

"Yes."

"What does it look like to you?"

"Trees. What else."

I ignore his brusque reply. "What kind of trees?"

He huffs his impatience. "You haven't bothered to learn the names of the trees that are your neighbors?"

"What kind of trees, Jerry?"

"When we got here, I thought they might be some kind of fir."

"That's what I think they are too."

"Why are you asking me these useless questions?"

I stay silent, letting the barbs of his words fall to the ground.

Keet steps closer to his uncle. "Maybe you could be more polite, Jerry."

I lay my hand on Keet's shoulder. "It's not important, Keet."

"It is to me."

Jerry stalks away.

"Where are you going?" Keet follows his uncle and the dogs, but I stay where I am. I hear Jerry's distant reply.

"To sleep."

ELEVEN

Keet sits at the edge of our bed, frowning. "I'm ready for this night to be over."

I take his hand in mine and kiss it. After we're in bed and the lights are out, I get up again and open the curtains.

"I think we should let the Salmon Moon help us sleep."

He holds out his hand and pulls me into bed beside him, but sleep doesn't find us until the ghost of dawn is a only a few hours away.

The click of nails on the floor wakens me, and I open my eyes to two black noses and two pairs of inquisitive eyes. Fae's tongue darts out and touches my forehead. Keet is on his side, still asleep. I reach for my phone and swipe it open. It's four in the morning.

After letting the dogs out in the backyard, I tie my robe around me and pad into the kitchen, opening the curtains and enjoying the approaching light of a new day.

"Good morning."

Startled, I turn to see Jerry sitting at the table, dressed in the clothes he was wearing last night, an empty glass in front of him.

"Good morning. I thought we'd let you sleep a little longer."

He stares out the window as I make my way to the sink.

"Do you want some coffee? Water? Tea?"

He gets up and lumbers over to where I'm standing, putting the glass down with a thunk.

"Coffee'd be good."

A thin wire of anxiety stretches through me as he draws closer, but as I smile into his eyes, I realize that below the anxiety is a deep well of sadness. Almost without thinking, I touch his hand.

The shield he's had in place since his arrival raises itself again, arranging his face into a well-practiced neutral blankness. I wait. He looks down. I take my hand away from his.

"I was a pain in the butt last night. Sorry about that." He attempts a smile as he sits down at the table and folds his hands.

After I put water on to boil, I sit across from him. "We're all a pain in the butt sometimes, Jerry. Being around family just makes it easier to be that way." He rumbles out a quick burst of laughter and shakes his head.

"My family isn't the problem, Nolee."

"Is something bothering you?"

He looks at me again, and if it weren't for the wrinkled and darker skin around them, I would swear those were Keet's eyes gazing at me. There's more worry and grief in their depths; no matter the color or shape, unguarded eyes tell me what the mouth won't, or can't.

"I'm not moving to Juneau just for a job."

The kettle boils. "Just a moment. Let me get the coffee and tea sorted out."

I grab three mugs and two French presses, filling one press with ground coffee and the other with loose-leaf green tea. As I pour water into each press, I see Jerry watching dawn's light skip across the waves.

I put two mugs on the table, move one toward him, and sit down. "Milk or sugar?"

He shakes his head.

"So, you're not moving to Juneau for a job. Why *are* you moving?"

The first open smile I've seen warms his face with its light. His heavy brows relax, his eyes half close. Whatever it is, it means more to him than staying in Sitka.

"I met a woman."

"Ah." I sip my tea, the heat and tang waking me up. "She must be important to you."

"She is," he nods. "She laughs a lot, knows how to have fun. I've done more things with her in a year than I've done in the rest of my life."

"What's her name?"

He smiles again, and when he answers me, his voice is soft. "Saila Muckpa."

"That's a gorgeous name. Where's she from?"

"Alaska. She's Inuit. Moved to Juneau more than thirty years ago. Has three kids. Her husband died when they were little, so she raised them herself. She's a watercolor artist."

"She sounds amazing. More coffee?"

He holds his mug out.

As I pour, he speaks again.

"When Keet called last month and let me know you were moving in with him, and the cabin was available ..." he looks out the window again. The day is brighter, the sea changing from gunmetal gray to a deep blue green. I lean forward.

He gives me a quick look, sips his coffee, then sets the mug on the table with care.

"I knew I needed to go to Juneau. I've liked having Mom live with me, where I can keep an eye on her, but she's one tough woman."

"I got that impression," I say, tilting my mug and letting the last of the green tea spread its fading warmth down my throat. I hear the clatter of paws outside.

"Need to let the dogs in. Be right back."

They follow me into the kitchen, watching as I fix their breakfast. I ask them to sit, then set their bowls down at opposite ends of the kitchen, calling Fae first, then Wallace. When I return to the table, Jerry says, "They're more polite than half the people I know. Looks like they eat better, too."

"They deserve it. You were telling me about moving to Juneau?"

"Yeah. That's about it. Except ..." he sighs. "I don't want to lose control of myself like I did last night. If I do, it will wreck what Saila and I have."

"Jerry, Keet told me you're a Vietnam vet. That you had some trouble when you got back?" His laugh has a bitter edge.

"I've never been in combat ..."

"It was a war. Don't sugar coat it."

"I've never been in a war, or even close to one. But I do know what trauma looks and feels like."

He looks up at me, his hands still on the table, the morning light on his expressionless face.

"I grew up on a ranch. There were a lot of rules; one of them was that I wasn't supposed to go in the hog pen, especially when the sows were farrowing." Seeing his confusion, I say, "When they had babies."

"When I was thirteen, my mom and dad had to leave the ranch for a couple of days. A sow had just had her babies that night. On the day my parents left, I snuck into the pen to pet the piglets. Before I knew what happened, the sow who had been lying down had me pinned in the corner. I had my hands on her snout. I'd swear to this day her eyes were red, but that may have been my fear."

"What did you do?"

"I didn't do anything. One of the ranch hands was working nearby, and he yanked me out of the pen. That was scary enough, but the scarier thing was that he wouldn't let go of my arm."

"What happened?"

I sit back in my chair and look out of the window at the brightening morning. No matter how many times I've told this story, I still feel a faint wave of nausea course through me.

"He dragged me to a dark part of the barn. He pushed my shirt up and was getting ready to unbutton my jeans. I think I was screaming, but I couldn't tell if it was me or the sow. My brother Frank came in. He was eleven at the time, and he ran up and punched the man in the back, hollering fit to raise the roof. He let me go."

"You have a brave brother."

"He's all of that. I didn't talk about it, but Frank told my parents what happened. The man was fired."

Jerry drinks the last of his coffee, setting the mug down on the table in silence.

"Jerry, I'm not saying that what I went through is anything close to what you endured." He traces a whorl in the wood with one finger.

"But trauma is trauma, and I've done a lot of work with animals who I swear had PTSD."

"You sound like the VA doctors my family wanted me to see."

"Maybe. What I'm saying is, last night, it looked to me like you were having a panic attack."

He meets my eyes, and I feel the shield being raised back into place, the fragile trust we'd built being pushed away.

"What if I was?" He squints at me, pursing his lips, then looks down at his mug.

"Is that the thing that worries you about being with Saila?"

He's quiet, hunched into himself so completely that I start to get up to give him some space.

"Yes," he whispers. He clears his throat before speaking again. "I can't control those attacks. And then I think of my crazy sister …" he trails off.

"Keet's mom?"

He waves my question away with a large hand. "She couldn't control herself either. I promised myself I'd never be like her, but when I got back from Nam, I was *exactly* like her. Couldn't control my emotions. Made everyone around me miserable. Felt like being dead would be better than being scared all the time."

"Can I offer something?"

He nods.

"Keep in mind I'm only a dog trainer."

A smile breaks through the clouds on his face, and I take a moment to notice what a handsome man he is before trying to explain what I know about trauma.

"When people feel their life has been threatened, a place like a mudhole begins inside them. In that mudhole is a bunch of dark stuff. A path leads right to it, a path wide and smooth as a highway. At any sign of threat, which can be as routine as meeting new people, starting a new job, moving, their brain jumps on that highway, and they fall right into the mudhole. It takes someone with a tow truck to pull them out."

His expression softens, and he laughs. "That's the silliest thing I've ever heard, dog trainer."

I smile. "Good. Then you'll remember it."

"Who has the tow truck?"

"A therapist, usually. Or it could be an understanding family member."

"Is therapy what you did?"

I nod. "When I was a teenager. And when I was an adult. It helped me get through my divorce better than alcohol, which I also tried."

Jerry's surprise shows on his face. "I don't know about the whole therapy thing …"

"Tell me about it," I say. "It's not my idea of a good time, either. But it helped."

He drums his fingers on the table, a deep timpani of his nervousness.

"I'm not saying you have to go, only that it worked for me."

He nods. "Our Nation brought me into ceremony."

"When was that?"

"When I got home. I was reminded of who I was, and who I would always be. That I wasn't just a soldier returned from battle. I was more and could be again."

"It helped?"

Jerry nods. "I didn't kill myself, so I'd say it helped a lot."

The shield is dissolving. I get up to fill the kettle again, turning on the burner underneath it, hoping that giving him space and time will allow him to speak the words he needs to hear from himself.

"Why did you drag me out last night? It wasn't for a walk and to talk about trees, was it?"

I smile at him. "Movement helps the panic attack move through more quickly. Looking at your surroundings reminds your brain that there's a way out of the trauma mudhole."

Jerry nods. "I'll remember that. I guess I could find someone to talk to, for Saila's sake."

"That would be a good start. Will you do me a favor?"

"Sure."

"Will you text me sometime, let me know how you're doing?"

He pushes his hand into his pants pocket and takes out a phone, swiping it open and handing it to me. "Yes. I'll do that."

I send myself a text before I remember that my phone's by the bed. Its distant ping is followed by a soft knock on the door.

Sylvie, wearing jeans and a blue blouse, hair in a tidy bun, says good morning and sits at the table next to Jerry, patting his hand with hers.

"Coffee, Sylvie?"

Before she can answer, Keet is beside me. "There's green tea in the press," I say, my arm around his waist.

"I'll get it. I'll make Grandmother's coffee, too."

We move around the kitchen in tandem, making food and conversation. Each time I catch Jerry's eye, he smiles. The storm of tension has blown itself out, and breakfast is easier than dinner had been last night.

Keet drives us to the ferry landing and after hugs and tears, we watch Jerry walk downhill toward the waiting ship, his gait slow, his step sure. Keet is on one side of me, Sylvie on the other.

"Think he'll be all right?" Keet says.

I wait, seeing if Sylvie will answer. When I look at her, she has tears running down her cheeks. I put an arm around her shoulders, squeezing her to me.

"I think he'll be great."

After a stop at the market, we go home and Sylvie drives her pickup into Keet's garage, where she wipes it down with a soft cloth, then closes the door. She turns and looks at both of us. "I'll go unpack."

"We can help if you'd like." Keet steps closer to her, and she looks up at him.

"I'll do it myself. I'll text if I need help."

He gives her a brief hug. "I'm glad you're here, Grandmother."

She looks at him a moment longer, pats his arm, then turns and walks back to the cabin.

Keet and I are in the house when he says to me. "Do you think she's okay?"

"You know her better than I do. I think she needs time to absorb the shock of the move. Has she ever lived by herself?"

He takes my hand, rubbing my knuckles with his thumb. "I don't know." He gives me a quick kiss. "Let's get these groceries put away. I need to swim."

As the cold water swallows him, Keet feels its chill on his fingertips first, then on his wrists, arms, shoulders, ribcage, hips, and feet. He closes his eyes, ignoring the slick slide of a jellyfish along his back. Feeling the push and pull of the current, he slows, dives, spins.

The first sensation that reaches him as orca is warmth, a rippling curtain of heat as his body lengthens. The second is a stream of pictures, a tide of information about the landscape beneath him, other whales far and near, and the familiar pull of his pod that he feels in his chest.

Surfacing, he draws a deep breath. The heat of the sun along his back and dorsal fin brings a shadow memory of the same heat he felt when he was trapped in the tank. Arching his back, he dives, sounding for his pod, hearing the chatter of boat engines and the splashes of birds above him. Feels his back and dorsal fin cooling.

An echoing cry, a falling arpeggio of notes, flutters under his jaw and into his head. A picture flashes of his pod feeding to the west. He pushes air through his head, siphoning the notes, bouncing them off the sloping seafloor beneath him. Whistles cascade around him, and the picture of a river of salmon runs through his head. Muscling his flukes through the murky water, he points himself away from the sun, rising to drink the air, leaping, feeling the joy of a fleeting moment of weightlessness.

By the time he reaches the other orcas—after they swoop over and under him, George over his back, Poppy and Tia swirling their bodies around his—he knows they're aware of his concern for his grandmother. They have no answers for him, but as they swim and hunt and eat together, they stay close to him, touching him with their flukes or tails, nudging him with their heads. George encourages him to race, and Keet leaps over him and swims under, spiraling around the young orca who's more than doubled in size during the past year. It won't be long before George can swim faster than Keet, but this day, Keet absorbs the force of his smaller body with his own.

As night moves across the sea, Keet nuzzles each member of his pod, staying longest with Nana. He's happy that she ate well, but notices that she hasn't been swimming as fast or as far as she used to. He senses her steady heartbeat, the rush and gurgle of blood through her veins. Looking into her eye, he sings her name, a quiet ululation of gratitude. She rests her head against his, skin warm where they meet, and sings his name back to him. Before he returns to Osprey Bay, he catches salmon for her, feeding her until the moon is high in the sky. When he turns to swim home, the pod goes with him, leaping and sleeping in turns.

TWELVE

A lithe woman with black hair rises from the sea and walks onto the beach in Osprey Bay. Wobbling and unsteady in the gentle current, she looks first at her feet, then at the sky. Taking another step, she splays her hands in front of her, moving her fingers one at a time, then raises them to push tendrils of dripping hair away from her face. As the sun warms her skin, she slowly turns in place, and a small smile appears on the stillness of her face.

Inside her head, she still hears her mother's cries when she swam away. Now, looking back at the channel, she sees a triangular dorsal fin rise out of the water, sees an exhale blown away in the breeze. Then, the dorsal fin disappears into the sea. The woman drops to her knees in the surf, letting the water run through her fingers.

We pass Sylvie on the road by the airport. She swerves toward the yellow line as she waves out the window.

"Where's she going?" Keet asks.

"I introduced her to Chena and Ava. They're meeting for coffee in town."

"I'm glad she's making friends. She was saying last week that her friends in Sitka were dead, dying, or had moved away."

"Sounds like she was lonely up there."

We've turned onto Osprey Road, the pockmarked dirt track that takes us home. As we reach our driveway, I see a naked woman with black hair so long it looks like a cape. She's staring at her outstretched hands.

"Keet, stop!"

The SUV lurches to a halt, shooting a spatter of gravel from under its tires.

"What is it?" Keet looks out my open window. "Who …"

I jump out and trot toward the woman who's wobbling to a standing position. Before my thoughts can get in the way, I stop, breathe out, drop my weight into the rocks, and will my heart to slow its thunderous beat.

She's young, but looks older than Abbie … so, late twenties, early thirties. Her hair, which reaches past her waist, is draped around her light brown body like a cloak dripping with sea water. She continues to hold her hands in front of her face, her dark eyes examining them in wonder.

"Hello?"

In slow motion, her eyes find mine, and her hands drop. The tide swirls around her ankles. Fae and Wallace watch through the fence, tails still. The only sounds are the sea and Keet's footsteps behind me.

"I think she's our mystery female," I say.

"How do you know, Nolee?"

"I recognize her face. She's the woman who was watching me out by the buoys."

We look at each other, then at her, standing, hands by her sides, unself-conscious.

"Are you alright?" Keet asks. He leans forward, as if to move closer. I put my hand on his arm.

"Wait a moment, Keet."

The young woman looks at both of us, then drops her head and bends over, touching her knees. When she straightens, she takes a step, then stops, looking at us again.

"Do we both go to her, Nolee?"

I take another deep breath. "Why don't you park the car and grab some of your clothes for her? She's way too tall to fit into anything of mine."

"I'm not going to leave you. We don't know who she is or what she wants."

"True. I also know that whatever her reason for being here, she won't hurt us. I'm safe, Keet."

The rocks shift under his feet as he walks away. Getting back in the SUV, he drives the rest of the way up the driveway, parks, and goes into the house. The dogs are still whining to be let out of the yard.

"I'm going to come closer to you now." I'd usually ask without words, but besides the sense that her presence isn't malicious, I can't read her at all. I'm not sure we can communicate like I do with dogs, or even with Keet's pod.

She watches as I take my time walking closer. When I stop, she puts her arms out again, balancing as she walks toward me. Now her feet are in the sand and she's striding fast, eyes locked on mine, arms lowered. Her hair hangs around her, too heavy with saltwater to move. I can't see her expression, but as she gets closer, I hear her breathing—not regular breathing, more like Morse code tapped out in air.

She stops inches from me and touches her face, feeling her nose as she breathes in that odd staccato pattern. Her eyes—dark brown, the iris outlined in a thick lavender ring—meet mine and she moves toward me. When she places her hands on each side of my face, I freeze.

I hear Keet running across the rocks and put my hand out behind me. "Keet, stop. I'm all right."

"I don't know what she's capable of, Nolee."

Still holding her eyes, I say, "I know. Give us a minute."

The woman's touch is gentle. She looks over my shoulder at Keet, then at me again. Taking longer breaths, she touches my lips. The waves of confusion that began rolling through my body get smaller after hearing Keet's voice. His voice often calms me down too, but I recognize the ebbing confusion's source as the woman who has her hands on my face, not my own. My own relief courses through me as I realize that we can communicate, but it needs to be through touch.

"Keet, I think she likes the sound of our voices. Talk to her, would you?"

A hesitant smile blooms across her face. Her lips are full, her teeth small, square, and very white. She takes one hand from my face and touches her own lips and teeth.

From behind us, Keet says, "Nolee, I'm going to stand beside you." Before I can reply, I hear his slow steps and feel the warmth of his arm against mine. The woman's hand hasn't left my face; her warm fingers touch my nose, then my eyebrows. Her fingers move to the hair above her eyes, jet black against skin the same shade of brown as Keet's.

I break away my gaze and look at Keet, standing next to me with clothes bundled under one arm.

"Here, hand me that t-shirt." I hold it up so our mystery guest can see it.

"I'm going to show you how this goes on, okay?" She puts both her hands by her sides and leans in closer. Her breath smells of fish.

"Why is she breathing like that?"

I see him smile for the first time since we got back. "She's trying to talk."

"With her nose?"

"With air. Like an orca would."

My short laugh startles her, and she moves away, watching us.

Keet's black t-shirt in my hand catches her eye. I hold it up, put my head through the opening and pull it down. Then I take it off and hold it out to her.

Her hand finds the cotton, and she strokes it with one finger. Taking a small step closer to her, I gather the shirt's material around the neck opening and hold it out to her. She looks at me through the ring of material and pulls at it. I move closer again, sliding it over her head much like I dressed Abbie when she was a baby.

The woman stares at me, her hair dampening the fabric. I guide first one arm through a sleeve, then the other. Finally, I pull the material down and reach behind her to draw out her sopping hair. It feels heavier than the soaking horse tails I was made to wash after they'd been out working cattle all day in the mud. The sharp crack of my father's voice echoes in my head, chiding me. "If you can't take care of your own horse's tail, maybe you'll learn by taking care of all the riding horses' tails. Start washing them." I remember it was a summer evening and I was hungry. But I couldn't have dinner until nine other horses' tails were washed. My hands were blue with cold by the time I got into the house and mom fed me supper. She put gloves on my stiff hands so I could hold my own fork.

"Nolee?"

Keet's voice brings me back to the present, and I refocus on the woman in front of me, dressed only in Keet's t-shirt, tilting her head at the sound of our voices, pushing air through her nose.

"Can I have those sweatpants, please, Keet." When nothing meets my hand, I turn to look at him.

He's staring at her ankles as though he's seen a ghost, shock in his eyes, body rigid.

"What is it?"

He points down. "What do you see, Nolee?"

Her legs are smooth and hairless, and circling each ankle is a black line that rises and falls like waves.

"Are those tattoos?"

"I don't know what they are, but I've heard about them. Those circles connect her to a different branch of our Keykwin family: the People who live under the waves."

"You've not mentioned them before."

"I haven't heard from them—no one has. My grandmother and mother spoke of these people, but I didn't remember until now."

"Seems like some of them are still around. I wonder what those markings mean?" Looking into her eyes again, I'm both fascinated and nervous. Turning from her to Keet, I hold out my hand for the sweatpants.

I slip off my flip-flops and put a foot into a leg of the sweatpants, then take my leg out and hold the opening for her. Her hand resting on my back for support shakes as she leans over and pushes her foot quickly through the hole and back into the sand. We repeat the process with the second leg. Her hand on my back is steadier this time.

I stand and pull the sweatpants up over her hips and around her waist, then cinch the drawstring. When I look at her, she's still smiling, and I smile back. Her eyes are darker than Keet's; the lavender ring around each iris is startling, and beautiful. My nervousness evaporates.

"I don't know what they mean, or I've forgotten. What next?" Keet's voice reaches me from a distance.

"One foot in front of the other, as my mom used to say."

Keet pauses, looking at the woman now dressed in his clothes. "What's your name?" She tilts her head when he speaks, her eyes darting between him and me.

"Does everyone in your family under the waves speak the same language, Keet?"

Still looking at the young woman, he shakes his head. "I don't know."

"It appears she doesn't know either. Let's bring her in. If she's Keykwin, she'll be hungry."

Once we're in the house, I leave the young woman sitting on the sofa, staring out the windows as though she's waiting for someone. She rubs her knees in concentric circles. Keet walks into the kitchen to get her a glass of water and I open the laundry room door and call the dogs in.

They skid to a halt on the wood floor and turn to sit in front of me, wagging their tails. I put them on leashes, intending to take them outside while Keet settles our guest.

Before we get to the living room, both dogs whine. I look at Wallace, then Fae; their tails are whipping back and forth, their feet tap dancing across the floor. I feel their rising sense of excitement and expectation. The young woman stands up and stares at the dogs. Then her eyes find mine, and she sits down again, gathering her limbs close to her.

"Do you think that's a good idea?" Keet says.

"I won't introduce them yet; they need to get some exercise first. But," nodding toward our guest, "she's just as interested as they are." I walk the dogs past her and watch her eyes follow them. Wallace strains at his leash, wanting to get closer. I make it to the door when I hear Keet's voice behind me.

"I'll get lunch ready if you want to give them a run. I'm not sure what level of interest she has. Maybe she wants to learn about the dogs, maybe she wants to eat them."

A shiver runs up my spine as I'm reminded of the reality that she's most likely a mammal-eater, and that assuming human form doesn't mean her tastes have changed. However, this conflicts with the ease I feel around her—not quite my usual knowing, but a close neighbor. I can't imagine her hurting any of us.

"We'll eat out on the deck," Keet continues. "We can watch the dogs, and they'll have plenty of room to run."

When I return, I see they've started their meal. She watches Keet's hands as he uses his fork to spear salad and a bit of salmon, then puts it in his mouth and chews. She looks down at her fork and picks it up, imitating him, then puts the food in her mouth. Her expression is like a light going on in a dark room: illumination, chasing away the shadows. I smile, and she turns to me, smiling as she chews with her mouth open.

"Looks like she's pleased with that salmon salad, Keet. You sure she eats other mammals?"

"I'm not sure of anything about her."

A volley of barking from the beach gets my attention and when I turn, I see two unfamiliar dorsal fins spiking through the bay outside the buoys. Both Keet and our guest scrape back their chairs and stand at the railing for a better look. She looks at Keet, then me, then back to the dorsal fins.

"Do you recognize them, Keet?" He's frowning as he moves closer to me.

"I don't. Two females. Do you have the binoculars close by?"

I grab them from a hook by the door, taking off the lens caps.

He takes them from me and looks out at the dorsal fins. Only the tips are showing as they swim east, west, then east again, the orca equivalent of pacing a small room. Keet lowers the binoculars. "Females, a mother and sister maybe…" he trails off, thinking. "If I could see more of their dorsal fins, or saddle patches, I might recognize them."

Our guest frowns, turns her back to the bay, and sits down again with a thump; it reminds me of the way Wallace throws himself on the floor. She starts to eat again, concentrating on her plate, using the fork with care.

"I thought for a minute…" He doesn't finish what he was going to say, shrugging instead. "I've got lunch for you, too." He hands me the binoculars, and I catch a glimpse of their angular dorsal fins and the gleam of one black eye. A black eye containing longing and fear. And the fear has the distinct edge that only comes from a mother. I gasp, feeling as though a spear has pierced my belly. The dorsal fins disappear. The dogs, trotting away from the house, are busy sniffing the tide line.

Keet interrupts my thoughts. "What is it?"

My voice sounds as though it comes from a great distance. "You're right; they're both females. One is our guest's mother." We hear the clink of a fork against a plate, rhythmic and slow. Keet hands my lunch to me and we sit down at the table with our silent guest, eating and staring out at the bay, where floating logs and cormorants bob on the surface.

"Do you want to follow them?"

He shakes his head. "I need time to sort this out." He looks at our guest. "Maybe she'll go back where she came from after she eats."

I'm almost done with lunch when I notice the young woman looking at me. I smile at her, and she smiles back, then reaches out and touches my face. A fleeting feeling of curiosity uncoils in my chest. I take her hand and guide it back down to the table.

"Keet, what are we going to call her? 'Our mystery guest' and 'the young woman' aren't names." Her hands are now in my hair; when I move them away, she starts touching her own hair, fanning it through her fingers, looking at it. She holds it up to her nose, inhaling.

Keet gazes out at the bay, filled with rolling waves and the lonely cries of gulls. "She might have a name, but she can't say it."

I hear the dogs climb the stairs to the deck and the click of their nails as they trot over to us. I turn in my chair, intending to intercept them before they rush up to the young woman, but Wallace reaches her first, leaning against her leg, thumping his tail against the deck. She reaches for his head as though she's touching something fragile, running a finger along his ears. He nudges her hand and licks her wrist, and she laughs, a deep current of mirth.

The sound surprises her, and she places her fingers against her throat and laughs again.

Wallace lays his head in her lap, ears up, tail brushing against the sun-warmed boards. As I watch them, I can tell that Wallace is entranced by our visitor. Keet's looking at them as well, a small smile on his face.

"Looks like Wallace has made a new friend," he says.

"He likes her. She feels safe to him. I guess that tells us all we need to know."

She looks up at me, eyes dancing, and takes my hand. A rush of pictures slams into my head—like watching a movie on fast-forward. Images that mean something to her are stretched out, seconds, rather than flashes: soft dunes of the land underwater, sunlight through kelp, seal flippers, the flash of a lighthouse beam. And there are sounds as well: boat motors and thunderstorms, the hiss of rain on choppy water, dolphins' chattering clicks and whistles, the fizz and thrum of schooling fish.

Through it all are orcas. They touch her with their pectoral fins and rostrums, the white of their eyepatches, like the lighthouse beacon, guiding her. A female who shares each meal with her also escorts her mother, an aged orca who doesn't swim quickly, who carries scars on her right side.

As quickly as the images hit, they stop. Our hands are still wrapped together, hers warm, mine sweating. In my head, letters come into view, as though rising from deep water. Her name sounds in my head, whistles and notes, each one corresponding to a shape, each shape a letter. I frown with concentration, trying to decipher what she's telling me.

Our faces are inches apart. Her expression is quiet, unperturbed. "Say that again," I whisper. She blinks her eyes and once again I hear the sounds and notes, see the shapes ... I capture the first five letters in a name that stretches out of sight. It's like looking for a road in the dark beyond the reach of the headlights.

"Zelka?"

She lets out a single breath and smiles at me. Without thinking, I put both my arms around her and hold her to me, feeling the echo of her heartbeat in my chest. One last image surfaces in my head, as though seen through a dirty window: the mother orca, the same one I saw outside the buoys. A jagged scar bisects her eye patch, and another one forms a rough seam on her right pectoral fin. A final sight pulses behind my eyes and then fades: an overturned blue car on a beach.

"Keet, she has a name. I also saw her mother. She has scars on her right eyepatch and right pectoral fin. Sound familiar?"

He shakes his head.

"I also saw an overturned blue car on a beach. That image came from the mother orca."

Keet catches my eye, looking as though he's taken a sudden hit to the head.

"The car my mother and dad drove was blue. That's the car they died in."

THIRTEEN

Hearing the roar of his grandmother's truck and the bang of a door as she gets out, Keet turns away from Nolee and Zelka. Leaving the deck, he walks toward her where she stands by the cabin's porch, one hand on the railing, the other shielding her eyes. She looks at him as he puts his hand on her arm.

"Grandmother." He stops, unsure, realizing he doesn't have the words to tell her that the young woman sitting on the deck may be family. Keet knows her hope that her daughter still lives will rekindle, and any fragile peace she's found over time will be disrupted. He sees his grandmother waiting for him to speak. She will not make this easy by drawing it out of him.

"A new family member is here. She might be my sister."

Sylvie blinks twice. Breaking away from him, she sits down on the steps. "Is this true?"

He nods. His grandmother rises; she's unsteady on her feet, but with each step, regains her strength. By the time they reach the table, Nolee and Zelka are standing. Nolee moves, putting the young woman behind her. Keet reaches for his grandmother's hand, but she walks away from him, toward the two women standing close together.

A breeze runs through the forest, over them, and out to sea. Keet smells the tang of trees mixed with the salty musk of the sea. His grandmother stops in front of Nolee, who puts her hands on Sylvie's shoulders.

"Sylvie."

His grandmother, staring at the young woman standing tall behind Nolee, doesn't respond.

"Let me see her ankles." Sylvie's voice is firm.

Nolee, unsure, turns toward Zelka. When his grandmother kneels,

Keet hears her knees creak with the effort. Sylvie pushes up each pant leg and looks carefully at the undulating gray lines around each ankle.

"Sylvie." His grandmother looks away from Zelka, standing to look at Nolee and then Keet.

"I don't know if she's related."

"Why do you say that?"

"We are the last line of women descended from She Sings Two Worlds. Our Keykwin cousins under the water carry these markings, but those of us from the land do not."

"Which means we don't know if my mother is still alive."

"Maybe she is." Sylvie pauses. "Maybe not."

Keet wants to tell her what Nolee saw and felt. He stays silent, watching Nolee take her hand away from Zelka and lay it on his grandmother's shoulder. Green eyes stare into brown eyes. He can feel the crackle of energy, like air thickening before lightning strikes.

"Your daughter may be alive, Sylvie. She was here fifteen minutes ago, as orca, with another female. She's scarred on her right side, and I saw a blue car flipped upside down on a beach. Keet tells me that was his mom and dad's car."

After staring first at Nolee, then Zelka, his grandmother turns away, strides to her cabin and shuts the door. Keet looks at Nolee, and they both let out a breath.

Fae barks. Both dogs are on Sylvie's porch, wagging their tails as she emerges again, a bundle under one arm. The three of them sit on the deck and wait for Sylvie to reach them. Keet, who thinks he knows what his grandmother's holding, has an all-too-familiar heaviness in his chest. When Sylvie reaches them, she thrusts a bundle of clothes into Keet's arms.

"These were your mother's clothes. I have more. Give them to her." She thrusts her chin in Zelka's direction, turns, and walks back to her cabin. Keet sees no way around his grandmother's request. "Let's go inside and you can help her change."

When Zelka and Nolee come out of the bathroom, Keet stares, his stomach dropping into his feet. For the second time that day, he feels entirely unmoored. Her black hair in a long, shiny braid, his sister—if that's who she is—is wearing a denim skirt with a frayed hem that falls below her knees and a teal t-shirt. It's as though he's seeing the mother of his early childhood, flesh once more. A memory of his mother standing on the shore in Sitka, staring out at the ocean in the twilight, flashes through his mind.

"Keet, do you think she'll sleep here?"

His reply is slow in coming. "Why can't she go back with her pod? Is she planning on staying for a while?"

Nolee gives him a puzzled look. "I don't know. I'm not going to take her to the dock and pitch her back into the sea."

He realizes that she's protecting Zelka, that she wants her to stay, family or not. "Let's talk with Grandmother. We can figure out what's best."

Nolee nods and takes Zelka's hand. The young woman reaches out with her other hand, and once again touches Nolee's lips.

"She keeps doing that. I think she's trying to figure out how to talk."

"Maybe."

Nolee allows her exasperation to show. "Keet Noland. She could be your *sister*. Aren't you even a little happy to see her?"

"I wish I knew why she was here." Hearing the heaviness in his voice, Nolee turns away from Zelka and comes to stand near him.

"I forgot what a shock this must be for you. If you want to find the two female orcas, I can take her to see Sylvie."

Keet cups her face in his hand. "I'll go with you. I can wait until I don't feel so whiplashed to figure out what to do."

Nolee takes his hand. "We'll figure out this whiplash together."

Sylvie meets them at the door and motions them inside, and Keet sees the small stack of folded clothes on the table. Most are blue, all of them hold memories.

His grandmother speaks, holding out a hand to Zelka. "Come here, child."

Zelka considers Sylvie for a long moment, then looks at Nolee, who gives her a smile.

Hearing the dogs whining at the door, Nolee asks Sylvie if she can let the dogs in, and Sylvie nods. Bounding in, the dogs circle the small group. Fae sits by Nolee and Wallace leans against Zelka's leg. She reaches down and rests her hand on his head, then straightens and holds out her hand to Sylvie.

As Keet watches as his grandmother and Zelka touch for the first time, he knows they're related. Time stretches and compresses much as it does when he dives and spins, transforming from human to orca. He doesn't know whether his mother is alive or dead, but the uncertainty feels like lead in his gut.

The two women hold hands, and Zelka's serious expression softens. She leans closer to Sylvie, touching first her shoulder, then her face.

"She needs to stay here with me," Sylvie says, while simultaneously moving Zelka's fingertips to her throat, over her voice box.

Nolee looks from Sylvie to Keet, then back to Sylvie.

"She seems comfortable with us. She's welcome to stay in the guest bedroom."

Sylvie doesn't look away from Zelka, who still has her fingertips on Sylvie's throat. "She's never slept alone. She's never experienced sleeping as a human."

"We'll be in the same house, Sylvie. She won't be alone." Nolee crosses her arms in front of her.

Sylvie looks from her granddaughter to Nolee. Neither woman breaks the silence, each waiting for the other to speak. Finally, Sylvie sighs.

"She will be alone all her life. She's the last of a dying race. If she's my granddaughter, it's up to me to teach her."

Nolee interrupts. "Then I'll—"

Keet puts his hand on her shoulder. "Lia."

Moving closer to her, he softens his tone. "Grandmother is right. Until Zelka knows more about being human, she's safest in the cabin, close by. No one's saying you can't spend time with her."

Nolee lets out a loud gust of air, nodding. "Okay. I don't agree, but I want Zelka to feel safe. Sylvie—" Keet tenses as Nolee steps closer to his grandmother. "No secrets."

His grandmother looks at Zelka, straightens, and gives Nolee a single nod. "No secrets."

As his grandmother and Zelka climb the stairs, Keet touches Nolee's shoulder. "What's going on?"

She shakes her head, looking at the floor. "I know we've just met her, but somehow Zelka feels like she belongs with us."

I follow Sylvie up the stairs, hearing their creak and taking comfort in the view overlooking the ocean from what used to be my bedroom. I don't see the chest the movers brought in, but the closet door is closed and even I draw the line at asking Sylvie about that mysterious chest.

"Sylvie, the sofa downstairs pulls out into a bed. Is she sleeping there?"

"Sleeping downstairs is too far away."

"Will she sleep in your bed, then?" The double bed is roomy for one person, but Sylvie is broad and Zelka is tall. I can't imagine either of them would sleep much.

Keet takes Zelka to the sliding glass door. Keet opens it, and they step out onto the small balcony. Seeing the Salish Sea from what must be for her a very great distance, Zelka gasps.

"Nolee, help me move this." I look back to Sylvie, who's gripping the nightstand between the wall and the bed.

"Where do you want it?"

"On the opposite side of the bed. We'll push this bed against the wall, then go to town and get a single bed that will fit. The nightstand will be the only thing between the beds."

I don't argue about Sylvie's plans, but I'm still not happy. It occurs to me I'm feeling something very close to the way I felt when Abbie was born. My heart has opened to Zelka because she's let me in with the innocence of a child. I want to shield her from the world but realize that it makes little sense to shield her from her own family. I also realize that I now trust this "felt sense," as Keet calls it, as much as I do my eyes or ears. I've trusted it with dogs, and have sometimes had flashes of it with people, as I did with Jerry. But to be allowed into this Keykwin woman's interior was life-altering. She has no barriers against me when we touch, which makes me wonder why I can't reach her when we aren't.

"Keet." Sylvie's voice breaks through my musings.

Keet leads Zelka back inside, closing the sliding glass door behind them.

"Take me to town so we can get a bed for her."

I look at Keet. "I can stay here with Zelka."

He nods and follows his grandmother downstairs.

While they're gone, I walk along the beach with Zelka and the dogs. Her arm bumps into my shoulder or rests there as she watches the sea, and she laughs as the dogs take turns fetching the ball. She doesn't speak to me in that strange language of shapes and sounds again, but our silence on this sunny summer day tells me all I need to know. I like her, and I'm glad she's here.

When Keet and Sylvie return, we help them set up the bed, then go back to our own house. Even though she's next door, I already miss her.

Hearing a whoosh of an incoming text, I pick up my phone and smile. "Good news?"

"Jerry says he and Saila found a place together, and that he's found someone to talk to."

"That's great news." Keet wraps his arms around me and rests his chin on top of my head. "It's been a weird day."

I lean into him. "I'm happy Zelka is here, Keet."

He squeezes me against him, then turns and walks into the kitchen. Looking around aimlessly, he says, "I can't think about making dinner. Let's go out."

FOURTEEN

Home for the first time in three days, Keet hears the ping of a text and looks at his phone at the same time Nolee pulls into the driveway. With a puzzled look on his face, he walks outside, where Nolee's letting the dogs out of her car. As they race to the water's edge, she walks quickly to him, wraps her arms around his neck, and kisses him. He forgets everything except the woman in his arms.

"I feel like I haven't seen you in forever, Keet."

He caresses her cheek. "It definitely feels longer than three days." Leaning over, he kisses her again.

Hearing another text come through, he remembers the first one, and they go inside.

"How did the charter with the Germans go?"

"Good. They were thrilled, especially since we saw Bigg's orcas all three days. We planned on camping on a different island every night, but they liked Patos so much that we stayed there the whole time."

The dogs clatter in and Nolee herds them to the laundry room. Keet picks up his phone and looks at the texts from his grandmother.

Come over when Nolee gets home.

Then. *I saw her drive by. Come over soon.*

He sighs as he types. *Be over in ten.*

As Nolee refills the dogs' water bowl, she sees Keet staring at his phone.

"What's up?" she asks.

"Grandmother wants us to come over."

"Now?"

"I let her know we'd be there in ten minutes. How were *your* three days?"

"Busy. Two shifts at Chena's store, and today was volunteer intake day at the shelter. And I spent time with Sylvie and Zelka. What's so important that we need to rush over to Sylvie's?"

"I don't know. She didn't talk to you about anything while I was gone?"

Nolee shakes her head.

"Let's go find out, then."

"Let me grab a snack first."

Through the open door, Keet sees Zelka and Sylvie sitting at the table. Sylvie motions them in and they sit with them. Keet hears Nolee take a bite of the apple she brought with her.

"I need to take my granddaughter to get a birth certificate."

Silence follows her announcement.

Nolee is the first to speak. "Is that a good idea? She's been human for less than a week."

"Grandmother, Nolee's right. She may never need identification," Keet says.

Sylvie juts out her chin and looks past them, through the open door. "She needs to take care of herself in this world. She cannot do that without being documented."

"I don't like it, Sylvie. Why can't we wait?"

"Wait for what? I'm the only one who can testify that she is the daughter of my daughter. Keet, your mother has a birth certificate, a driver's license—"

"And a death certificate." Keet clenches his jaw. "How do you know she's your granddaughter?"

Sylvie looks at Zelka. "I considered what Nolee said she saw. I know Zelka is Keykwin. And I know that Zelka has the same smile as your mother, Keet. You didn't see it enough to remember it."

"My mother had two expressions. She was either angry or crying."

Sylvie nods, looking down. "By the time you could make your own memories of her, that is true. But before that, when my daughter was happiest, she had the same smile as Zelka gives us. I have no doubts in my mind or heart that she is the daughter of my daughter. Zelka needs a birth certificate that tells everyone she is our family. She needs that soon."

"Grandmother, is there something you need to tell us?"

"I'm old, Keet, not dying. At my age, you learn the best time for most things is now."

"She's not even talking yet, Sylvie. She's not ready for the world." Nolee reaches across the table to Zelka, who takes her hand.

"I'll be with her. I know how to help my granddaughter."

"Do you want me to go—"

Sylvie's gaze stops Nolee from talking.

"It's best that she and I go by ourselves. You can help us by finding out what we need to do."

Nolee takes a breath, ready to object, then studies Zelka, who's moved her other hand to Sylvie's shoulder. Conversation stops, and Keet feels a wave of calm taking over. He looks at Zelka closely, realizing that even if she's not speaking, she understands what's being said.

"As long as we're making plans," Keet says, "I'd like to swim out and see if I can find out if my mother is still alive."

Zelka gives him a sharp look and drops her hands into her lap.

"I'm not saying I'll bring her back here. But I need to know if it's her, and why she never chose to find me again when she survived that wreck."

"I'll find out where you need to go," Nolee says. "It'll probably require staying overnight, so I'll also book a room for you."

Sylvie nods, watching as Nolee taps her phone.

"There's an office in Bellingham. You'll need to take the ferry to Anacortes and drive up. Do you want me to print out the directions for you?"

"I have the GPS. We'll be fine."

"I'll step outside so I can call and get an appointment."

Looking at Keet, Sylvie stands up. "Go find your mother, if she's out there, Keet."

"I'll swim out this evening."

Minutes later, Nolee strides back in, slipping her phone into a hip pocket. "They can see you on Wednesday morning at ten. I'll use my laptop to arrange the rest of your trip." As she turns to leave, Zelka goes to her and takes her hand. The room is silent, then Nolee speaks.

"It's not like here, Zee. It's loud and fast and there are a lot more people. I worry you'll be scared."

Zelka takes Nolee's other hand, holding both in her own, then steps closer and smiles. Nolee's face relaxes, and she gives a small chuff of laughter.

"Okay. You're right." Kissing Zelka on the cheek, she waves to Sylvie. "I'll bring the rest of the details of your trip over when I've completed everything." She leaves before anyone can ask any questions.

"We'll come back, Grandmother. Nolee and I need to talk about my plan."

Zelka follows him out the door, then picks up a dirty tennis ball and trots to the beach with the dogs. When she flings the tennis ball, they turn and give chase.

Behind our house, the hardwoods are flaunting their yellow leaves in a show of late summer preparation of the colder weather to come. Zelka's outside, throwing the ball for the dogs, but instead of being out there with her, enjoying the gorgeous day, I'm in our office, printing out reservation information for Sylvie.

This time last year, I was in a state of panic—Keet had left me, and I felt worthless. As I'm ruminating about what a difference a year has made, Keet walks in. I close the laptop, giving it a tap with my fingers.

"What did Zelka say to you, Nolee?"

"That she's curious about the world. That she's only known a small part of it and wants to know more."

He nods, watching her through the window. "I understand your concern, though."

"She reminded me that she's Keykwin and comes from a long line of people who were brave."

"Can't argue with that."

"I didn't even try."

"I think her presence here means one of two things," Keet says. "Either my mother is dying or ..." he pauses, looking away from the sea and into my eyes. "My mother is still alive and Zelka doesn't want to be with her."

"Your mother is alive, Keet, I'd swear it was her swimming outside the buoys when we found Zelka."

"I know, and I trust what you felt. But until I see her for myself, I can't swear to it."

"What do you need to do?"

"Eat some dinner before I swim out to find her. I may be away for a couple of days."

My breath catches in the cage of my ribs and rattles around in my chest.

Keet takes my hand. "Nolee? Lia?"

I will my eyes to focus on his.

"What's going on?" He cups my face in his hands.

I take another breath. "I'm scared."

"Tell me why."

"The last time you said that, you were gone for months. I didn't know you'd been captured, that you were trapped in that awful tank. I just knew you'd left me. And then when you got back, you left me again."

He leans over and pulls me to him. Closing my eyes, I ground myself in the sound of his heartbeat and the whoosh of breath in and out of his lungs.

"If it *is* my mother, she won't be far away. I'll find my pod, and they'll help. I won't do this alone."

"But you don't know you won't run into trouble."

I feel him nod. "You're right. And I still need to go."

"Would Zelka go with you?"

He pulls away from me.

"Why?" His tone's not angry, but there's a warning note, an edge to his tone.

"She can show you where she last saw her. Your mother."

"You were the last one to see her. Right here, in the bay."

"She—" I let go of his hands.

"Nolee, Zelka isn't your daughter, but you're acting like she is. Why are you so protective of her?"

"She's most likely your sister, and you're treating her like a stranger."

"Because she is!"

"Not to me. She's here for a reason. Our job is to give her a family until she can tell us what that reason is."

"She has a family–they're out there right now." He gestures toward the window, as if he could conjure orcas from sea and sky.

"If she wanted to be with them, she'd still be out there. She's here. With us. I won't treat her any differently than I have been. I like her. The question is, why don't you?"

The silence between us is an anchor holding us against the rising swell of our emotions.

"I'm going to let the dogs in." I step outside and whistle for the dogs, who are with Zelka on Sylvie's porch. I wave to her as Fae and Wallace trot to the house. Once they're inside, I take extra time wiping off their wet paws. When I go back to the office, Keet is still sitting near my desk.

"Do what you need to do, Keet. My fear isn't your responsibility. Find your mom if she's out there."

It feels as though the swells are growing larger. Keet is silent, although a storm of emotion plays across his face. Looking away from me, he gets up and paces the room. He's usually the living definition of equanimity, but since his family started showing up, his agitation surprises me.

"Your fear isn't my *responsibility*, Nolee? Is anything my responsibility? Or am I absolved of anything to do with you at all?"

Jolted out of my train of thought, I feel a rush of heat run through me, thawing the freeze. Fae, who'd been lying on my foot, shifts, putting her weight across both of my feet. I take a breath, waiting for the heat to pass. The fiery words I want to say could burn down everything he and I have rebuilt.

"What I meant was, it's important to you to find your mother. I don't want my fear to stop you."

He paces, his long strides making a short distance between the room's walls. Finally, he stops in front of the desk and puts a hand on its smooth surface, as if to draw strength from the wood.

"Keet, what's going on?"

"I thought everything was in its place," he mutters before walking back to the armchair and sitting down. "My grandmother would stay with Jerry, and I'd swim north twice a year to visit her. My mother and dad, dead. No siblings. No family. Just you and me, beginning our lives together." A wave of compassion pushes against my anger as I realize what Keet has been struggling with.

Fae stands, walks to Keet, and lays her head on his knee. He scratches behind her ears.

"Instead, my grandmother lives next to us with a sister I didn't know existed until today, and my mother has been alive for thirty years without my knowledge. Jerry has a girlfriend in Juneau, and now it's not you and I starting fresh together. It's all this family drama I don't want!"

"It's a lot when you put it that way."

He nods. "On top of that, you want to make sure I don't feel pressured by anything you feel."

"Wait. What?"

"You told me your fear isn't my responsibility."

"Yes, and it's true."

"Maybe. But what *is* my responsibility, then? Are we living together because it's fun? Convenient? I thought…" He blows out a breath. "I thought that by taking this next step—by moving in together—it signifies that we *do* have a responsibility for one another. I choose to live my life in relation to yours, and I hope you choose to live yours in relation to mine. I'm not interested in being roommates with benefits."

The words I want to say freeze inside me. Keet waits, his eyes on Fae as he pets her head. The images in my head are on a reel that moves like clockwork: following my father's orders, even when I was scared; marrying Nathan and ignoring my gut telling me we would be better friends to each other than spouses; scenes of my life with him, pretzeling myself into different shapes, trying to be a person he would pay attention to before finally realizing that I could love our daughter so much that Nathan could disappear. Those images, like watching a silent movie of my life, unfreeze the words I need to say.

"You're talking about how everything has changed with your family, and how it's taken you by surprise, right?"

He nods.

"You've taken me by surprise. Our living together is a huge surprise. I find myself in my old habit of not being a pain in the ass, of not causing you to look at me without that light in your eyes, all so you won't leave me. It's the only pattern I know. Just like your pattern with your family."

Fae leaves us, and I hear her drinking from her water bowl in the kitchen. Keet takes my hand, his eyes brimming with tears. "I *want* to live my life in relation to you, Keet, but I don't know how to. Can you be patient with me while I change my habits?"

He leans over and kisses me, then whispers "yes," against my lips. He ends the kiss, placing his forehead against mine as he says, "Can you be patient with me while I figure out my family? Let's help each other, Lia, instead of pushing each other away."

We both stand, holding each other. "I'm happy to help you, Keet, and happy to be helped. Now let's get you something to eat so you can find your mom."

FIFTEEN

That evening, after leaving Nolee and diving into the rising tide, Keet whistles for his orca pod. He sends out waves of sound through water, listening for their presence. After many breaths and a long swim, he hears his orca family feeding. They reunite in a jubilation of frothy water, leaping and touching, long and short whistles mingling with the sound of boat motors, distant whale cousins, and the sea's susurration. His youngest cousin, George, refuses to leave Keet's side, bumping him, rolling over his broad back, inviting him to swimming games. They play, then Keet hunts and shares salmon with his family.

The following day, not long after sunrise, Keet feels his mother before he sees her, and a shadowy memory of her arms around him when he was still small enough to curl up in her lap crosses his mind. Keet sends out the soft burst of clicks and whistles that is her orca name. His family pod surfaces, then dives beneath him.

Against his jaw, like the slippery tickle of kelp, he hears his own name in a creaky, whistle-filled static. He dives deeper in the dark-green water, searching for the familiar thump of her heart. Then she swims into view, her heartbeat slow and labored. He bursts her name to her again, along with a flow of memory pictures of their time in Sitka. She sings back to him with visions of their cabin, visions of their first swim together as orca.

As she glides closer, Keet flips over, white belly to the surface, then twists right side up. He sounds along the right side of her body, touching her with clicks as gentle as mist on skin. Floating toward her, drifting on the swell of the tide, he sees the long, dark scar that bisects her eyepatch, and the jagged cleft of her right pectoral fin. He touches her rostrum with his own. His heart slows in time with hers as he lays his giant head along the scarred eyepatch. Closing his eyes, he sounds soft chirps and cries that spiral to the surface in a cloud of bubbles.

Keet hears his pod rising and falling, breathing, remaining close; their calls reassure him. Swimming behind and below him, they reveal the presence of his mother's small pod, silent and out of sight. The low hum of a passing boat fills the water.

When Keet drifts close to her again, his mother noses along his side, along his back, up his dorsal fin, where she touches his pectoral fin with hers. Then he's drifting in her wake as he did when he was small, and her voice guided him into the world of orca.

Before he can ask any questions, she erupts in a volley of triple notes, whistles that pierce his ear. They both surface, and the air against the top of their bodies feels warm in comparison to the chilly water. After simultaneous inhales, they dive together, and she opens the book of her life after the car accident to him. Her images are in his head, her sensations wash through his body. He sees her right hand, slippery with blood, is missing the first finger; a jagged point of bone rises from the knuckle where the finger used to be. The picture changes and now he's looking through broken glass at a human man—his father, head brutally twisted, brown eyes sightless.

A throbbing begins deep inside Keet, and he knows his mother is worrying about the baby she carries. Another jab, and through a wash of red, he sees her swollen belly, then the man again. Sirens wail in the distance, but his mother's high keening is much louder. His own heart vibrates with the strain.

Another pull, as though he's being punched from the inside. Cradling her belly with her undamaged hand, she uses the other to wipe the blood out of her eyes. Her feet are cold. She stumbles toward the water, unthinking, wanting the pain in her body, and in her heart, to stop. She's in the water, wading, fighting contractions, pushing deeper, groaning as saltwater sloshes against her wounds. Taking a breath, she lowers herself into the water, the drumming in her belly throwing her into panic.

Deep within her memories, as she swims out into the sea, he sees her twist into orca, ribbons of blood trailing after her as she swims—swims away from the man she loves, with no elders to bid her goodbye, to usher her into her Walk Into the Water. Pushing against the current with her weak fluxes, she surfaces and looks back toward the beach, where the people are swarming around the overturned car. When the gripping pain in her abdomen lessens and then goes quiet, she thinks she's killed her daughter.

As Keet surfaces and inhales, retreating into his own body, he hears the family pods exchanging information, their clicks and trills bouncing against the seafloor. As he and his mother dive and swim away from their pods, his mother drafts in the current created by Keet's large body. They swim through sunset and moonrise, nudging one another, reassuring one another, each taking joy in the other's existence. When Keet paints sound pictures of Zelka as a human woman, his mother receives them first in silence, then a single whistle. Keet hears, *my daughter*. Behind them, their pods are sharing the locations of salmon and the best parts of the day and night to hunt.

Keet's mother stops and floats to the surface, and he joins her; they bob together, warm sides touching. She nudges him, sings his name in double descending notes, and swims away. He knows she's returning to her pod. It's time for him to return to Nolee.

As he waits for the others to catch up, he scans for salmon, which he locates ahead and beneath him before his pod joins him in a flurry of black and white. Rollicking through the water, George bumps into him, flipping over his back and under his belly. Nana rests her pectoral fin against his and they dive together. They swim and eat and watch over George as he drifts next to his mother, napping and lazily flicking his tail.

By sunrise, they're floating outside the buoys in Osprey Bay. Keet nudges each of them, staying with Nana the longest and rumbling the low notes of her name. He feels the quiet peace that emanates from her.

Then he dives, twists, and rises again as a man. As he swims to the dock, he sees Nolee and the dogs waiting for him. She has a towel in one hand and is pressing the other against her heart as though to keep it from leaping from her chest. Pulling himself up onto the bobbing dock, slick from last night's rain, he smiles.

The dogs and I have been awake since the early hours of the morning. I'd like to think my dream of Keet and Nana, George, Belle, Atma, Tia, and Poppy swimming together in a companionable black-and-white knot was a portent of their coming—an antidote to the fear that engulfs me every time Keet swims away from home.

As I lie dozing on the sofa in front of a fire, I'm snapped awake by the sound of Keet's voice inside my head, saying my name. I rub my eyes and see the dogs at the window; Fae's wagging her tail. In the gray light, I jump up, pull a jacket on over my nightgown, and grab a towel from a hook by the door. The dogs and I race across the deck, and I know they'll reach the dock before I do.

Out in the bay, dorsal fins appear and disappear in the early morning light. The largest, next to Nana, sinks, then Keet comes up, black hair slicked against his skull. Knifing his arms through the water, he reaches the dock where I wait for him. He shakes the water from his face and pulls himself up. I'm so eager to hold him that I almost send both of us into the cold water.

"Welcome home," I breathe into his chest, warm and damp beneath my cheek.

He strokes my head, holding me tightly. Stepping away from him, I hold up the towel. He kisses me, then rubs his hair and dries himself off; as he wraps the towel around his waist, I put my hand on the soft roundness of his belly.

Covering my hand with his own, he says, "I think I know what it's like to be pregnant."

Startled, I clear my throat. "What's it like to be pregnant?"

"Let's go inside and I'll tell you, though you're still the expert."

Washing dishes after our quick breakfast, Keet shares what he saw and felt when he met his mother.

"Let me make sure I understand this, Keet. Your mom was thrown clear of the car when it landed near Samish Bay, but your dad died. Your mom was at least eight months pregnant. She was injured and in early labor when she went into the sea and changed into orca."

Keet nods. "And she was worried about her baby—"

"Your sister," I interrupt.

He gives me a long look, but I hold my ground.

"She thought she'd killed her baby. She was close to giving birth when she was human, but an orca's gestation time is double a human's."

"How long?"

"Up to eighteen months. She didn't know when she'd give birth, or what it would be, or if it would even be alive."

"Do you think that's the reason you couldn't hear Zelka? Because your mom changed before the baby was born? Making Zelka different somehow?"

Keet lets out a long sigh. "Maybe. I don't know. When my mom took me into the water the first time, I was four. My grandmother was furious. I was supposed to have a ceremony when I was nine, to prepare me."

"Why did your mom do that?"

"Rebelliousness? Not thinking straight?" He shakes his head.

"What happened when your mom gave birth to Zelka?"

He looks at me again, his face more open, his eyes brighter. "I don't know. We didn't get that far. But I'm glad to know she's alive, even if I'm angry that she's stayed away so long."

"We need to tell Sylvie."

He nods. "We'll tell her tomorrow morning, when she and Zelka get back from Bellingham."

Zelka sits motionless in the front seat of her grandmother's pickup, eyes wide, hands tightly clasped in her lap. The noise is deafening, but she's adapted to it, as she has to the sight of cars speeding past them faster than she's ever been able to swim. Swiveling her head, she looks at her grandmother—Sylvie—who needs a cushion to see over the steering wheel. They're almost at a place called Anacortes, where the ferry will take them back to Camas Island. Back to Osprey Bay. Back to her brother and Nolee.

When they got on the ferry yesterday, there were too many cars and too many people making too much noise. Zelka was halfway out of the truck and heading for the churning water when Sylvie caught up with her; she would've jumped had her grandmother not stayed beside her. At first, she had to close her eyes and put her hands over her ears. Then Sylvie took one of her hands and started talking. She told her stories of ravens and stories of trees, stories of all the different people on the earth. She talked about cars and boats, about where they were going, and when they would return home. Once Zelka was calmer, Sylvie led her back to the truck, still holding her hand.

They ate and slept in a tall dark building. Sleeping as human was easy for Zelka, and in some ways, more refreshing. She listened to her grandmother's breathing and let it soothe her into sleep. Sleep was a black place, deeper than the underwater canyons into which she and her mother used to swim.

After waking up and eating, they drove to a short square building. Once again, Grandmother took her hand. She walked them both into a room where other people were sitting in chairs and staring at the wall, watching a square covered with moving pictures. Letting go of her grandmother's hand, she rushed to the square, touching the giant face of the person talking. He had white hair and very blue eyes. She put a hand on his throat, trying to feel what he was saying.

There was a loud noise of many voices behind her, then her grandmother calmly guided her away from the square and back to her seat—a wobbly chair that made a good sound when she rocked back and forth in it. Sylvie sat still beside her.

They were called into a smaller room by a person shaped like Zelka, but shorter. This one had a desk smaller than the one in Nolee's office, a funny shaped box that had lights and made noises, and three places to sit. The person had bright, spiky hair and something shiny in her nose. Zelka reached to touch it, but her grandmother stopped her.

The person said, "How can I help you today?"

Her grandmother and the person exchanged many sounds. Zelka couldn't stop staring at the person's hair, its beautiful color. She pulled her own hair over her shoulder, remembering that Nolee had called it a "ponytail"—*What is a pony, and what is a tail?* —and looked at it. Not the same. *This person comes from a distinct line of people*, Zelka thought. She points to the other person's hair, then to her own.

"Doesn't she talk?" the woman asked Sylvie.

"She's not been around many people. She's from rural Alaska and only speaks the language of her family."

Zelka keeps pointing at the person's head while holding her own hair in the other hand.

Sylvie gives a low chuckle. "I think she wants to know the color of your hair."

Zelka nods, then smiles.

The woman smiles back. "This is amethyst. Purple."

Zelka flips her hair behind her. "Amah-thist. Purr-pull." Her grandmother stares at her, then smiles and pats her knee.

The purple-hair person rolls her chair away from the desk, pulls open a drawer, and hands papers to her grandmother, who takes a pen and fills them out.

They leave the small room and go through the big room. Zelka looks at the square, but the man with eyes like the winter sky is gone. In the truck, Zelka hears sounds—words—in her mind. She remembers the words "birthday," "identity," "next appointment," but she doesn't know what they mean.

Her grandmother says, "You are brave for coming with me out into this world. I'm proud of you." Zelka returns her grandmother's gaze and nods as she's seen her family do, although her version brings her chin to her chest and back up again. Her grandmother starts the truck, joining the river of cars going back the way they came.

At first, she thought she'd never figure out the strange sounds coming from throats and through mouths. But within two suns, she'd begun to understand, particularly names. Smiles and laughter and feelings in her chest that faintly echo her orca sensations are also recognizable. Some of the music that Keet plays reminds her of kin under the waves, the small and large singers, the hyper-chatter of her dolphin cousins. Relaxing her hands in her lap, she takes as big a breath as her small lungs allow and touches her grandmother's shoulder.

"Yes, child?"

Zelka lays a hand on her stomach and touches her mouth.

"I am hungry too. We'll get something to eat on the ferry." After her grandmother pays the ferry fee, they join a long line of cars. Zelka's nose fills with exhaust fumes. She reaches for a handle, looking at it, then her grandmother.

"Do this." Sylvie puts her hand on the crank and moves it in a circle, rolling her own window up, and Zelka does the same, watching as the window rises in fits and starts. Pleased with her accomplishment, she smiles at her grandmother. Sylvie puts a warm hand on her shoulder, then drives forward as the line of cars moves.

Home again, Sylvie pulls up in front of Keet's garage and Zelka opens the pickup door before her grandmother has rolled to a stop. Keet and Nolee and the dogs are on the beach, moving driftwood up to the tree line. Wallace sees Zelka and races for her, ears back, mouth wide, tail wagging. She sits on the ground, and when Wallace knocks her backward, she laughs. "Gooboy."

She stands as Nolee walks up to them. Smiling, Nolee says, "He *is* a good boy, isn't he?"

Zelka hugs Nolee, and as memories of the trip begin unspooling behind Zelka's eyes, Nolee stops rubbing her back. Zelka can feel Nolee sharing in her experiences and it's so close to how she feels when she's orca that she squeezes Nolee tighter before releasing her.

"That was a big trip, Zee. I'm glad you're home." They both turn and see Keet and Sylvie talking by her truck.

"You found her?"

Keet nods. "I did. She explained many things."

"But she didn't come back?"

"She swam away with another orca pod. I don't know if she'll ever come here."

Sylvie grunts, shuts the truck door, and turns toward her cabin. "I'm going to go lie down."

Zelka watches the stooped form of her grandmother, then goes to stand next to Keet. She and Keet are the same height, and when she touches his shoulder, he's aware of flickering images at the edges of his vision. Giving her a small smile, he removes her hand and walks down to the beach. Zelka watches him go.

Nolee calls out. "C'mon, Zee. I need a snack before dinner. Are you hungry?"

"Hungry."

"I thought so. I haven't met a Keykwin yet who wouldn't eat when food was offered."

SIXTEEN

The dogs' whining sounds distant, noises encased in cotton batting. Only half awake, I wonder if I'm dreaming. But when I crack my eyes open, I see the soft light of an early fall morning, the solid line of Keet under the blankets, his ribcage rising and falling with each slow breath.

The dogs whine again. It sounds like they're in the living room. Swinging my legs out of bed into the early-morning chill, I put on my robe and slippers and shuffle down the hall. Fae and Wallace are standing by the front window, tails low, ears forward. I stand at the window with them, my hand resting on Wallace's broad head.

A white shape is floating by the dock, but I can't tell what it is. I'll need to go out on the deck to see better.

"Dogs, stay inside." As I step out, they watch me, curious, and I feel their bubbling anticipation of a run, of something new to investigate. The white shape changes, comes into focus. It's the head of a woman, her hands gripping the dock. Dawn bathes both her and the water in its soft reflected light.

Almost without thinking, I hurry to the dock. Now that I'm closer, I see that the woman's face is lined, and her skin is a darker shade than Keet's. Any lingering doubts about her identity are erased when I see her eyes. It's Keet's mother.

Torn between helping her or going back to the house for Keet, I hear the dogs scrabbling across the deck and down to the beach. They stand, one on each side of me, raising their noses to the wind. Keet's not far behind them.

Dressed in only the shorts he sleeps in, he runs across the dock and drops to his knees, holding out his hand. Looking into his face, the woman reaches for him with her left hand. By the time I join them, she's kneeling on the dock's swaying surface, head lowered, white hair lying like tendrils of bleached seaweed along her back. I throw my robe around her, and Keet and I help her stand.

"Let's give her a minute," Keet says.

We look at one another, and I see the shock move across his face as she straightens to her full height.

"Nolee. I'd like you to meet my mother, Hazel Noland."

At the sound of her name, Hazel's eyes, blank and dim, meet mine. She pulls away from us, trying to break free.

"Mother, you need to let us help you at least to the house."

She scowls at him, takes a couple of shaky steps, then stops and pulls the robe closed. I tie the belt for her, careful to avoid her eyes. By the time we reach the deck, she's almost able to walk on her own. Looking down at the arm I'm holding, I see the scarring that runs up her hand disappear under the robe's sleeve. The first finger on that hand is missing, an uneven stump the only indication of where it had been.

Once we're inside and she's sitting down, wrapped in a blanket, I see another scar, a puckered, jagged line pale against her brown skin. It runs from under her hair above her right ear, down her neck, and ends at her collar bone. She feels me looking at her, and turns away, sinking more deeply into the sofa.

"Nolee, can you go get Grandmother and Zelka, please?" The tension I can feel running through his body tells me this won't be a simple family reunion.

When I open the door, I see Sylvie rushing across the grass, Zelka close behind her. When the dogs greet them, they give each of them a distracted pat on the head. Sylvie looks up, spotting me waiting for them on the deck. Her hair has escaped her bun, and she brushes it away with a trembling hand. Zelka, her face pale and frightened, stays behind her grandmother.

We meet on the deck, and Sylvie grips my wrist with her gnarled hand, the tremble gone. "Is it true?" she whispers. "Is she here?"

I nod, unable to form words.

"I've been dreaming of her arrival every night since Zelka came to us."

"It's not a dream anymore, Sylvie."

Keet looks up when he hears the door bang open. His grandmother grips the doorframe, her face blank with shock, her eyes wide. In the next moment, she rushes across the room and drops onto the sofa next to Hazel, who looks at her mother but doesn't speak; her lips set in a hard line.

Looking over his shoulder, Keet sees Zelka standing in the doorway, her face expressionless. Nolee takes her hand and leads her to the table.

Rooted in place as the past and the present crash into each other, Keet feels himself being tugged in opposing directions. He feels Nolee's hand on the small of his back as she directs him into the kitchen, turning on the burner underneath the kettle.

"Let's give them a moment."

Keet wants to go back, to demand an explanation, but Nolee's hand is still on his back. As he looks into her eyes, he hears a small gasp behind them and turns to see Zelka, fists clenched in her lap, watching her mother and grandmother. They sit without speaking, holding one another's gaze in stony silence. Keet waits for the pressure to break and scatter the emotional detritus of the storm his mother has brought into their home.

He looks back at Nolee; her eyes, as they always do, anchor him.

Taking down two presses, Nolee says, "We'll need coffee and tea. Maybe a few things to eat." As he moves to the refrigerator, he hears the hiss of coffee grounds settling into one of the presses and the flutter of green tea leaves in the other.

While assembling a meal of leftover fish; a plate of cheese, crackers, olives, sliced apples, and bananas; and a half loaf of sourdough bread and stick of butter, he dares a look at the two women on the sofa. His grandmother has wrapped Hazel in her arms, her back shaking as she cries. Hazel's face is blank, her eyes staring into space. Keet sighs, resting his hands on the worn wooden countertop, counting its cuts; he's up to fifty-three when he feels a light hand on his shoulder. Zelka's watching him, her pupils small in the brown and lavender of her eyes.

He puts his hand over hers, smiling. "It'll be okay, Zelka. We'll figure it out."

He isn't sure she understands him, but she smiles back. The kettle whistles and Nolee pours the steaming water into each press and sets the lids in place. Remembering the platter of food, he puts it on the table, then walks to the sofa and rests a hand on each woman's shoulder.

"Let's eat something. I've made coffee, Grandmother. Mom, do you want coffee or tea?"

She glares up at him, gathers her hair in one hand, and swings it behind her back.

"Clothes." Her voice is harsh, a chainsaw whisper in her throat. She clears it. "Then coffee."

Keet's grandmother rises. "I have your clothes."

Hazel stands and takes a hesitant first step, pushing Sylvie away when she tries to help. "Let me be. I'll go with you."

After they leave, Keet, Nolee, and Zelka stand at the window, watching them make their slow way to the cabin. At Nolee's whistle, the dogs skitter into the house, slobber and dirt and wagging tails. Nolee pets both, then Wallace settles himself next to Zelka while Fae shadows Nolee.

Keet pours two half-cups of coffee, adding milk to the brim and putting sugar in his mom's. Next, he pours the green tea into three mugs. Nolee comes back and sets plates on the table, along with a handful of silverware. The last time he had this many dishes on the table was when she first spent the night with him. He smiles at the memory, letting it remind him of his present life, letting it soften the jagged edges of his past. He laughs, remembering what he said about edges to Nolee, thinking of Creator's sense of humor, returning Keet's own words to him on the dented platter of family history. Nolee looks over at him, relief on her face that he's found something to smile about.

They sit silent at the table, Zelka between them, waiting for Hazel and Sylvie to return. Keet, restless, gets up. "I need to walk. Be right back." Half jogging out to the beach, he rolls up his pant legs and walks into the cold water, feeling the rocks settle under his feet. He wonders how he can feel so empty and so overwhelmed at the same time.

On his way back, he hears the bang of a door and sees his mother and grandmother leaving the cabin, making their way to the house. His mother wears a sweater over a long dark dress, and her hair is in a braid that hangs past her waist. Quickening his stride, he arrives behind them. Nolee hands him a towel and he brushes the sand off his feet, a shifting sense of unreality tugging at him still. Smoothing down his pant legs, he takes a breath and stands, facing the two women he's known the longest. He says the first words that feel safe.

"Mom, Grandmother, your coffee is on the table. Help yourself to the food."

They take turns filling their plates. He tries not to watch his mother as she remembers how to move her body. He knows how it feels, the hesitation between thought and action; being human after being orca is like swimming through sludgy water. His grandmother doesn't eat. She sits close to her daughter, sipping coffee, looking out the window.

Keet realizes that as strange as he finds this, it must be even stranger to Nolee. He places his hand on her thigh and she covers it with hers; a tight smile contradicts the worry in her eyes.

"Why are you here, Hazel?" Although his grandmother has phrased it like a question, to Keet, it sounds more like a command for his mother to explain herself.

The cuff of the sweater rolled away from Hazel's wrist reveals a bold highway of veins across her left hand as she puts food on her plate; her right hand remains in her lap. She pauses, taking a sip of coffee and closing her eyes.

"I'm here for my daughter. She's coming back with me. We don't belong here." Finishing her coffee, she bangs the mug on the table and eats the last of the food from her plate.

Hearing the menace in Hazel's voice, my grip tightens on Keet's hand.

"She belongs wherever she wants to be, Hazel." At my words, Hazel turns her eyes on me, her black gaze intensifying. I sit straighter, refusing to be cowed by the menace she projects. I thought Keet's uncle was intimidating, but he could take lessons from Hazel.

"You're not Keykwin. You're not even family."

Feeling Keet release my hand and half-raise from his seat, I touch his arm. "Keet, it's okay." Turning back to Hazel, I lean toward her.

"This doesn't have to be decided right now. Let's wait until Zelka can speak for herself. Meantime, we can get to know each other."

My attempt to calm the situation skips across Hazel like a flat rock on water. She leans away from me, motioning toward Zelka.

"She can't speak for herself. She's never been human—"

I interrupt when I hear her raised voice, which is winding into a tirade.

"Zelka is human now, and she showed up for a reason. She needs time to tell us what that reason is."

I turn to Zelka. "You don't have to decide right now. You're welcome here with us."

The chair creaks beneath Keet's weight. His voice quiet, he addresses his mother. "Mom, Nolee's right. Let's slow down and get to know one another again."

Hazel turns her head and looks out the window, then moves more food onto her plate. Sylvie watches Hazel, then puts her arm around her shoulders.

"Daughter, it's good to see you." She takes her arm away and fills her own plate with the rest of the food.

I glance at Zelka's empty plate and touch the rim. "Zee, do you want more?"

A sudden smile brightens her face. I hear her push air through her teeth, then she rests a delicate hand on her throat. "Zee."

In the silence, I feel tears fill my eyes. Slicing an apple, I put it on Zee's plate and watch as she uses a fork to eat it. The crunch of apples between her teeth is the only sound in the room.

After a meal thick with unsaid words, Keet and I walk with his family to the cabin. Pulling out the sofa, we make it into a bed for Hazel. As I tuck the sheets under the mattress, Zelka stands beside me and touches my arm. She nods at the mattress, wanting to help.

"Yes, why don't you tuck that side in?" She walks around to the opposite side, watching what I'm doing and mimicking me.

I hear the thump of three sets of feet coming down the stairs. When I look up to get a read on how things are going, I see Sylvie and Keet. Hazel's rubbing her forehead.

"Hazel?"

She avoids my eyes. "I need to sleep."

"We've made your bed."

She sits on the edge of the bed, staring at the floor.

"Granddaughter," Sylvie says. Zelka looks at her, then at her mother. "We'll go outside so your mother can sleep." Zelka turns, smiles at Keet and me, and walks out onto the porch. As Sylvie passes us, Keet touches her arm and she stops.

"Remember what we talked about? Please give it some thought."

Sylvie nods. I go outside and wait as Keet draws a blanket over Hazel, who's lain down still in her clothes. Sylvie and Zelka walk toward the cove.

Watching their retreating forms, I wait for Keet. When I feel him beside me, I turn to him. "What do you want Sylvie to think about?"

He pauses, takes a deep breath. "I'd like my mom and grandmother to introduce Zelka to my family pod."

"Is that a problem?"

After a burst of bitter laughter, he shakes his head. "Only that my mom can't wait to get back to being orca, and my grandmother hasn't been one in five decades."

I look at my watch. "Keet, I need to be at the shelter in a couple of hours. Did you say you have a tour today, too?"

He nods. "I think my grandmother can handle things here."

I take his hand and we walk back to our home, where the rubble of the meal waits for us on the table. After cleaning up, we undress in the bathroom and step into the steaming shower.

Keet watches the water stream in rivulets over the round curve of Nolee's hip. It starts in her wet hair, sleeked back, shimmering where the sun hits it through the skylight. The water races from the ends of her hair, down the groove of her spine, over her hip, and down the length of her leg muscles. Her skin is pale in the places that she keeps covered, but her arms are soft and tan. He can't keep from tracing the crystalline water's path: down back, down flank, down hip. A need to be close to her overcomes him, especially after the chaos of his family. He puts an arm around her waist and pulls her to him. She turns in his arms, wiping water away from her face.

"Keet? I'm a little—" she gives a huff of embarrassed laughter. "As sexy as being in the shower together is, I'm feeling out of sorts. And..." She stops talking as he kisses her words away. "... I could do shower sex when I was twenty-five, but I'm no longer twenty-five. Hell, I'm not even forty-five..." Her voice trails away as he tastes the water on her neck.

He kisses her again and brings his hands up to feel the curve of her skull. He wraps his arms around her waist, then straightens and lifts her off the tiled floor. "Is it too much?"

"I don't want you to stop, but I also don't know how I feel after everything that's happened this morning." She sighs and then, feet still off the floor, kisses him.

He sets her down. "I don't have any ulterior motives other than enjoying this moment with you. I'm harmless, remember?" He kisses between her breasts, inhaling her scent as it mixes with the water. When he pulls back, he sees the confusion in her eyes.

"Don't you need time to process everything that's happened?" she asks as she moves away from the hot water that hisses over them.

"I need you, *especially* after everything that's happened. You're my calm in the storm, Lia."

She steps back under the flow of the water, not taking her eyes from his. Keet moves toward her, kissing her as water cascades over them. He backs up, guiding her to the shower's tiled seat. The steamy glass makes it feel as though they're the only two people in the world. Now one, the steam swirling between their faces, he wonders again how he found her, and why she stayed. He sees only the green of her eyes, like an emerald expanse of water he could swim in for the rest of his life.

Once out of their shower, he dries her back and kisses her between her shoulder blades. "I love you, Magnolia Burnett."

She turns and kisses him. "I love you too."

At the end of my workday, Wallace and Fae wait in the back seat of my car as Andi and I talk.

"So Keet's family is all there?" She gives me a wry smile. "All the in-laws. How's that going?"

"About as you'd imagine," though I don't think she *could* imagine beings who are both human and orca. "Tense. But I think we'll get things worked out."

"If you need a referee, let me know. I got plenty of practice with my kids."

I laugh, hugging her. "Thanks, Andi. When's our next Casa Mariachi night?"

"I'll text you next week. You might need a marg to yourself after all that family time."

"Maybe so."

Arriving home, I don't see Keet's vehicle. When the dogs and I go inside, I'm startled to hear footsteps in what I thought was an empty house.

"Zee! You took me by surprise." I put my hand on her arm. "Everything all right?"

Looking out the window toward her grandmother's cabin, she gives me her formal nod.

"Needed to get away from your mom?"

She nods again, then points at my chest.

"Me? Good. I was working at the shelter this afternoon." As I speak, she puts her fingers against my throat, then against her own. I hear her breathing before I hear the words.

"Me. Good."

"That's a great start!"

She folds me into an embrace, with no squirming to get away or self-consciousness about being close. I wonder if she misses her orca family and their tactile togetherness. I rock her until I feel her heartbeat slow, then give her a squeeze. "I'm making tea. Do you want some?"

"Yes."

"Fabulous." I can't stop the grin that lights me up from the inside. Letting the ginger brew for fifteen minutes, I take her around the house and name everything I can find. As the dogs curl up on their beds, Zelka pours our tea, then stands at the window, watching the evening sky change colors. I take the mugs from the counter and hand one to her.

"Are you sure you're okay, Zee?"

She leans toward me and lays her head on my shoulder, and I feel a small nod. Then she straightens up and sips her tea, the steam curling around her face. I hear Keet's 4Runner pulling up to the house.

"Your brother is here."

When Keet walks in the door, Zelka says, "Brother. Keet."

He looks from her to me and back again. "When did she start talking more?"

"Since about a half-hour ago."

"I guess I shouldn't be surprised. She's Keykwin. Being human can't be completely foreign to her."

I shrug. "I think we need to stop being surprised. She's capable of more than we think."

"What makes you say that?" He walks over and kisses my cheek, squeezing me against him with one arm. I flush as I remember our shower that morning.

"Give me a minute, and I'll tell you." I set my mug on the table and take Zelka's hand.

"Zee, can you put the mug down?" As I'm saying the words, I picture her placing her mug on the table.

She sets her mug beside mine and I take both her hands. Without speaking, I ask if she has anything she'd like us to know.

I feel the breath leaving my lungs and blink. Zelka's brows are pulled together, a rare frown on her face. Keet moves closer to us.

I look at him. "She's afraid, and the feeling is new to her." I look at Zelka, who's watching our conversation. Before Keet can reply, I ask her, "Who, or what, are you afraid of, Zee?"

A picture of Hazel as she is now—long white braid, hard black eyes— swims into focus.

"It's our mother, isn't it?" Keet's voice is as hard as the vision I just received.

"You felt that?"

"I felt something, something that feels the same as when I was a kid and Mom was around. Not a big leap to guess it was about her."

"Do you feel safe staying in the cabin with her and your grandmother?" Smiling again, she gives a slow nod. "Yes."

"If not, you're always welcome to stay with us." I look at Keet. He steps closer and puts a hand on her shoulder. Their profiles make it clear that they're brother and sister. The same tilted eyes, the same high cheekbones, the same strong chin. How Keet could've denied that for as long as he did puzzles me.

Keet says, "I look forward to the day when you can tell us your story."

Releasing my hand, she rocks forward and hugs Keet hard. He's startled, then puts his arms around her shoulders and embraces her. When she steps away, they laugh, and both have tears in their eyes. When she feels the wet track of the tears on her skin, she gives me a puzzled look.

"Those are happy tears, Zee."

As the three of us stand in the kitchen, laughing and hugging one another, I no longer doubt that I'm truly home.

SEVENTEEN

The next day while Nolee's at the market, Keet splits firewood, enjoying the heft of the axe, the sharp crack of the wood, the deep *whunk* as the blade cuts through the wood and into the stump. He hears his grandmother's truck before he sees it. As it rumbles to a stop, he buries the axe in the stump and gathers up smaller pieces of kindling. Looking at the woodpile by Nolee's former cabin, he admires its height, but it also makes him a little uncomfortable; he knows she split and stacked it trying to erase him from her memory.

Sylvie and his mother slide out of the truck, and his mother goes into the cabin. Sylvie pauses, watching Hazel, then turns toward Keet. He gives her a small wave and she makes her way over to him.

"Do you need help with the groceries?"

"We didn't make it to the store. Hazel wanted to sleep."

His grandmother takes in the pile of wood, the axe, and Keet, his black jeans flecked with woodchips.

"We never got to talk about your and Zelka's trip to Bellingham. How was it?"

"Not bad. I showed the government lady my birth certificate, then both your parents' birth and death certificates, and the copy of your birth certificate. I told them most of the truth: that Zelka's parents were dead and she was born at home in northern Washington; that her mother wasn't mentally capable of making a record of her birth before they moved to Alaska. When her parents died, I raised and home schooled Zelka and later, we moved here from Sitka."

"You think they'll be okay with that?"

She shrugs. "They will or they won't. Not much I can do about it."

"Do you have another appointment?"

"No. They'll call. They kept copies of everything I brought."

"I guess this means we'll have to figure out a legal name for Zelka. And her birthday."

She looks back at the cabin. As though she'd heard them talking about her, Zelka walks out and joins them.

"Hi, Zee. Grandmother and I were talking about a legal name for you. Do you have one in mind?"

She tilts her head to one side, which reminds Keet of Fae when she hears a word she likes. Looking from her brother and her grandmother, she shakes her head.

"No rush. Do you know when you were born?"

She looks out at the incoming tide, punctuated by whitecaps and foam. "When the ocean was angry."

"Your parents had the car wreck on Mother's Day, Keet," Sylvie says.

"I remember. That year, it was May eighth."

"She would have been born as orca about nine months after that."

He smiles, looking at his sister. "'The month the ocean is angry' is called February, Zee."

"Febberary," she says.

"Close enough. Wait until you have to spell it."

"She told me the same thing," Sylvie says. "When I filled out the form for her, I wrote the fourth of February 1991."

"Nolee's birthday is the twenty-eighth. We have two reasons to celebrate now." He pats his sister on the arm.

She points at the woodpile.

"That? It's wood to keep us warm this winter. If you want, you can stack it in the pile there." Keet points at the stacked wood by the garage. When she smiles her assent, he places several pieces in her arms and she turns and walks away, her thick black braid catching the sun like a raven's wing.

Sylvie looks at Keet. "Can you text Nolee and ask her to pick up a few things for us?"

"Sure. Let me get my phone."

Home from the market, I take a couple of bags of groceries over to Sylvie and Hazel. As I approach our house, I hear the roar of classical music. Hands full of bags, I walk in and see Keet and Zelka with their heads bent over a book. They look up in unison and give me the same smile. "Nolee!" Zelka says, standing up.

Keet closes the thin book, then turns down the volume. As I set the bags on the kitchen counter, he asks, "Are there more groceries to bring in?"

"There are." He gives me a peck on the cheek as he passes on his way to the car. Zelka, who's behind him, also kisses my cheek, then peers into each bag.

As Keet's stowing items in the pantry, I ask Zee if she wants to help us put away the groceries. Reaching into a small canvas bag, I pull out an apple. "This is an apple. It goes in that bowl."

"Apple. Go in that bowl." She carefully puts each apple in the large ceramic dish on the counter.

When Keet comes back into the kitchen, Zee touches his arm and points back the way he came.

"I think she wants to know the names of the food."

They turn, and I hear the pantry door glide open and the murmur of their voices.

"Soup," Keet says, then the clink of a can being put down.

"Soup."

"Ketchup," he says.

"Catch up."

"No, that's something you do when you fall behind. You catch up."

I hear her laugh, then "Ketch-up."

The music ends, and in the silence, I hear Zelka say, "More music."

A few clicks, a moment of silence, then the deep vibration of cellos sounds a singular note, followed by the high notes of violins soaring above it—like birds singing in a thunderstorm. Zelka rushes over to the speaker and stands in front of it with her eyes closed. Keet looks first at Zelka, then at me. "She discovered classical music today."

"Looks like she's a fan."

"She is. I figured out that if it has violins or other stringed instruments played with a bow, she's mesmerized."

"No guitars?" I fill the kettle turn on the burner underneath it.

"Not so much."

"Does she like modern music?"

"She found the eject button when I played an Eagles CD."

"Sacrilege! Abbie would say the Eagles aren't 'modern.'"

"Another sacrilege."

We laugh, then notice that the volume has increased on the music.

Keet puts my face close to my ear. "We're talking too much!"

"What's she listening to?"

"Mozart's Violin Concerto Number Five. She's had it on repeat for the past two hours."

As Keet and I move around the kitchen and talk about what to have for dinner, the concerto ends. Zelka joins us, carrying the slim book I saw them looking at earlier. She holds it out to me.

"*A Brief History of the Violin*. Nice, Zee. I'm glad you found music you enjoy. I love music too."

She turns and sits at the kitchen table, flipping through the book.

"Don't tell me she knows how to read."

Keet shakes his head, laughing. "Not yet. She likes the pictures and colors."

"So her orca sight isn't technicolor?"

"Not even close. Shades of black and gray, at least when seen with human eyes."

"Does sound give you a sense of color?"

"Not much."

Closing the book, Zelka looks up at us. "Color?"

I sit next to her and open the book. As Keet makes dinner, we talk about primary colors, then shades of color. By the time dinner's ready, she can find and name the colors we've talked about throughout the house.

"Impressive, Zelka." She gives him a smile and points at her arm.

"Brown."

"Yes, your skin is light brown."

She nods, then looks at me and touches the back of my hand.

"No color."

That makes me laugh. "Not much. I've always been pale."

She covers my hand with her own and points at them.

"Why different?"

"People come from different places. Skin tone comes from everyone in our family before us, and where they were from."

She nods, squeezes my hand, and continues eating.

Keet and I look at each other.

"Purple hair lady. Amethyst."

"What's that Zee?"

She points to the cabin. Mimics driving.

"Oh! I get it. The lady in Bellingham had purple hair." We laugh. "Talking with you is easier in some ways when there aren't words."

"Yes." She chews and swallows. "The lady in Bellingham had purple hair. Why?" Zelka asks.

Fork halfway to his mouth, Keet looks at me. "Great. We've gone from a race discussion to people's personal choices about their looks."

"Abbie also asked these questions once she realized people looked different."

"You've had these talks before?"

I nod my head. "And discussions about why some kids at her school had two mommies or two daddies, or more than one mom or dad. It all comes down to respecting people who aren't like you."

As Keet resumes eating, I turn to Zelka. "Some people like to put different colors in their hair. It makes them happy."

"What is happy?"

"Aaaand, on to philosophy," Keet mutters.

"Give me your hands, Zee. It's easier to show you."

We hold hands across the table, as I look into her eyes. I've grown accustomed to the lavender ring that circles the dark brown of her iris, but still find it both startling and beautiful. Closing my eyes, I send her how I feel when I see Abbie or Keet, or the dogs, or the sea. I show Zelka her own face. When I open my eyes, she beams at me and whispers, "Happy."

Suddenly, in my mind, pages from a different book start flipping. There's a broad expanse of sunlit ocean, and I feel power coursing through my body as I dive, feel the touch of other orcas beside me, the comfort of feeling another heartbeat in time with my own. A gliding, a push against water, and I catch a salmon and eat it. I feel the joy of sharing seal meat with a pod member. Keet sees my expression when I look at him.

"What is it, Nolee?"

"I think she just showed me she eats both fish and mammals."

"That's not possible. Zee," he touches her hand on top of mine. She looks at him.

"Keet."

"You eat fish?"

"Yes."

"Nolee, what did she show you?"

Catching a salmon and sharing seal meat with her pod."

"Zee, do you eat seals?"

"Yes."

She removes her hand and picks up her fork, finishing her meal.

"Keykwin, or even regular orcas, don't eat both fish and mammals, Keet?"

"Not that I know of."

"I eat fish and seals," Zee says. She takes a bite of bread, then finishes her salad.

Keet, hearing his mother's heavy footsteps on the deck, turns to see her opening the door.

"Daughter, it's time to come back to the cabin with me."

In the time it takes him to breathe deeply, Nolee says, "Hazel, do you want to join us? We have plenty of food."

Hazel, who only has eyes for her daughter, walks around the table and puts her hand on Zelka's shoulder, but Zelka shrugs it off. "Eating now."

"I'll wait until you're finished." Hazel yanks a chair out, sits next to her daughter, and looks at Keet. "We have dinner at the cabin. Why is she eating here?"

Keet blinks. "Mother, Nolee asked you a question."

Nolee touches his arm. "Keet, it's okay—"

"It's not okay with me that she ignores you in your own house."

Hazel grunts. "Now it's her house, too?"

The clatter of fork against plate cuts through the silence. Zelka stands. "We go back to the cabin, Mother." She puts her hand under Hazel's elbow and steers her toward the door.

"Thank you, Keet. Thank you, Nolee."

"You're welcome, Zee. See you tomorrow."

After the door shuts, Keet gets up, agitation coursing through him. It's an old feeling, one that he thought he'd laid to rest along with the memory of his mother. Although he grieved his parents' death, he'd quickly buried the feelings of shame and anger he felt every time he thought of his mother. He puts the dishes in the sink, watching the soap bubbles slide across their surface.

"Why aren't you giving your mom a chance, Keet?"

"All she's had is chances. She had years of chances. I'm done waiting for her to be the mother she can't be."

"That's in the past. You can't rule out the possibility she's changed—"

Keet interrupts. "You know what she said to me before they moved to Nebraska without me, when I was eleven years old?"

"What?"

"She said, 'Don't become like me.'"

Nolee steps closer to him, takes his hand. He squeezes it in return, then releases it and starts to pace. "Not 'I'll miss you,' not 'I love you.' Nothing. It was always about her. She was a miserable person, and I spent my childhood thinking it was my fault."

"You've told me you know it wasn't."

"I know that. But somehow, part of me is still that little boy when she's around." He sits, rubbing his head until his hair stands up in different directions.

"You didn't feel that way when you met her as orca?"

Keet shakes his head.

"What's different?"

Keet sighs. "As orca, we don't make choices in the present based on the past hurts. We have knowledge and we share it, but we don't use it against each other. When I found her, all we felt was relief and joy. We listened to one another's stories. It wasn't until she got here as my human mother that I realized how mad I still am at her. And how hurt. Human emotions are messier than orca feelings."

Nolee hugs him and he feels the reassuring presence of her body against his. "I spent most of my childhood terrified I'd be like her."

"You're not." She pulls away, holding his eyes with hers. He looks into their green depths for a way to pull himself out of the dark cave of his thoughts.

"I thought I was. In the years before you and I met, and after my escape from OceanMagic …" he swallows, hears a clicking in his throat.

Nolee steps back, her hand on his face, looking at him.

He turns his head, kisses her palm. "I thought the same illness that took my mother away from me was taking me as well. I'd felt trapped in its teeth for years, like it was devouring me, piece after small piece. That whoever I was, I would disappear into the same belly of the beast that took my mother."

"That sounds terrifying." Nolee takes his hand in her firm grasp. "That beast is long gone from you, Keet. You came back here. You chose a life at peace with both realities."

Keet's shoulders drop as he lets out a breath. He kisses Nolee. "I know your mother was good for you, Nolee. But mine wasn't. She still isn't."

Against his lips, Nolee says, "You aren't your mother, Keet."

EIGHTEEN

"How long have I been here, son?"

Keet looks up from the onion he's slicing. "A couple of weeks. Why?"

Hazel closes her eyes and sways in place, grabbing the counter for support. Keet knows she's incapable of any genuine emotion, and that she's always feigned illness to gain attention. But seeing her do it again makes him both sad and angry—sad for the innocent little boy he was, and angry at being forced to deal with it, to deal with her.

"Because it's time for your sister and me to return to where we belong." She moves to the table, where she runs her hand across its smooth surface.

"I know you don't want me here, Keet. I know you haven't forgiven me for leaving you when you were still a child."

His laugh is bitter and short. "I can forgive you for leaving, and I have. I forgive you for choosing to live in the sea. What I can't forgive you for—"

"The clock won't stop ticking." He looks at his mother, who's rocking back and forth in her chair.

"What?"

"It's louder every day. Tick tick tickticktickticktick—"

"What are you talking about?" Her tone alarms him; he knows she's winding up into one of her disconnections, the point at which he recalls feeling his mother leave and a dark threat take over.

"The clock in my head. When I'm human, it's so loud it makes me deaf. And when it stops, so do I."

"You don't hear it when you're orca?" Keet can't remember her ever being this articulate about what happens to her.

"The clock, Keet! Ticking, ticking, ticking, counting down the minutes of my life, never stopping."

Keet, stunned into silence, freezes. Her words extinguish his ancient anger.

His mother doesn't notice. Hands wrapped around the edge of the chair seat, she rocks it until the legs lift from the floor. "It won't stop. Tick. Tick."

"Mother, you're not making sense."

She yells at the floor, "Because you're not listening!"

He lowers his voice and walks closer to her. "I'm listening, but I don't understand. You want me to stop what?"

"You can't stop it, I can't stop it. If the ticking stops, it never gets back to the place it belongs." She lets go of the chair and holds her head.

"Mother. Mom!" Wrapping his arms around her for the first time in decades, Keet feels her labored breathing and high-pitched keening move through his own body. He strokes her rough white hair and wills his voice to stay low and soothing. "Mom, I want you to be at peace. I'm okay now. We'll figure everything out. We're together again."

She looks up at him, eyes swollen and red, mouth slack. "Keet. I can't do this. I can't be human. The clock is torture. I'm in a prison and no one can hear me scream."

"We can help. Please, let us help."

"Son, you can't help me if you can't forgive me."

"What..."

"You can't forgive me." She stands up and moves away from Keet.

"I said I've forgiven you—"

Her hands on the windowsill, Hazel gazes out at the darkening sea and the sun setting over a distant island. "I haven't."

"You haven't what?"

"Forgiven myself. Everything is my fault. Getting pregnant, taking you into the water as Keykwin when you were too young, leaving you, your father's death..." Her tone is flat, as though she's telling him what to get at the market.

Then his mother is silent, the storm of her discontent blown out. But Keet feels freezing water lapping at his chest, almost to his heart. "My life is your fault, mother? My existence is something you can't forgive yourself for?"

"All the pain you've been in, it's also my fault. I should've taken my Walk Into the Water at my Keykwin initiation. But your father..."

"My father what?"

Turning from the window, Hazel stares at Keet with dull eyes.

"You *cannot* stay silent about this. Talk to me!" Something inside him roars to life, melting the ice that threatened to freeze him into a man still haunted by the ghosts of his childhood.

"You are just like your father. Soft-hearted, gentle. Gave me hope that wasn't mine to have. He wanted to have a child with me. A child he thought would anchor me to the land. He thought moving away from the water would bring me back to him."

Standing near the bonfire of his anger, ready to incinerate what's left of his feeling for his mother, Keet retreats from that dangerous heat by pulling a deep breath into his lungs, then another. Memories flood his mind: Nolee, his grandmother, Zelka, his pod and their inability to doubt their value or the value of life. Finally, the realities he knows both as orca and as human align: He belongs in his life, as does his mother, even if she's half out of her mind.

He takes another breath. "Did moving to Nebraska help?"

She shifts her eyes from his and back to the sea, then shakes her head. "My head was quieter. But the nightmares kept your dad and me awake."

"Nightmares? What were they about, Mother?"

She looks at him again and wipes her eyes with her lean left hand, leaving her right hidden in her pocket. "The sea is devouring me. I fall in and can't change to orca, and the darkness drags me down until it takes the breath from my body. Like it's doing now."

Hazel sits again, massaging her forehead. "When I was pregnant with your sister, the nightmares stopped. It was the happiest your dad and I had ever been, and I was looking forward coming home, to sharing the news that you had a sister."

"You knew she was a girl?"

"I knew from the moment she was conceived, Keet. As I did with you."

"And then the wreck happened."

Hazel nods, wrapping both arms around herself. "The sea was so close, and your father was dead. I couldn't stop crawling toward it. I couldn't stop the cramping, telling me your sister was in danger." She rocks back and forth. "And now you can't forgive me…"

Keet sits in front of her and tries to catch her eyes again. "I forgive you for all of it. But I can't forgive you if you force Zelka into the sea when she doesn't want to go."

Hazel finally smiles, tears running down her cheeks. "She's my daughter. The only thing I've got right in my life."

Keet hears footsteps on the deck, and turning, sees his grandmother stride through the open door. "That's enough, Hazel. Enough of your misery. You dump it where it does not belong. Your son has always loved you, but you have always loved yourself more. If the Walk Into the Water is what you want, we will give you that last ceremony and bless you as orca."

Hazel stands tall, her eyes shining. "My daughter will leave with me."

"Your daughter will decide for herself."

Towering over Sylvie, who holds her ground, Hazel's voice rises. "I can't be both! I can't walk as Keykwin, I can only swim as orca." Without waiting for a reply, Hazel rushes through the door. Keet sees Nolee and Zee in the distance, throwing a ball for the dogs. Keet and his grandmother follow, watching as Hazel bears down on the group.

Wallace is the first to see her. Returning to Nolee and Zelka, he positions himself in front of them, facing Hazel; his hackles are raised, his tail is high and vibrating. As she continues to stumble toward them, Wallace pins his ears and shows his teeth, and a low rumble comes from his chest. Before Hazel comes within reach, Keet catches up with her and grabs her arm. "Stop this, mother. You're safe with us. We want to help."

Nolee and Zelka turn, surprise and shock on their faces as Hazel reaches for Zelka. "The clock won't stop! We must return to its waters. The clock in the water ..." She covers her ears with her hands, and the high-pitched keening starts again.

As Keet, Nolee, and Sylvie hold Hazel, Zelka sits on the ground, the dogs at her side.

Over the top of his mother's head, Keet looks at his grandmother. "She's going to self-destruct. What do we do?"

Sylvie sets her jaw in a hard line; Keet can almost hear the snap of her teeth when they meet. "We help her back to the sea."

"What's this 'clock in the water?'" Nolee asks. Keet and Sylvie exchange a look. "Do either of you know what she's talking about?"

When neither Keet nor Sylvie answer her, she directs her irritation at Sylvie. "No secrets, remember, Sylvie?"

Hazel raises her hands to the sky. "Tickticktickticktick" she screams, swaying back and forth between us before exhaling and sinking to the wet rocks.

Resigned, Sylvie looks at Nolee. "It's an ancient story, even for our people." Keet feels the urgency pulling at him, needing to get away from his mother.

"Nolee, we need to get my mother into bed. Resting might calm her."

We lift Hazel from the ground, but Zelka stays behind, kneeling on the rocks, holding the dripping ball in one hand and wrapping another arm around Wallace. Fae trots behind Nolee, darting glances over her shoulder, her white-tipped tail low. She briefly stops and turns toward Wallace and Zelka and whines, then runs to catch up with us.

After we put Hazel to bed, Nolee says, "Is Hazel in some sort of danger? Why does this clock in the water upset her so much?"

Sylvie touches her sleeping daughter's shoulder before looking up at us. "Let's talk outside."

They walk to the beach, joining Zelka and Wallace, who's lying beside her. After settling herself, Sylvie explains. "The water clock is made of two wooden bowls. One is large," she holds her hands away from her body, "and the other is small. The smaller bowl has a hole in its bottom. We fill the large bowl with water and place the small bowl inside it."

Nolee says, "That sounds beautiful. Why was it used?"

"We used it to keep time at councils, so everyone had equal say." Sylvie rests her hands in her lap. "They started speaking when the small bowl was placed in the water and when it sank, they were finished. We had different-sized water clocks for different occasions. The storyteller water clocks were the largest; if the story wasn't over when the small bowl sank, it would be continued at the next gathering."

Keet watches as Zelka pets Wallace, doing his best to not feel slighted. "Each water clock had a different purpose?"

Sylvie nods, tapping her fingers against each other. "There was the council water clock, the children's water clock, the storyteller's water clock, and a water clock for women's full moon time."

"Every community had these?" Nolee asks.

"The ones I've heard about, yes. Our Keykwin ancestors made their own once they found their home in the north."

Sylvie brings her hands together so tightly that her knuckles turn white.

"What is it, grandmother?"

"I am the keeper of the women's full moon water clock, the *S'gah-heenah*. Your mother was next in line. Now it passes to Zelka."

At the sound of her name, Zelka stands and walks toward the water. Nolee turns to Sylvie. "What else?"

Sylvie motions to her granddaughter. "We'll wait until Zelka comes back."

Zelka pauses at the shoreline, looks back at them, bends down to pet Wallace, and returns to sit down. She places herself beside her grand-mother, closing her eyes.

Sylvie continues. "On council days, or storytelling days, or days when women freed their blood into the earth, the keeper of the water clock—always a woman—would fill the large bowl at sunrise and put the small bowl inside it. When the small bowl began filling, she would strike a wooden bell.

"I've since learned that other cultures also used water clocks." Nodding at Nolee, she continues. "Our word, *S'gah-heenah*, translates to "clepsydra" in your language. Keepers of the water clocks trained with their mothers or sisters or aunts, polished the clocks and took care of them, sometimes even slept with them by their side."

"I remember you showing me the women's full moon water clock," Keet says.

"Yes. I chose that role from my mother, who chose it from her mother. An unbroken line of Keykwin women have given their lives to its care."

"If Mother was next in line, why did you show it to me, Grandmother?"

Sylvie reaches across Zelka and pats Keet's knee. "Because it's our way to share knowledge. Nothing belongs to only men, or only women, or only children, or only old ones. We each do and provide where our talents lead us. Among the Keykwin, some men would cook, and some women would hunt. Some children were wise and some old ones foolish. But each person has a rightful place within the Nation."

Nolee, sitting on the other side of Keet, says, "You said the…" She tries to pronounce the Keykwin word, then gives up and smiles. "… the clepsydra are only kept and watched by women, though?"

"It has always been our way. My mother told me that as a woman holds the fullness of creation of life in her womb, so does the water clock hold the fullness of the passing of time."

Nolee pauses. "The water clock is visual. Someone watches the water rise and the bowl sink?"

"Yes."

Keet looks at Nolee, understanding where she's headed. She looks at him, then speaks to Sylvie. "Then how could Hazel hear ticking? Do you think her human memory of clocks got mixed up with the water clock?"

"I don't know."

Taking Nolee's hand in his, Keet asks, "Grandmother, could you tell Nolee about the *S'gah-heenah*?"

"As the water clock keeper spends her life with the water clock, the women teach her how to listen to its rhythm, how to know where the water is without looking at it. Few knew how to do this, even during the time of my grandparents. Once she no longer needed to watch its progress, she escorted the clock to rituals, to story-tellings and councils. Over time, she served as the water clock for her village, only displaying the actual water clock at clan councils, to show respect and declare honor. At that point, she let go of her name and was known as *S'gah-heenah*, or Clepsydra."

"She *was* the water clock?" Nolee says.

Sylvie takes Zelka's hand. "What my own *S'gah-heenah* whispered to me is that we are all water clocks filling with sacred life water. The basin of each soul is a different size and fills at a different rate. But at the end, which is also a beginning, we sink. We become a part of the water, emptied, then refilled."

Zelka covers her face with her hands. Wallace looks at her, then licks her arm, and Nolee touches her knee.

"Zelka? Do you have something to say?"

She moves her hands to her lap. "Not yet."

NINETEEN

We walk Sylvie back to her cabin and check on Hazel, then Zelka and the dogs follow us home. As Wallace takes a long and messy drink from his bowl, Zelka waits outside the door, and I invite her in. She sits on the sofa, Wallace curled up at her feet.

Connecting my iPhone to the stereo, I choose a Dan Fogelberg playlist, and smile as the first notes and his silky-smooth voice pour from the speakers. When the chorus comes on, I start singing, needing to shake off the heaviness of the day, "*There's a warm wind blowing the stars around…*"

I hear Keet ask, "Who's that one by, Lia?"

"Since I chose him as the artist to stream, I'm going to go out on a limb and guess Dan Fogelberg?"

"Huh. Close."

"If it's not him, are you going to tell me who?"

"Two 'whos,' actually. England Dan and John Ford Coley. It came out in 1976."

"And?"

"It was written by Parker McGee."

"And?"

"It made it to number two on the Billboard Hot 100 chart. Stayed there for two weeks."

"I've always liked that song."

"Sing the lyrics again?"

Giving him a sideways glance, I ask, "Why?"

"I like your voice. And I'd like to hear your version."

"Right. *I'm not talkin' about the linen, and I don't want to waste your time, there's a warm wind blowing the stars around…*"

Keet stifles a laugh.

"What?"

"I think I like your lyrics better than the original ones."

"I got the lyrics wrong too?!"

"It goes like this," he clears his throat. "I can't sing as high as they do."

"Go on, let me hear the real lyrics." I nudge his shoulder.

"*I'm not talkin' about moving in, and I don't want to waste your time, but there's a warm wind blowing, the stars are out—*"

I burst out laughing. Keet stops singing and laughs along with me.

"And here," I gasp for breath, "I thought they were being poetic. Or metaphorical."

"Turns out, neither. The guy in the song was trying to get laid."

The song ends and another begins, one with quiet violins and strummed guitar chords. The single notes of a guitar run along my spine like fingers on a piano keyboard.

"Now, *this* is Dan Fogelberg," Keet smiles. "One of my favorites."

"What is it?"

"*The Reach.*"

He takes me in his arms, and we dance in the kitchen. Closing my eyes, I forget about everything except the man who's holding me. The song, and the dance, ends with a kiss. A movement nearby reminds me that Zelka is here.

Looking at Keet, she asks, "What does it mean, 'get laid'?"

Swallowing our laughter, Keet and I move apart. I give the chili another stir and put the corn bread in the oven. When I turn around, I see Keet smiling at Zelka. "That whole conversation, and you focus on 'get laid'?"

When Keet opens his eyes, he hears Lia snoring beside him. Turning his head, he sees her comforter-wrapped shape in the early-morning light. Outside, the birds are singing the reluctant autumn sun into the sky.

His contentment fades as he remembers his mother and the weight of her darkness. He knows he needs to check on her, but he also wants to stretch out this moment: the birdsong, the light, and the woman he loves sleeping beside him.

He rests his hand on the curve of Lia's hip and she turns toward him, eyes still closed, settling into the space between his arm and ribcage, sliding her leg over his. He closes his eyes, holding her close and feeling the slow and steady thud of her heart, the weight of her body. When he feels her lips on his jaw, kissing him good morning, he returns her kiss, then realizes how hungry he is.

"I'm starving, Lia. Let's get up and eat."

After a quick breakfast, they walk over to Sylvie's cabin.

"Think Hazel will be better this morning, Keet?"

"I hope so. She couldn't be much worse."

When his grandmother opens the door, the smell of frying eggs and sausage wafts out. Keet sees his mother sitting at the table, head in hand, eyes closed.

"Come in," Sylvie says, opening the door wider. "There's hot water if you want tea." Sitting next to Hazel, she takes a sip from her mug.

"Thanks, Grandmother." Keet lays a hand on his mother's back. Her muscles are taut, and her spine is distressingly prominent. "Did you sleep?"

Head still in her hands, Hazel nods.

Nolee sits down across from her, then turns to Sylvie. "We wanted to check in before we go to work."

Keet hears the stairs creak and looks over to see Zelka coming to join them.

"Good morning." Her voice is soft and clear and she doesn't put her hand on her throat or lips to form the words.

"Good morning, Zee." Nolee pats the chair next to her. "Come sit a spell."

After fixing her tea, Zelka sits next to Nolee, who puts her arm around her and gives her a squeeze. "Did you sleep well?"

"Yes." Zelka says and points at Nolee.

"Me? I slept great."

"I slept great also," Zelka says, as though feeling the words as they leave her mouth. Her singular concentration impresses Keet, and he remembers for the dozenth time since she arrived that he has a sister. But this time, the thought warms rather than confuses him.

Looking up, Hazel reaches across the table toward Zelka, taking her daughter's hand in her own.

"I've never told you your birth story, daughter," Hazel says. Without waiting for a reply from anyone at the table, Hazel speaks.

"I'm alone. I eat to sustain my daughter, a child who might not survive my transformation to orca. I hear a distant pod feeding on a run of salmon. I sing to them, but only the pulse of the ocean and the whir of fish flash pictures inside my head. I'm alone.

Weeks pass. I eat and rest in short bursts and I follow the sounds of this faraway pod. One bright and windless morning, the picture of them is clear and strong. I pulse my name toward them, diving and swimming as fast as I can to the last place I hear them.

The orcas I seek range up and down the coast, keeping distance between themselves and the inland mammal eaters. I know I'm close to the open ocean; sounds return pictures of the seafloor far below, long furrows covered in dim shadows. The water pushes and pulls my body more, and the singing whale song and conversations are clearer.

One dim morning, the orcas I've followed are waiting for me: a small pod of a mother, her daughter, and a son who's in his fifth or sixth summer. They rise to the surface, and I follow at a safe distance, waiting. I'm overjoyed to feel the vibration of their clicks running along my body. Inside my head, I see what their clicks reveal: a tiny heart and the beginning of a small tail. I'm so relieved, and I swoop downward, then up again, breaking through the surface in a shatter of spray, landing and sinking and swimming. Finally, the pod joins me, touching me with their pectorals and tails. I'm no longer alone.

After months of being fed by my adopted pod, I feel the first pulls in my midsection, a clenching that causes me to swim in tight circles. The female orcas hover nearby as I swim in the grip of birth pains. The sounds of my adopted pod show that my baby's heartbeat is strong.

The sun rises, reaching for the middle of the sky, but still I labor, rotating first one way and then another. I'm panicking. I ask the water to take away this pain, to pull my baby from my body. I pray.

As I spin, human memories rush in: lying flat on my back on a white bed, pushing; the voices of men telling me not to push; pain that threatens to rip me in half. I remember a mask over my face, and then, when I wake up, the round face of my son looking at me from his blankets. I remember the flaccid emptiness where once I felt full.

Surfacing from these memories, I surrender to the exhaustion, resting on the surface, breathing, my tail hanging low in the water. The female orcas float nearby. They are silent.

Hours pass as the pod send me pictures, until I see a tiny pair of flukes emerging from my body. I dive once more, fast, pushing down, using the last of my strength, then feel a tug and hear a small pop. As I turn, I see, through a cloud of my own dark blood, the pale markings of my daughter, floating and motionless.

I rush to you and settle my head under your chest, gently guiding you up to air, to life. A flicker of movement against my head tells me your heart is beating, and I feel the moment the first rush of air inflates your lungs. Beneath the waves, I hold you above them as you grow stronger with each breath.

I vow never to let you go; never to abandon you as I did my son. I will never be alone again."

"You know the rest, daughter. Until earlier this month, you and I have never been apart. I will never let you go."

The numbness Keet feels when his mother is around has engulfed him. Even Nolee's touch on his arm goes unnoticed as he stares at the table, not hearing the birdsong outside the windows.

Nolee looks from Zelka to her mother. One set of eyes is bright and shining, the other is dull. Zelka removes her hand from her mother's, stands, and looks at Nolee. "Wallace and Fae?"

"We can let them out before I take them to work with me."

Once they're outside, Nolee turns to Zelka. "I know it's difficult to understand, but your mother loves you."

Zelka nods, looking at the ground as they walk. "Too much."

The month passes in a blur of trips to the market, meals, and work. Keet's sailing schedule is full, so Alex joins him on the weekends. Each day, Zelka surprises us with the number of words she's able to speak and understand. Free of the constraints of learning a language from childhood, including what's "right" or "wrong" to say and do, she often brings us to laughter, and occasionally tears. But behind her questions, I sense a young woman who is enjoying exploring the fullness of who she is.

One rare day off together, Keet and I take the double kayak past the Point. Returning flushed with sun and wind and exercise, we drag it up onto the beach, and I bend down to clean the kelp off my legs.

Keet comes closer to me, the smile gone from his face. "Lia?"

Picking the last slick green strand of kelp off my skin, I answer absently. "Yes?"

"What do you think about getting married again?"

My head snaps up. "What do I think about *what*?" I'm sure I've misheard him. I *hope* I misheard.

"What do you think about getting married? To me."

I feel like a horse ready to bolt, and probably look like one too. "Keet, where is this coming from?"

"Is that a no?"

"It's not anything other than a question about your question, which I'm shocked as shit that you're asking."

I step away from the tideline, which brings me closer to Keet, who's also moved closer to me. Taking my hand, he speaks to me in low, soft tones, much as I used with nervous ranch horses back in Texas.

"This isn't a proposal. I'm curious. I know your first marriage wasn't good for you. I haven't forgotten that." He moves his thumb in circles on my palm, something he knows breaks down every bit of sense I have.

"And?" I look up into his eyes and see the sun sparking in their brown depths.

"And I've never been married, and I'd like to be. To you."

My breath leaves my body in a rush. As I try to inhale, I hear Keet's voice. It sounds far away.

"Lia? Here, sit down, head between your knees."

I follow his suggestion. The warmth of Keet's hand rubbing my back calms me, then a burst of nervous laughter escapes. "If it wasn't a proposal, I don't know what is." I look up and he brushes the hair out of my eyes. "After Nate, I told myself never again. No name change, no ring, no being the brunt of someone else's bullshit. Besides, not being married and wanting to try it isn't really a compelling reason."

He's quiet, his face soft, his touch on my back softer.

"I don't expect you to change your name, or wear a ring, or put up with my bullshit. You never have. What would change?"

I can see he believes nothing would change, when in fact I know all too well it does. That kind of commitment changes everything.

"Do you want to date other guys?"

Stunned, I shake my head, as though a very loud bang has gone off next to me.

"How did we get from marriage to dating other men?"

He's smiling, which rockets me to my feet; his hand falls away as he stands up too.

"It's an option, Nolee."

"It's *not* an option, Keet. I have no interest in swiping right or left or whatever the hell people do these days. Why are you still smiling?"

"Because you're calling me on my bullshit. I'm sorry. I just wanted you to know that I don't think I own you."

"Of course we don't own each other, Keet. I've told you I'm yours. I've told you with my body, with my words, with my moving in. You're it for me. Since we're asking questions, do you want to date other women?"

He's laughing, and now an urge to punch him washes over me. He takes a step back, his hands in front of him, warding off the threat of blows, trying to stop his laughter. "No, I don't."

I pick up a rock and hurl it into the water. "You're infuriating, Keet Noland!"

"I know. And to answer your question, I'm not interested in other women. I don't know what you mean when you say, 'swipe right.'"

This surprises a laugh out of me, and I wipe my hands on my jeans, noticing a piece of kelp stuck to my palm. I'll be damned if it isn't the one I thought I'd washed off.

Brushing my palms together, I look at Keet. "Let's shelve this conversation for another time."

Like a woodfire, my waning anger and confusion still radiate heat.

"It was an idea, one that I'd like to include you in instead of putting you under pressure with a proposal."

"If we're being honest here, Keet, I can tell you I'll live with you for the rest of our lives. Marriage, though?" My eyes meet his without a waver. "Means nothing." I move closer to him and take his hand. "But you do. You mean everything to me."

TWENTY

Zelka looks out the window toward the beach, where she sees Keet and Nolee holding hands, the kayak beside them. She turns back to her mother, who has, in Sylvie's absence, told Zelka all the reasons she can't remain a human woman.

"It's too dangerous here, daughter. Too many bad things happen. You need to come back as orca, live in the ocean with me, forget these human ways."

"I like who I am, mother. Stop telling me who you want me to be." Her usually radiant smile dims as she looks out the window and away from the frowning woman beside her. She watches Keet and Nolee carry the kayak up from the high-tide line, wishing she could join them.

"I'm not telling you who I want you to be. I'm telling you that this isn't your place. Your place is with me. Your place is where you're safe." She places a stiff hand on her daughter's tense shoulder.

"I want my own life."

"You don't know any other life except the one you have. I do. I know what you're choosing isn't right for you."

The sound of the sea, retreating and approaching the shore in a heartbeat of shifting stones, fills the silence between them.

"I can't help you if you stay here, daughter. You'll be alone. It's dangerous to be human, to be a woman—"

"I won't be alone. I have family here, too."

"They don't know how to help you. How to teach you. They don't know you the way I do."

"Mother, if I stay with you, I'll always be your version of me."

Hazel stands, then turns to the window to watch the sea as it fades to black at day's end. Her daughter's voice is far away when she hears her say, "I'm staying here. At least for a while."

Nolee, Hazel, and Sylvie join Zelka at the table on the deck, where she sits with a notebook open in front of her, its pages fluttering in the breeze. When a sudden burst of wind rolls her pen to the ground, Wallace picks it up and, wagging his tail, returns it to her. After taking it and giving Wallace a pat, she puts it on top of the notebook and pushes both toward her grandmother.

Sylvie draws the notebook closer, then takes the letter they received from Bellingham out of the pocket of her red jacket, unfolding it and tucking it under the notebook.

Nolee, who had gone inside to help Keet with drinks and food, comes back with a pitcher of water, lemons floating on top. The bright yellow half-moons catch Zelka's eye and she leans over the pitcher, closing her eyes and inhaling the sharp citrus tang. As Keet brings out the glasses, he hears her say, "It smells like sunshine."

Zelka looks at her mother, looming on her right. "I don't agree with you taking human names, daughter."

Zelka sighs. "I know. But this is my choice, not yours."

She turns to her grandmother again. "I shared my name with Nolee when they found me. Why do I need another one?"

"For your birth certificate, Granddaughter. It's what this country wants, so they know who you are."

"Then I'd like to be named Zelka Wallace."

Nolee chokes on her water and Keet pats her back. When she recovers, she says, "Zee, I'm sure Wallace is honored, but he already has that name."

Hazel sits straighter and nudges her daughter. "It's a boy's name."

"I don't understand," Zelka says. "I'm supposed to have more names, but they can't be names someone else already has?"

"You are a woman, and you need a woman's name, a Keykwin name," her mother tells her.

"Grandmother told me my Keykwin name is between us, not to be said outside of the family."

"She's right."

Zelka looks at Nolee. "Who is Wallace named for?"

"William Wallace, one of many Scottish people who fought for his country's independence from Great Britain. He was very brave, which is why I gave Wallace his name."

"Then I want my name to be Zelka William." She hears her mother huff in agitation. "That's not a woman's name!"

"Having man or woman names means nothing to me, Mother! It's my choice."

Her grandmother writes two names on the paper.

"Do you want that as your full name, or as a middle name?" she asks.

"I need more than two names?" Bringing her braid over her shoulder, Zelka runs her hands across the thick plait.

Sylvie sighs. "I don't agree with this either, Zelka." She taps the paper with her pen. "They want to fit us in boxes so they can make sense of us. But still, it's required. Choose a name you can feel proud of when you say it."

"Do I have to have the same last name as my mother and brother?"

"It would help."

"Help the official people, or help me?"

"The official people."

Nolee leans toward her. "Zelka, do you remember when we were talking about different colors of skin, and how that links to our ancestors?"

"Yes."

"In our culture, last names are similar. It tells you who your father is."

"What about my mother? Or my grandmother? Why can't I take their names?"

There's silence around the table as they sit with her question. After taking a sip of water, Keet speaks. "You could. But we've given children the last name of their fathers for so long that no one questions it. Mothers' names have been lost."

Zelka asks Nolee, "What is your last name? Where did it come from?"

"My father's last name is Burnett. I was married before and I took my husband's name of Evans. But I changed it back to Burnett when we got divorced."

Zelka shakes her head in confusion. "None of this makes sense." She taps the paper in front of her grandmother. "Please write Zelka William."

She watches as her grandmother makes a scribble of lines and dots in dark ink, then puts down the pen and removes the letter from Bellingham from under the notebook.

"Granddaughter, they've already listed your last name as Noland.

We can choose your other names, and you can change your last name at another time, once they know they can identify you. For the time being, can you accept your father's name?"

Zelka's hand rests on the bench, and Wallace shoves his broad head under it. She smiles, stroking his ears. "Wallace." In saying his name, she realizes it is a small sound for how big she feels about him, and he feels for her. A name is a starting point in the story of herself, but it's nowhere near the ending.

"Yes, Noland can be my last name." She hears the scratch of the pen on the notebook paper. "What is the Keykwin word for 'ocean,' Grandmother?"

Hazel answers before her daughter has stopped talking. "Eils."

Zelka looks from her mother to her grandmother. "I want my name to be Zelka William Eils Noland." She smiles down at Wallace, who grins back, putting all his teeth on display.

Smoothing out the form, Sylvie fills it out, then folds it and tucks it back in her pocket. "I need to go to the cabin for a minute. Please meet me by the water."

They file off the deck behind her, then walk to the beach, waiting for Sylvie to return.

When she does, she's barefoot, pants rolled up to her knees. She motions for everyone else to do the same. Sylvie walks into the water and holds out her hands to Hazel and Zelka, who join her. Nolee completes the circle; she's the only one who shivers.

Zelka listens as her grandmother speaks in Keykwin. Some sounds are familiar, many are not. But she likes the rhythm, the words spoken with precision, a music all their own. Her grandmother asks her to kneel, then places her hands on Zelka's head and says the same four words nine times. When she finishes, she's silent for a moment, then brings scissors out of her pocket and shows them to Zelka.

"Granddaughter, you have received your Keykwin name. It is custom that we take a little of your hair and give it first to the sea, then to the land." Zelka nods, and Sylvie lifts her braid, cutting off hair from the end. The sharp snick of the scissors announces Zelka's place in both worlds.

When her grandmother asks her to stand, Zelka sees that her mother, tears on her cheeks, holds a small length of hair in one cupped hand, and hugs her.

"I'm happy to be here, on your naming day, Zelka."

Each member of her family takes a few strands from Hazel and drops them into the water. Back on land, they scatter the remaining hair to the wind. The breeze speaks its own sibilant language, but Zelka knows it also carries her name, circling above the earth for the first time.

"The summer Keet was seven, we had his birthday party at our home. This was when we were still living by the ocean. Kids from his school were there, and they were daring each other to go in the water, seeing who could stay the longest."

Hazel takes small bites of her dinner. We're seated around our table, a celebratory meal in honor of Zelka's naming. Everyone but Keet seems interested in the story his mother is telling.

"Keet kept winning, and his friends were getting mad. The next time I looked out the window, the kids were standing on the shore, pointing. I don't see Keet. Running out of the house, I yell, 'Where is my son?' Some kids cry. One boy, Keet's closest friend, points out into the water, and he says, 'The blackfish ate him.' I look out into the water, and I see Keet, as orca, watching me. My mom came out with towels, dried off the kids, and took them into the house for cake.

"I waited on that beach, so mad because my son endangered us. We had fought hard to be accepted in the community. He was making friends at school, and then it was gone. By the time he swam back to the shore as my boy, his friends were leaving. He opened his presents with only his family there."

Hazel, looking down at her plate, continues eating. The rest of us are frozen in place; forks rest on plates, eyes don't blink. Saying, "That was a happy family memory. Anyone for dessert?" Keet stands and goes into the kitchen.

Zelka and I start to clear the table, and Keet stacks everything in the sink. Busying myself with the kettle, I sneak a glance at the table. Sylvie has Hazel's hand in her own in front of their empty plates. When Keet reaches for the plates, Hazel takes her hand from her mother's and lays it on Keet's arm, stopping him from turning away.

"I know I've been swimming in dark places, son. I can't find anywhere to surface or to breathe. Every time I think there's clean air, it's smoke. I've been human too long. It's time for me to return to the water, live out the rest of my life as orca."

"Do you have a family pod?" Keet asks.

"They're gone."

"Gone where?"

"We swam with a female and a mother and son, but we separated when my daughter chose to change into a human. An orphaned female stayed with me until I chose to also change to a human, to reclaim my daughter."

"Do you want your Walk Into the Water ceremony?" Keet looks down at his mother, her hand still on his arm.

She forces a smile. "There's no time."

"We could do it tomorrow," Sylvie says.

Hazel turns to Sylvie, taking her mother's hand. "Mom, you've given me so much." A pained expression crosses her face. "You've been a mother to Keet. More than I ever could be."

She looks up at Keet. "I'm so sorry ... for almost everything."

"What do you mean?"

"I'm not sorry for having you. You brought me so much joy."

Keet drops into the empty chair next to her. "But—"

"Forget what I said when I was drowning in darkness. My heart is always with you. I'm proud of who you are, and all you have done, Keet. The darkness will never take that away." She looks at me, smiling at her for the first time. "Thank you for loving my son, Nolee."

In the silence around the table, I hear Hazel take a deep breath, then begin to speak in the Keykwin tongue.

"What's she saying?" Zelka asks Sylvie.

"It is the blessing we sing when one of our people takes their Walk Into the Water."

The sun sets on these two arms
The sun sets on these two legs
I will smell the moon no longer
I will smell the trees no more
I give up my clothes
With happiness
I give up my hair
With happiness
I give up my human skin
With happiness
Joining the waves as one.

Hazel jumps up as though someone is pulling her and, with a guttural sound, pushes chairs and her mother aside and runs out the door, shimmying out of her clothes as she heads toward the dock. We follow, Keet reaching her first. He grabs her arm.

"Mother!"

I see her turn to him, eyes blinking, saying something under her breath, pulling away. He slows Hazel down until Sylvie can catch up, then they follow her out onto the dock. I hope being closer to the water will calm her. Zelka and I remain on shore, watching as Keet and Sylvie grapple with Hazel, trying to stop her from jumping into the water. Sobbing, she finally slumps in surrender. Keet and his grandmother look at one another, and I hear Keet.

"We need to do something, grandmother. She's having more of these disconnections, not fewer, the longer she's human."

"We need to let her go."

"If we give her the Walk Into the Water ceremony, would it help?"

"Grandson, we cannot wait another day, even another hour. She needs to be released now."

I look at Hazel, naked and weeping. Even from this distance, I see the long-healed burn that mottles her skin. My heart gives one aching thump, then another.

"I need to go with her, then." He looks into his grandmother's eyes, and she looks back.

"Do what you must, Keet."

"I can guide her to my family pod. They know her, they'll look after her."

Sylvie nods. Nods again, deciding.

"Then I will go with you as well."

"Grandmother—"

She holds up her hand, then places it on Hazel's back. "Keet, whatever you're going to say, I've already thought of it. But she is my daughter. I must be with her."

Keet looks into her eyes, at the bright dagger of pain that knifes through them.

"We need to go. There's no more time." He turns and looks at Nolee and Zelka, holding hands as they watch the scene unfolding in front of them.

"Nolee. We need to get Mom into the water. Grandmother's coming with me."

"Keet!" Nolee strains against Zelka's hand, but Zelka doesn't let go. Nolee turns to her, says something Keet can't hear, and then jogs to where they huddle on the damp dock.

"We have to get her to my pod, and make sure she's safe. And it needs to happen now."

"I know. Can we say goodbye to her?" Keet nods, and after giving Hazel a quick kiss on her head, which Hazel doesn't notice, Nolee gestures to Zelka.

"Zee. Do you want to say goodbye to your mother?"

The wind catches Zelka's hair, blowing black strands across her still face. Taking small steps, tears running down her cheeks, she walks the length of the dock, kneels, and kisses her mother on her cheek.

"Goodbye, Mom. I love you."

At this, Hazel stops her endless whisper of ancient words, the last of the day's light reflecting in the whites of her eyes. Raising her hand to her daughter's face, she soundlessly forms the words "I love you too," then crawls to the edge of the dock. Taking her hair in her hand, she holds it out to Keet, who uses his knife to cut through it with a sound like ripping paper. He then hands it to Sylvie. After calling into the sky, "She Sings Two Worlds, we give you back your daughter," Sylvie releases it to the wind. Some strands disappear. Some strands lie on the rippling water like cobwebs.

Nolee kisses Keet and Sylvie. "Come home soon." As she watches, Keet dives into the water without a splash; the next thing she sees is his large dorsal fin. Then Hazel drops into the water in silence and goes under. After a rush of bubbles on the surface, her smaller dorsal fin appears.

On land, Nolee and Zelka hold each other. As Zelka cries, Nolee whispers into her hair. "Zee, you can join them. You can swim with your mom."

The young woman steps back and shakes her head. "I can't. I don't know who that woman is. She doesn't feel like my mother, just some …" She stops, her face tense with pain. "She's a stranger to me. I'd rather remember her as I once knew her."

"You won't be alone. Your grandmother and brother are there. You've never been together as an orca family. You could do that for your mom."

Zelka shakes her head again, putting a hand to her mouth, stopping the sobs caught there. She looks out at the dock, where she sees her grandmother undressing and piling her folded clothes next to Keet's.

Once done, she sits hunched on the edge of the dock, praying, the strong expanse of her back rising and falling, then slides into the water and bobs on the current. Keet, in his orca form, swims closer to his grandmother, surfaces with a whoosh, then dives again. Sylvie submerges; Nolee sees the pale underside of her feet as she kicks down through the dark green water. Outside the buoys, two dorsal fins rise far behind a third: a lone female orca, swimming away from her family as fast as she can.

TWENTY-ONE

Zelka and I stand on the beach, the wind in our hair, tears on our cheeks.

"She's all I've ever known."

I wait a moment, giving her time, wanting to offer support. "Creating your own life is scary. But you're not alone, Zee. We're here with you."

She drapes an arm over my shoulders and leans into me. "I wouldn't have had the chance to know myself as human if it weren't for you and Keet."

Out in the bay, there's no sign of her orca family. The sun sets in a sky tinged orange and yellow. An eagle flies overhead, banking into the wind. I can see his pale head tilting to the side, searching for his evening meal.

"Let's go inside, Nolee. I need to sleep." I show her the guest bedroom, and as she sits on the edge of the bed, I tell her about the ocean quilt, and how I hope it will help bring her some peace, too.

"I'll leave my door open, Zee. Let me know if you need anything." She looks at me and nods, then lies down on top of the quilt and closes her eyes.

"C'mon dogs. Bedtime." Fae follows me, but Wallace hangs back, ears up, body straining between Fae and me and the woman on the bed.

"Good boy, Wallace. Stay here with Zee."

I feel my own tension ease when Wallace sighs and curls up on the rug by the bed, eyes halfway closed, large ears alert for her sounds.

Flicking on the porch light, I gather up glasses, pitcher, and the notebook with Zelka's name on it: Zelka William Eils Noland. I trace Sylvie's spidery handwriting, feeling the indentations in the paper, the shapes that make up the name of a young woman who is crafting herself with the same courage as her unknown ancestors.

"Nolee?" Hearing my name spoken in a whisper, I struggle to open my eyes, blinking away their heaviness in the dark hour before sunrise. Dressed in shorts and a t-shirt, Zelka sits on the bed beside me; I see the shine in her eyes, the tears coursing down her cheeks.

"Zee?" My voice crackles with sleep. "What's wrong?"

She touches my shoulder. "I'm going to find my mother, and I didn't want you to worry."

"Let me get dressed and I'll walk with you."

She nods, then wipes her face and looks at the dampness shining in her palm. "I'm still not used to this crying stuff."

I sit up straighter, rubbing her back, feeling the angles of her shoulder blades beneath my hand. "If it's any comfort, most humans aren't used to that crying stuff either. Myself included."

She nods, then rises. "I'll be in the living room."

As I pull sweats and a hoodie on over my nightgown, I hear the dogs' small woofs as they greet Zelka. Judging by the click of their nails, they're doing their happy dance for her. When I join them, I kneel and rub their ears as they snuffle my face. Zee stands in the middle of the room, hands clasped over her stomach.

"Zee, do you want me to fix you some breakfast before you go?"

"No, thanks. I'll catch something to eat ..." she trails off, looking out the window at the water brightening from black to light blue, mirroring the pale sky. Turning toward me, she steps closer and takes my hand. "I need to go."

The dogs fly out of the house, dancing around us as we walk onto the cold beach. I give Zelka a hug, feeling compelled to say something but have no idea what that something is. Her collarbone is round and smooth beneath my forehead. Finally, I share my happy thoughts: Zelka throwing the ball for the dogs, Zelka dancing with me in the living room, Zelka watching the sunset. Her arms around me tighten, and in response, a tidal wave of her emotions wash over and through me, stretching my heart between the earth and the morning sky. I realize that she has, once again, shared with me the magnitude of herself and how she holds her beloveds. What I call happiness, she feels as a vast world of belonging.

We release one another. She smiles and walks out on the dock. Standing with her face to the east, she raises her arms to the sky, her body bathed in the shell-pink light of the rising sun. I hear her singing, her voice pure and unselfconscious, like a rare bird gifting its song to the air. When she lowers her arms, her are eyes still closed and her face is upturned, as though she could drink the light of this new day.

"Zee?" She opens her eyes.

"You always have a home with us." I swipe at my eyes, feeling a sharp tug in my heart as I remember what she said about "this crying stuff."

She walks along the bobbing dock as though she's floating, then turns back. She buries her face in Wallace's neck and holds a wriggling Fae with her other arm. Then she stands up, and her beautiful lavender-ringed brown eyes look into mine. We hug again, and under the currents of pain and loss and sadness, I feel a deep well of joy, of life, of family.

She touches my face, then walks to the end of the dock and removes the elastic holding her hair in a braid, letting the morning breeze lift it. As I've seen Keet do, she stands with her back to me and undresses, laying her clothes on the dock. She looks over her shoulder at me, smiling, her hair billowing like a cloak around her. I raise one hand. She nods, turns, and with one graceful movement, dives into the water, which is now as blue as the sky it reflects.

The ripples have disappeared before I see her rise again as orca, far beyond the buoys, a small triangular dorsal fin speeding away. I send out a silent prayer that she finds her family before it's too late. Before Hazel does something while Zelka isn't with her.

With a nose bump to my calf, Fae recalls me to the present moment, then nudges my leg again, wagging her tail. Wallace, out at the end of the dock, snuffles Zee's clothes, then sits and looks out at the water.

"Let's go make some tea, dogs. And some breakfast." Fae trots ahead of me, but Wallace stays on the dock, lying on Zelka's discarded clothing, looking out into the bay, waiting for her return.

Keet, his grandmother, and his mother find Keet's pod after four days of slow swimming. Zelka, who had caught up with them the previous night, joins Keet in the hunt for food, feeding the older females a steady supply of salmon. His grandmother helps by swimming beyond their sight, sending bursts of click trains that he adds to his own, narrowing the area where the fish might be. His mother is silent, her heartbeat erratic and slow. He wonders if she's regaining herself as orca, pushing away the madness of being human. Zee swims first beside her mother, then to him, then to her grandmother.

Keet's family pod is music to his heart; in their touching and splashing, they express the joy of reuniting. They welcome his grandmother, and now the two matriarchs—Sylvie and Nana—swim together in harmony. His mother lets the others touch her, nudge her with rostrum and pectoral and tail, but he feels not even a ripple of response from her. Zee hangs back, unsure of these new orcas, until George, swooping around her in bubbling spirals, draws her out to play.

A week goes by as the pod makes its way west, providing food for Hazel and their matriarchs. One moonlit night, Hazel leaps out of the water, crying and wailing, making noises none of them have ever heard in their lifetimes. Her cries scatter fish and seals, jellyfish and birds in a widening arc away from them. With no warning, she rams Atma, flails her body against Poppy. George speeds away, taking shelter behind Keet. Keet swims him to Belle, who places him under her pectoral fin and swims them away from the melee. Crying in alarm, Zee follows Keet, Belle, and the rest of the pod.

Suddenly, Keet feels a tug and a sharp pain on his pectoral fin. Tilting his head, he sees that his mother has taken the fin in her worn teeth. With his blood floating around Hazel's head, Keet tries to swim up to the air, but is unable to rise. When she finally releases her grip, he sees that she's opened her blowhole; the air rises in large bubbles as it escapes her lungs. Her next breath will be her death.

Tilting his head again toward his mother, he stops his push for the surface. His grandmother and Nana are trying to glide underneath Hazel, trying to force her to the surface to breathe. Keet is silent, saving the air dwindling from his lungs. He surfaces, gulps a breath and sends out a call for his family, finally locating them huddled around George. Zee swims between the two groups, heart racing, head filled with her mother's cries.

As he dives again, singing his mother's name, he sees the flash of two white bellies pass him on their way up. Keet's click trains bounce off of his mother's slowly sinking body, watching as she rolls onto her back and begins to settle, mouth open, eyes closed, on the bottom of the Salish Sea. As he hovers, singing a song of mourning, blood from his pectoral fin swirls in a slow spiral dance through the moonlit depths.

Zee appears through the murk, her heartbeat growing closer, until she's floating next to him, her head against his body. He feels their combined grief; his own cavernous, Zelka's piercing. On his other side, angled downward, his grandmother sings her grief as the white of his mother's belly finally fades to black. The three of them send click trains into the depths, seeing behind their eyes Hazel's limp body, as silent now as she was in her last days.

The need for air forces them to surface, where they swim in a close circle high above Hazel's body, rising and falling, touching and singing. The rest of the pod members join them, making a second circle, exhaling in the moonlight.

Taking a large breath, Zelka dives and swims around her mother's body, nudging it, resting her head against its cold skin. Throughout the night, she repeats the pattern: breathe, dive, touch. But she no longer sings her mother's name.

For a couple of days, I relish the silence that greets me when I return to the house. But then I feel the emptiness. For someone who thought being alone was ideal, I'm surprised that the longing for my family is so strong. I've always believed that the people we choose to bring close to us are our genuine family, and that family related by blood is happenstance. I feel lucky that Abbie and I are family in both senses. I glance at my phone, where the last text from my daughter tells me she's got a date tonight. I smile, reminding myself I need to text her later. Right now, I need to get out of this empty house.

I wasn't scheduled to work at the shelter this morning, and I take Andi by surprise.

"Nolee! What are you doing here?" Her hand flies to her mouth. "Oh my god, that sounded so ungrateful." Pulling me into a hug, she continues. "What I meant to say is, 'It's great to see you and what a delightful surprise.'" I laugh and she releases me.

"Everyone is still gone sightseeing and I'm knocking around Osprey Bay by myself. I got lonely … there's only so much beach walking the dogs and I can do."

"Did you bring Fae and Wallace?"

"They're in the yard at home, chewing on bones."

"Make yourself comfortable and look at these adoption applications. I still have some hot water in the kettle. Tea?"

"Do turkeys stampede at dawn?" My smile feels forced.

"I have no idea, but I'll take that as a yes." Pouring hot water into a mug and adding a tea bag, she sets the mug in front of me as I begin thumbing through the stack of paper.

We spend the next few hours approving applications; noting which dogs are suitable; and then, when Andi finishes filing, checking on the kittens. I'm closing the door on their playroom, brushing off the hair from my jeans, when Andi waves me over.

"I'm famished. How about lunch at the Camas Café?"

"Sounds good."

It's a sunny October day, and on our walk to the café, the crisp autumn breeze blows away some of my mental fog. As we finish our lunch, Andi leans toward me. "You've been a little distracted, Nolee. What's going on?"

I take a moment to think about my answer. "It's funny, Andi. I was alone in my marriage. I was alone when I first arrived. Now, my family is away, and I'm alone again."

"What's funny about that?"

"That we can use the same word for different experiences. I'm realizing that I'd rather be physically alone than go through the emotional neglect of my former marriage."

The waiter returns and Andi asks for the check. After he leaves, she says, "It's like that as we get older, though, isn't it?"

"What do you mean?"

"Life comes in layers of experiences. We have to go through most of them before we know how to make sense of it all for ourselves."

"True. But when *do* we figure it all out, Andi? When do we have the answers?

At this, she laughs so hard that she needs to wipe her eyes. Finally, she reaches out and puts her hand on mine.

"We don't. Ideally, we have our best guesses and the certainty of our limited time, our mortality. And enough maturity to recognize both."

"When you put it that way, Andi, I feel so much better."

Seeing my expression, she laughs again, and this time, I laugh with her.

At the shelter, the twins are romping with the dogs in the play yard, so Andi and I get back to work in the office. Looking over at her—tapping on her keyboard, glasses perched on the end of her nose—I take comfort. "I'm glad we're friends, Andi Fox."

When she scoots her chair across the floor to give me a hug, the casters make a long squeal that reminds me of Keet. I swallow my piercing worry and wrap my arms around her.

"I am too, Nolee. It's going to work out, whatever it is."

TWENTY-TWO

Fae and Wallace are in the back yard with me while I clean up, when I hear them yipping and grunting and jumping against the gate. I rush over to the gate, standing on my tip toes, as if I could see farther in the dim afternoon light. I see two shapes huddled on the dock, heads bowed as though a great weight is pressing down on them.

Rushing to the dock with an armful of towels and robes, I see gauzy layers of steam rise from Keet and Zelka's skin as the cold air hits their bodies. Where is Sylvie? Why hasn't she come back?

I drape a towel over Keet and another over Zelka, whose face is hidden behind a curtain of wet hair. I can't tell if the drops hitting the bobbing dock are tears or seawater. I rub Keet's back, happy to feel the solid line of muscle under my hand.

Keet is the first to speak. "Help Zee." He stands, wrapping the towel around his waist and flicking the hair out of his red-rimmed eyes.

I look down at her, huddled and unmoving. "Zee, honey, let's get you dried off and inside." Gathering her hair into a heavy ponytail, I wrap a towel around her and rub her shuddering back. "Stand up, sweetheart. Let's get this robe on you."

Limbs heavy, she rises in slow motion. The towel drops to the dock as I help her into the robe and tie the belt around her narrow waist. Although she moves as though pressed down by a thousand-pound weight, I can feel her bones, light and fragile as a bird's.

A volley of exhales catches my attention and I look seaward to see seven dorsal fins, rising and falling with the current.

"Is Sylvie coming in?" I look at Keet.

He wipes his eyes. "Not yet. She wants to stay with our orca pod for a while."

"Let's get you both inside and fed." I glance at the gray clouds moving in. "We won't have sun much longer." Grabbing the dropped towel, I follow them back to the house.

I leave the guest room, where Zelka lies curled up under the quilt and Wallace sits with his head resting on the bed, watching her. Leaving the door open, I join Keet in the kitchen, standing near him as he slices vegetables for dinner. My throat feels constricted when I ask him, "How long can she grieve like this, Keet? It's been two weeks. She hasn't stopped crying, and she's barely eating."

Keet gathers the vegetables and drops them into a large bowl. "It's been seventeen days, actually."

I wrap my arms around his waist, his warmth and the familiar contours of his body bringing me comfort. I wish I could give Zelka some kind of comfort too. "How about you?"

"The sadness is heavy in a different way. Feels like I'm grieving for my mother a second time. At some point, I'll feel grateful that she isn't suffering so much. But not yet."

After an early dinner, we coax Zelka out to the beach. Wallace stays by her side, ignoring the ball and Fae speeding after it.

Handing her the drool-covered ball, I ask, "Zee, can you throw this for Wallace, please?"

I see her swollen eyes, her small and muted movements. Zelka takes the ball from me with delicate fingers.

"Wallace?" she says. The dog's large ears swivel toward her voice, his eyes brightening for the first time since Zelka's return. She throws the ball, which lands a short distance in front of them. Wallace walks to it and looks up at her, the tip of his tail wagging. A smile appears on her face as she retrieves the ball and throws it harder. The speed of Wallace's departure sprays them with sand and small rocks, but before they've wiped themselves off, he's back, dropping the ball at Zelka's feet. She grabs the ball, goes into a fast walk, then slings her arm back and throws, sending the ball down the length of the beach. Like furry speeding bullets, both dogs take off in happy pursuit.

Keet laces his fingers in between mine as Zelka and the dogs play, watching her break free from the petrification of her grief, hearing her voice and her laugh as Fae barks and Wallace's tongue lolls out of his mouth. She turns toward us then walks back and wraps her arms around us. We rock together, breathing and crying. I feel a warm weight against my leg, and when I look down, I see that Wallace has settled himself between me and Keet.

Home after working at Chena's store, I look at my phone when it pings. A text from Keet. *Grandmother came back this afternoon. We're in her cabin. Come join us?* I send a thumbs-up emoji and make my way to the bedroom to change out of my pet-hair-covered clothes, the memory of kitten-cuddling making me smile.

That warm and fuzzy feeling fades when I see Sylvie at the table, her face drained, her eyes shuttered. When she stands to greet me, I notice that her clothes hang from her shoulders; she's still broad-shouldered, but the rest of her has melted away. Keet and Zelka are cooking, chatting in low voices. Before I can express my concern, she places a hand on my arm. "It's good to see you again, Nolee."

I smile, uncertain, but am reassured by the strength I feel flowing through her hand.

"We're so glad you're home. This past month has been strange without you."

Keet joins us and kisses my cheek. "Halibut stew tonight. Grandmother made it; I still can't convince her to share her recipe."

Sylvie laughs. "Grandson, I would let you drive my truck before I'd give you that recipe." Keet widens his eyes and holds out his hand, palm up. "Deal. I'll take the keys."

Smiling, she gives him a small push. "Go check that stew. I think it's done."

Small talk and questions from Zee pepper our conversation as we set the table. Once we sit down, however, the only sounds are the tap of spoons against bowls. When Sylvie speaks again, I'm relieved to see she's eating her second bowl of stew. "It was good to be with our orca family. It is also good to be here, with my human family. Let's walk after dinner. Hazel's story needs to be shared."

Keet finishes his stew and takes my hand in his. Across from me, Zelka gets up, takes the empty bowls to the sink, and—shoulders tense, head bowed—washes them.

Keet closes the cabin door and follows the three women making their way to the rocky beach. There's no easy talking among them, no touching, nothing except three people caught in their own worlds. Zelka, Nolee, and Keet sit on their sea-bleached log. Keet takes Nolee's hand in his. It's cold. Sylvie lowers herself to the ground next to them and begins.

"Every twenty-eighth generation, a Keykwin child is born with a storm inside them."

"I haven't heard this before. Are you saying you think Mom might have been the twenty-eighth?" Keet asks.

Sylvie nods. "It hadn't happened in my memory, or even in the memory of my grandparent's grandparents. When Hazel was born, I'd almost forgotten about it. But as she grew, I asked my mother if she could be the twenty-eighth."

Nolee scoots closer to Keet. "What did she say?"

The light is gone from the sky and in the space between Nolee's question and Sylvie's answer, the air vibrates with the hiss of the rising tide hitting the shore.

"She'd seen Hazel's tantrums. She told me all children have tantrums, it's part of their growth. Even Keykwin children are still children. But Hazel screamed every day. It was like she was being thrown on a fire. I took her to doctors; I took her to medicine men. I accepted the burden that I had done something to her. The only way she could fall asleep was when she was in a warm bath."

"When did you realize she might be the twenty-eighth generation?" Keet asks.

"My grandmother reminded me. She spoke only Keykwin, and I spent much of my childhood with her while my parents worked. I learned most of the Keykwin stories from her." While Sylvie is silent, Keet wonders what memories are playing in her head. When she speaks again, her voice seems to come from far away.

"When Hazel turned two, I left her with my grandmother so I could swim as orca. I was exhausted from being in the storm and needed a rest from my daughter."

Zelka lays a soft hand on her grandmother's arm, then slides off the log to sit next to her and fold her into an embrace. Sylvie returns the hug, then, smiling and patting her face, moves away. When she speaks again, her voice is stronger.

"When Hazel was three, I took her into the water with me." She looks at Keet. "This was at the cabin in Sitka. I stayed human, and I held her with me in the ocean. She stopped screaming. She laughed."

Nolee looks at Sylvie. "That must have been a relief."

Sylvie nods. "Every day in the summer, we'd be in the water together. She was a happy baby. She could swim in the shallows by the time she was four, when the weather was nice." Sylvie pauses. "I decided she needed to know who she was. I talked to her in Keykwin and English, told her the story of She Sings Two Worlds, told her what I was going to do, and that I was still her mother. Then I changed."

"You changed to orca with her in the water?" Keet's surprise shows on his face.

Sylvie looks at the dark water, nodding. "Hazel was so happy in the ocean. I wanted to show her why."

Keet clears his throat, then puts his arm around Nolee's waist. "What did she do?"

Sylvie gives a small smile. "She swam out to me and changed, too. We spent the rest of that day together, in peace, as mother and daughter instead of enemies."

"Mother said she should've taken the Walk Into the Water when she was initiated as Keykwin."

"She was so strong, and so stubborn. I wanted her to experience life as a human, Keet. As she grew, I thought it would get easier."

"But being human didn't get easier."

Sylvie looks at Keet, shaking her head. "No. She met your dad, Charlie, when she was sixteen. Falling in love made the storm inside her go quiet. They got married and had you. But the storm began again after you were born."

"This must be the reason I have so many more memories of you and Great-Grandmother than I do of Mom. She was gone, swimming as orca, even before she and dad left."

"Yes. Sometimes she was gone for days, occasionally weeks. When she came back, she would be quieter, be able to be your mother. But the storm always came back. She said being near the water made her crazy."

"That's why she and Dad left, isn't it? Moved away from the sight of the ocean? But I didn't want to leave you."

Sylvie reaches over and pats Keet's hand. "I'm honored to be your grandmother, and I loved raising you."

"Keet, didn't you say the first time you swam as orca you were four?" Nolee asks.

He nods. He hears the rocks rumbling as the sea pummels them, feels the warmth of Nolee's hip against his, and squeezes her in gratitude for her presence during this conversation. His grandmother is watching the rising tide, watching the logs bobbing in the channel.

"I didn't want her to do it. She taught you the way I taught her. Keet, you were a quiet and happy baby, and the same as a child. A ceremony, Family under the Waves, is performed when a Keykwin child is nine years old. By that time, they know about their Keykwin ancestors, but the ceremony prepares them for the change into orca, selects their pod ..." She stops, rubbing her eyes.

"Grandmother, it's all right. It turned out better than I could've imagined. But what about Jerry?"

Sylvie says, "What about him?"

"He and I talked about some of his challenges. He mentioned nothing like what Mom went through."

Sylvie sighs. "Jerry didn't want his orca family. He's Keykwin but has never once been orca."

"I've not thought about it until now, Grandmother, but you're right. He's never spoken of it either." Keet leans forward, looking at his grandmother. She says,

"Jerry told me when he was twelve years old that when he grew up, he would never have children because he didn't want them to be like Hazel. The memory of his sister caused him to isolate himself."

In a flash of insight, Keet understands his uncle. Nolee leans into him. "Sound familiar?"

"My Uncle Jerry and I aren't too different, after all."

After listening to the sounds of the night and the sea, exhaustion catches up with them. Yawning, they return to their homes. Zelka walks with her grandmother, one hand under her elbow, and Keet and Nolee let the dogs out for a last run before going to bed.

"How are you feeling?" Nolee asks.

"More at peace than I've felt since my mother was here."

Taking a stick out of Wallace's mouth, Nolee doubles back toward the house, looking down at the ground. When she finds a bright yellow tennis ball, she throws it in the opposite direction, then joins Keet again. "I'm glad to hear that. It's been a tough time for you."

Keet sees the white tip of Fae's tail and the patchy white of Wallace's head heading toward them. When they get close, Wallace hesitates, looks between them, then walks up to Keet. With the ball in his mouth, he sits, tail whipping back and forth. Kneeling and reaching toward him with a slow and steady hand, Keet scratches Wallace on the chest. Then, in one fluid motion, he takes the ball, stands, and throws it. Ball and dogs disappear into the night.

Nolee's grin glows in the dark. "Looks like he's decided you're safe."

Closing the cabin door, Zelka turns to see Sylvie coming toward her with scissors in her hand.

"What are those for, Grandmother?"

"In case you want to cut off your hair. For your mother."

Zelka brings her thick black braid over her shoulder and holds it with both hands.

"I don't understand."

"It is a tradition. We cut our hair when we grieve. It is a way to honor the people who come before us and who are gone. We burn our hair with the grasses, and the smoke carries our prayers for our loved ones into the sky."

Zelka stands straighter, feeling the comforting bulk of her hair in her hands, connecting her to all she has ever known herself to be.

"All of it?"

Her grandmother nods.

"I won't cut my hair. My tears for my mother are enough."

Sylvie puts the scissors back in the bathroom medicine cabinet. "Remember, her last sound was of you, both as orca and a woman. She gave you her Blessing, Zelka."

TWENTY-THREE

"Do you want to know how I found you, Keet?"

Keet is driving Zelka to the market. They've survived the dirt road, the wet pavement hissing as the tires pick up the previous night's rain.

"I *have* been curious about that." He glances at his sister, wondering if that's what his eyes look like: dark and tilted, light shining in their depths.

"When I was fifteen, I began dreaming of human experiences. I didn't know that's what they were. One moment, I was floating next to Mom as she rested, and the next I'd feel myself above the water, looking down at trees and mountains. One time, I even felt warm ground beneath me. They were strange dreams."

"Did Mother ever know?"

"She knew something was bothering me, but my heartbeat was the only information she could reach. She stayed close to me; unless we were touching, she couldn't feel what I was feeling. It took me a while to realize that."

"That makes sense. As orca, we stay close anyway."

Zelka nods. Lacing her fingers together and looking down, she says, "It was almost morning. Mom and I were resting, and I had another experience, this time about walking through trees. Mist swirled in the branches, and I remember trying to breathe it in."

"Did you see yourself as human?"

"No. I had drifted away from mom, and her cry woke me up. After that, I started asking her about the things that happened when I rested."

"What did she say?"

"She said I needed to forget them. That they were bad dreams. It was the first time I'd heard her use that way of describing what happened, so I kept asking her what the words 'bad' and 'dreams' meant."

"Did she tell you?"

"She said they meant my brain was getting rid of things it didn't need."

As Keet signals a turn, he hears Zelka inhale deeply. Looking over at her, he sees that her head is raised, her eyes are closed, and there's a small smile on her lips.

"You know what still surprises me most about being human?"

"Tell me."

"Smells."

They laugh at the same time. "I know there are unpleasant smells, but I can't stop smelling all the time. Nolee told me that a dog's sense of smell is much better than a human's. I wish Wallace could share what he smells with me." She rolls the window further down, letting in the salt- and pine-laden air.

"How did you find me?"

"I never stopped asking Mom questions about my dreams. She wasn't as troubled when she was orca. She felt darker than the other orca we met, but I figured that was just her."

"It makes more sense now that we know about the twenty-eighth generation."

"It does. When she realized I wasn't going to stop asking her, Mom told me that she was different from other orca, that she came from a line of people who could choose to be human or to be orca. There were called Keykwin."

She turns her head away, and Keet sees her swipe at her eyes. Wanting to give her some time, he concentrates on his driving.

"The first time I felt anger was when she told me that she had made the choice for both of us, and I was to be orca. It's how I was born, and how I would live."

"She was that way as a human mother, too. Convinced her way was right."

"I didn't question her knowledge. But when I knew I could be human, I wanted to try it."

"This was before you learned about me?"

"Yes."

"Where were you? How did I miss hearing my mother?"

"We stayed out in the deeper waters. Mom refused to swim inland, said there wasn't enough food."

"What changed? How did you find your way here?"

"I knew if I swam away from her, she'd follow. I found the underwater river, the one that flows into … what's it called?"

"Puget Sound."

"We heard clicking in a canyon. She wanted to leave, but she wouldn't while I was there. I think that's what upset her again."

"What do you mean?"

"She called the noise we were hearing 'ticking,' but I didn't know what she meant. I know now that clocks tick." Lifting her braid from her neck, she closes her eyes again, then continues talking.

"Mom told me about you. Where you might be. How she and Dad moved away and left you with our grandmother. Up north. That you'd made a life here."

Keet tightens his grip on the steering wheel.

"So you knew who I was when you started showing up in Osprey Bay?"

She nods. "Mom refused to come with me. She said leaving you was the biggest mistake she made."

"It was for the best." Keet can feel his throat tightening.

"You never talk about our dad. Why?"

Keet darts a glance at his sister, her firm gaze, the strength of her question stifling him.

"The memories I have of him are good, but there aren't many. He left with my mom. She was it for him, it was always about her." Keet rolls to a stop as they reach Northsound, then turns left toward the Market.

Zelka's voice is quiet when she answers him. "I wish I could've known him. Even for a little while. What kind of person was he, that he could accept our mom?"

Keet says. "A good one. But if you'd asked me that when I was going through adolescence without my father, I would've said what he did was unforgiveable."

Zelka watches the cars and people moving through the parking lot of the market. They wait behind another car that is turning into the parking lot as well. Keet says, "Tell me more about this clicking sound, Zee."

"It was interesting to me, but for her, it was maddening. While we were swimming in the area, Mom told me old Keykwin legends, and stories about my human family. She wanted us to swim into the canyon and find our cousins."

"Did you?"

"Yes. From the time I was young, she and I practiced staying under the water for long periods of time. It was easy for me but difficult for her. Once we were above the canyon where the clicking was the loudest, we spent most of our time diving toward it. She had to stop, though; the clicks became louder the closer we got. I think that's when her storm got bigger. Those clicks opened something in her that she was trying to keep hidden."

"Did you stop swimming in the canyon?"

Zelka shakes her head, tucks a strand of hair behind her ear. "No. I went deeper. I discovered a house there; it had many corners, but only one entrance. I sang to it during the new moon, and the full moon, and daytime. But nothing happened. Just the knocking sound, like two rocks hitting each other."

Keet parks and shuts the engine off. "How long were you there?"

Zelka, who's not quite mastered the art of the shrug, lifts her shoulders and drops them. "Suns and moons beyond my count. You know that orca time is different than human time, Keet."

Shopping finished, Keet and Zelka buckle their seatbelts. Keet looks at his sister, who is still blushing.

"You aren't interested in Erik?" Keet teases.

"I don't know what to do when a man says those things."

"What things, Zee?" Keet nudges her arm. "He asked you if you wanted to meet for coffee sometime."

Zelka squirms. "I want to be around you and Nolee and Grandmother. I don't understand why I would drink a random liquid with a stranger. In a room with other strangers."

"Well," Keet says, stifling a laugh. "Meeting for coffee is more about getting to know you."

"I'm still not interested."

"I'm sure he figured that out when you walked away from him." Keet laughs. "When you were orca, didn't you get together with a male?"

"By 'get together,' do you mean 'get laid,' Keet?"

Keet laughs again, starts the car, and begins the drive back home.

"Sure, that's what I mean."

Zelka's silent for so long that he looks over at her. She's blushing again, the blood staining her cheeks a bright pink. She raises her hands to her face. "How do I make this stop?!"

He signals, turns, and heads toward Osprey Bay.

"You don't. It's part of being human."

"It's an annoying part. I feel like I can't have my secrets."

"You don't have to answer, Zee. I didn't mean to put you on the spot."

She rolls the window down and loosens her hair from the braid, rolling it into a bun like Nolee showed her.

"Do you know how old I am?" she asks.

Keet, used to her quick changes of topic, answers, "Twenty-three years younger than me, so that would make you thirty."

"How did we get so far apart?"

"Mom had me when she was seventeen. She and Dad got in the accident when I was twenty-three. They were coming to tell me about you."

Zelka turns, closing her eyes against the cool breeze that blows across her face.

"She wouldn't let me close to any male orcas."

"Why?"

"She said they were trouble, and to stay away from them. Mom and the other female were always with me. It wasn't difficult to keep every other orca at a distance."

"So, you've never …"

"Been laid? Yeah."

"That's actually a coarse way of saying that, Zee. As your brother, I now officially feel awkward."

"I'm not ignorant about the process. The other female mated a lot. She only had one baby, though."

Keet and Zelka sit with their own thoughts, the sounds of tires on wet pavement like background music. When they reach the dirt road leading to the cabins, Zelka speaks. "I need to tell all of you something."

Keet glances over at her. Unlike her usual open gaze, her eyes are clouded with worry. He pulls over and lets the SUV roll to a stop.

"Would it help to tell me now?"

She searches his face, opens her mouth as though to speak, then shuts it with a snap. "No. I'd rather everyone hear it. I don't know if I could tell it again."

Keet lets his foot off the brake. "Okay."

"Mom made me promise that I'd tell no one."

"Then maybe you need to keep that promise, Zee."

"No. This is one I need to break."

She raises her chin. "I know about the clock in the water, and I know where it belongs."

As I let the dogs out into the yard, I hear Keet call my name from the deck, and walk out to join him, Zelka, and Sylvie at the table. The fall breeze carries hints of the coming winter, and I'm glad I'm wearing a sweater. Keet, Sylvie, and Zelka, who seem to never get cold, wear short-sleeved shirts.

Keet starts the conversation. "Zelka has something she wants to tell us."

As I get comfortable, Zelka begins by describing how she and her mother found a house in a canyon under the ocean, and the sounds that came from it. She shifts her position, putting her shoulder against Keet's.

"This is the story of Janadsila's water clock, the one I told mom about. She told me to never speak of it. But I need to. The sounds we heard from the water canyon house told me a story."

One day, a young woman who is a Weaver from the land dwelling Keykwin Nation decides to visit her cousins under the waves. Her name is Janadsila, and she's a great-granddaughter of She Sings Two Worlds, the woman who gave her female relations the ability to be both human, and blackfish. Janadsila swims as blackfish to her cousin's village but enters the Water Canyon House as a beautiful young woman. Spending days away from her own family, Janadsila dances, tells stories around a fire, brings fish for their meals.

A burnished, dark-red bowl glows in the firelight. Her cousin Weshtay sits with it, cradling it in her lap, long arms around its rim. When Janadsila walks closer, she sees that inside the red bowl, there is a smaller, darker bowl with a hole in its bottom. Weshtay hums as water fills the small bowl through that hole. As Janadsila watches, she's first entranced, then jealous. She wants to sit with the bowl cradled in her lap, to feel the weight of it pressing against the inside of her thighs. When she asks Weshtay if she, Janadsila, can do this, her cousin shakes her head so her dark hair covers her face.

The rest of the day, Janadsila spends time with the others, but her eye is always on the bowl, and on her cousin, who, throughout the day, empties the small bowl into the larger bowl then replaces it on the surface with care. Janadsila hears Weshtay whispering to it, and sees her caress it like it is a loved one.

As Janadsila departs, spinning and swimming home as blackfish, thoughts of the red bowl spin even faster in her mind.

She bursts into her mother's dwelling. "I demand to know about the red bowl our family under the waves possesses!"

Janadsila's mother stands. Although curved with age, she is still taller than her tallest daughter.

"You can demand all you like, Janadsila. The water clock is theirs, as sacred to them as our cloaks are to us."

"A water clock? Why don't we have one?"

"It's not our way."

Frustrated, Janadsila turns and disappears into the forest, thinking about how she can make a water clock for herself. By choice, she isn't a weaver; sitting still for long periods of time and making small progress isn't her way. Janadsila wants to gaze into a water clock, to look down into its depths and hear what it says to her. She wants to see her own reflection in its water.

Anatshan, a young man from another village, is her age. Although he's quiet, she notices his eyes on her when he thinks she isn't looking. He is a carver, and Janadsila knows that he has the skill to craft a water clock for her. She must charm him into doing it.

Janadsila walks the trail to his village, looking at the red cedar trees around her with fresh eyes. She could have as many water clocks as she wants. Finding Anatshan, she gives him a branch polished by the ocean and allows her eyes to linger on his. "I thought of you and your skillful carvings," she said.

Chin tucked against his chest, he smiles and thanks her. "I hope I will be a worthy carver, to call the spirit from this wood."

Though it is the busiest season, the time when warm air and sun coax berries from the bushes and fish to the streams, every evening, Janadsila visits Anatshan. Her own weaving lies forgotten, as does her obligation to contribute to her family's food stores.

Occasionally, she swims to her cousin's village under the waves. Pretending to be interested in conversation, she sits beside Weshtay, burning for the water clock. Janadsila doesn't dance. She doesn't sing. She imagines what it would be like to touch the dark-red wood and have it touch her back.

When the ground is cold under her slippered feet, she meets Anatshan in the forest. He has promised to take her to a red cedar tree that lightning had struck down, and she means to convince him that this would make a powerful water clock. But Anatshan says no. "This tree is a gift. My grandfather will carve a Kootéeyaa, a totem pole, from this tree."

Janadsila leaves in a rage, dives into the cold ocean, spins into her Black-fish form, and swims for her cousin's village. She tries to calm herself. When she arrives in the house with many corners, Weshtay is gone. Janadsila hears singing at the end of the house, sees shadows flickering on the wall around the fire as they dance.

Walking to her cousin's bed, she throws back the covers, hoping to find the water clock, hoping to touch it, to stroke it, once only. But it's not there. Making sure no eyes are following her, she steps closer to the shelves above her cousin's resting place. The clock is not there. In a frenzy now, Janadsila throws aside blankets and furs, then scrabbles at the hard floor with her fingernails. On her hands and knees, in the dim light of the flickering flames, she sees a small door set into the wall. Holding her breath, she opens it.

There, wrapped in a woven cloth that Janadsila herself had given Weshtay, is the water clock. Janadsila's hands shake as she brushes the cloth aside and takes the bowls in her hands.

"It's warm," she whispers.

Her cousin's cries break her concentration. "Janadsila! Janadsila! Stop!"

But she doesn't stop. Janadsila jerks upright and flees the house with the water clock. She tucks it under her pectoral fin as she swims as fast as she can back to land. Once she's human again, she runs into the trees with it clasped to her chest, her dripping hair like long dark tears against her cheeks. She spends that night huddled in the trees, and the next, and the next. She spends many nights alone, holding the water clock tightly in her grasp. The clock is now as cold as the frozen earth under her feet.

For days, Janadsila walks and sings. After many short days and long nights, in the far north she finds a Keykwin village among the trees. Sheltered by her distant cousins, she eventually marries their leader. She shares her knowledge of the Blackfish, weaving a story about the water clock and how it was carved for her from a lightning-struck red cedar. Janadsila teaches her daughters this story.

Many seasons go by. Janadsila lies dying, surrounded by her children and grandchildren. Even as she takes her last breath, she clings to the water clock. Her eldest daughter removes it from her mother's embrace, an embrace that death has not loosened.

From the time Janadsila stole the water clock, it never glowed, never whispered its secrets to those who held it. It waits, listening for the song that will bring it home.

"No." Sylvie says, shaking her head, closing her eyes.

"No, what?" I ask.

She covers her eyes, shaking her head. "That is a Keykwin teaching story about why we don't take what isn't ours."

Seeing his grandmother's agitation, Keet asks, "Zee, are you sure about this story?

Zee nods. "I heard it with every new moon. Every new moon, we swam together down to the canyon under the sea, trying to get into our cousins' house. That is the story I heard in the clicking. It never changed."

Sylvie says, "No. This can't be."

Zee shrinks from her grandmother's declaration.

"I've been told that same story. But two things are different." Sylvie places her palms on the table in front of her and pushes herself upright. "The first thing is the name of the carver Janadsila tried to persuade. His name is not in the story of our water clock. But it *is* the name of the man who carved my cedar chest."

I glance at Keet, and seeing the question in my eyes, he shakes his head. I look back at Sylvie.

"The second difference is that Janadsila's cousin gave her the water clock, and she passed it down to her daughters. This has happened for centuries. My grandmother's grandmother gave it to her. That water clock is stored in the cedar chest."

Sylvie is silent, staring at her folded hands in her lap.

I lean toward Zelka. "Why could you hear the story of the water clock and your mom couldn't?"

"I've asked myself the same thing. To her, it was ticking. For me, those sounds told a story."

Sylvie looks up and motions for them to follow her.

TWENTY-FOUR

The three of us sit on the edge of Zelka's bed, watching Sylvie open the closet and remove the dark green sheet covering a chest, which looks as though it had been carved from the trunk of a cedar tree. After folding the sheet, Sylvie lowers herself to the floor in front of the chest and opens the lid.

The outer surface of the chest is weather-worn gray, but the inside is a soft shade of winter wheat. Sylvie sits cross-legged, murmuring, hands in her lap, head bowed. Then, after a moment of silence, she speaks.

"This chest comes from the Keykwin Nation. This is the story they gave me.

"Lightning struck down the forest's largest tree. For ten months, the carver Anatshan, an old man by then, worked to carve the chest, helped by the people of the forest and the people from under the waves. When it was finished, both Nations celebrated. Each year in the spring, during what we call the Seal Moon, one kin group would take it for their own and care for it.

"It would spend twelve moons on land and then an equal time in a village under the water.

"One year, the people of the forest refused to return it to the people from under the water. But on a night after the Seal Moon, a man in love with a Keykwin woman from under the waves gave it to her. She took the chest as her own and carried it out to sea. She met her brothers and parents and grandparents, and they took it down to their village. When she died, her grandchildren returned it to their forest cousins, giving it to the grandchildren of the man who had loved her. In this way, it came to me. The water clock has always been inside the chest."

The roar of waves rises inside me. Underneath the roar, I hear orcas and gulls and seals and whales. Rubbing my fingers together, I feel them sticky with salt. I have no desire to touch the chest. Sitting close to it is enough to drown me in its sensations.

Sylvie rises to her knees and leans over the cedar chest. When she turns toward us, she's holding a large wooden bowl; its dull surface is a deep red. Nesting inside this bowl is a smaller, dark-brown bowl.

As waves of dizziness move through me, I take a deep breath and let it out, then squeeze my eyes shut. Sylvie's voice breaks through the sensation, and I open my eyes as she speaks.

"This is the water clock."

Zelka, who's sitting opposite Sylvie, doesn't touch the water clock, but leans in, as though she too can hear it. Then she looks at the chest. "Grandmother, what else does this chest hold?"

Sylvie touches her granddaughter's knee. "Things that are sacred things to our people. You will know about all of them, in time. But now, we will discuss what to do with the water clock."

Sylvie hands the water clock to Zelka and removes the smaller bowl, which she places in her own lap.

"Can you please fill the bowl, Granddaughter?"

Standing, Zelka cradles the bowl and goes downstairs to fill it. Sylvie reaches into the chest and brings out a porcelain pitcher and a small cotton towel. Outside, the sun is beginning to set behind the islands. Inside, there is silence. When Zelka returns, she places the bowl in her grandmother's lap. Sylvie sets the smaller bowl on the surface, then looks at us. "Come sit with us, please."

Keet and I join them, each of us sitting at a point of the compass. We watch as the water trickles into the inner bowl through a small hole in its middle. In the small bowl, a tiny ripple disturbs the surface of the water, but the water in the larger bowl is placid.

Minutes pass as the small bowl fills, then disappears under water of the larger bowl. When the water is quiet, we all let out a long breath. Sylvie passes it across to Zelka, who settles it between her crossed legs. She looks at Sylvie. "May I empty the small bowl and set it on top again?" Sylvie nods. When the small bowl has once sunk again, she says, "Granddaughter, please pass it to your brother."

Zelka hands it to Keet, who caresses its surface. Sylvie smiles. "Now, please let Nolee sit with it."

I shake the tension from my shoulders and hold out my hands as Keet passes it across to me. My heart clenches and my throat feels thick with emotion. Settling the water clock in my lap, I rest my hands along its curves and bow my head. Underneath the echo of the ocean, I hear an other-worldly singing—as though human voices are reaching me through water. Behind that is a faint ticking, like a large clock in a distant room.

"It sings." I shake my head, knowing what I said isn't quite right. "She sings. Do you also hear the ticking?"

Sylvie, Keet, and Zelka nod their heads. Zelka says, "It sounds like the clicking coming from the house under the waves, but very far away."

I hand the bowls back to Sylvie. She tips the water into the pitcher, then uses the towel to wipe the inside of the water clock dry. Her movements are deliberate, and she handles the bowls as she would a baby. Folding the towel, she places it on top of the small bowl, then nestles the clock back into the chest and shuts the lid.

"What do we do with the water, Grandmother?"

"We share it, drink it with our next meal."

She pauses, her knobby hands massaging one another. "I have decided. We must return the water clock to her home, so she can sing with our cousins under the waves."

"Sylvie, how do you know this water clock and the one Janadsila stole are the same?"

"When my daughter was sixteen, my mother and I initiated her into the Way of the Water Clock. It lasted four days. We were not sure Hazel would accept the responsibility or be able to pass our tests. But she wanted the water clock—she said she heard it speaking to her at night."

"What did it say?" Zelka says.

Sylvie shakes her head. "Hazel said she would forget as soon as she woke up. But one morning ..." Sylvie bows her head and rubs her forehead, sniffs, then sighs. She looks at her granddaughter. "When you and your mother were close to the canyon under the waves, she heard the ticking of the water clock. Because we had already initiated her as the water clock's next guardian, she was reminded of her life as a woman. As a daughter and mother. And all the choices she made. What sounds like a story to you, Zelka, was a record of bad memories for your mother."

"I understand. Grandmother. Will you tell us what happened one morning?"

Sylvie takes her granddaughter's hand in her own. "Your mother told me she felt she had been swimming for many nights. She thought she dreamed, because when she looked down at her feet, both ankles had those marks on them."

"These?" Zelka stretches her legs in front of her, touching the gray symbols around her ankles.

Sylvie nods. "Hazel made me look at her legs. She was convinced the people from under the waves had given her their markings. But Hazel's legs were clean. That's when I told her she couldn't have those designs, that only our family under the waves have them."

Zelka traces the black wavy circles around each of her ankles. "Why do I have them if I'm her daughter?"

"I don't know, Granddaughter. But what I do know is that the water clock must return to its people."

"The weather won't hold much longer." Keet says, waiting for Sylvie to stand, then handing her the pitcher. "Zee and I should swim out to the water canyon where she heard the clicking. I need to know what the sea-floor looks like—to get an idea of what to expect before we try to return the water clock."

Sylvie picks up the sheet and shakes it out. "I agree. I'll stay here with Nolee."

"Wait a minute," I say. "Keet, why can't we sail out there? We can anchor and you and Zee can find the canyon. It would be faster."

"It's not a safe time of year to be sailing. The water out there is tricky even when the weather's calm. I'll be safer—and so will you—if I swim out with Zee, and you stay on land."

Though I want to convince him that my idea is better, I realize he's right. Plus, my inclination to argue is outweighed by the pleasure of Sylvie's companionship and her acceptance of me into her family. "Thank you, Sylvie." With a smile, she hands me the sheet. "Please cover the chest."

Early the next morning, with the sun hesitating on the horizon and the gray morning streaked with silver light, Keet and Zelka prepare to leave. Standing on his grandmother's front porch, he hugs her, then kisses her soft cheek. No words pass between them. He kisses her once again, then turns and walks to the dock.

Watching Nolee drag the kayak to the shallows, Keet remembers their lovemaking earlier that morning, the ways they moved together, still half asleep, wrapped in the blankets of their dreams.

"Are you positive you want to be out there with the sea like it is?" Keet asks. The water may be at its lowest, but it's still uncooperative. She nods, her focus on getting into the bobbing kayak. Stepping into the water, he holds it steady. "Climb in. I'll help you out into deeper water."

After being pushed out, she paddles to the buoys, where Zelka, in her orca form, waits. As he walks back to the dock, Keet sees Wallace and Fae at the gate in the backyard, standing with their ears back, squinting against the wind. Keet removes his clothes, stretches his arms above his head, and, pushing his feet against the dock's damp wood, dives in.

After spinning into orca form, he surfaces and sees Nolee bobbing in her kayak. Breathing and diving, he pops up next to her. She reaches out and touches his rostrum and together, they ride the current in the winter Salish Sea. He sings her name, a high-pitched whistle, strong and steady. His love for her floods through him, as does the sense that the two of them are inseparable, held within a vast, smooth bowl of mutual promise.

"I feel the same, Keet. You and Zee come home soon."

He exhales, rolls to his side for a last touch of her hand along the length of his body, then dives and swims to Zelka, touching her before they start their journey.

The first day's swim from the Salish Sea to the Strait of Juan de Fuca is a hard one. Pushing themselves high along the surface to avoid breathing in wind-carried water is tiring, and the extra effort slows them down. Periodically, they seek out calmer inlets where they can rest.

During one of these intervals, with Zelka's tail touching his, Keet receives a steady stream of images. Inside his head, he can see the beat of her heart, and oxygen making its slow course through her body. As this picture fades, he sees the upslope of seafloor underneath them, then feels a thin line of worry he knows isn't his. When they surface to breathe, images and feelings that seemed as close as his own stop, the cord cut. Then, deep underwater once again, Keet touches his pectoral fin to his sister's and sees her eye snap open. She whistles Nolee's name, and their shared picture of her blossoms into a larger feeling, the one of home, the one of companionship, and safety, and love.

Keet and Zelka swim through gray days, stopping only to catch salmon and dodge the ships and boats that growl through the turbulent water. Once through the strait and into the open ocean, the currents push them in all directions. Zelka, following an underwater ridge, tilts south into a swift-flowing current that carries the distant warbling echo of their humpback cousins.

Keet feels a high-pitched clicking; if he hadn't heard it before, he might've mistaken it for the clicks of another orca pod. He nudges Zelka, and they both rise to breathe. When they dive again, she points her rostrum down and swims past him. Feeling his lungs reach their limit, Keet hovers in the undulating current, watching with his sonar as Zelka's form grows blurry, then stops. She sings, then clicks, then sings again, and notes come back to him as a picture: dilapidated structures. Zelka, now a dark mass in darker water, clicks again, and in his mind, he sees a single long, low structure, all corners and angles. Letting her know he needs to breathe, he points to the surface, despite the efforts of the underwater river that seems to be trying to coax him along its path.

Keet stays on the surface, waiting for Zelka to return. The chilly wind whips across his dorsal fin and he sinks until the water protects it. He can neither hear nor feel his sister.

He takes several deep breaths, broadens his back, and dives down, down, down. The pressure of the water around his body feels like he's being squeezed by invisible hands. Closing his eyes, he sounds even deeper, his click trains bouncing back, providing dim pictures of a canyon far below him. There's a crack in the seafloor wide enough for him to swim through but too deep for him to stay there. Slowing his heartbeat, Keet again hangs in the water. And waits.

Two objects clicking deep in the crevasse flare inside his head. It's a regular beat, slower than his heartbeat. Ignoring his body's need for oxygen, he points his head down again and sends out another series of clicks, then waits for a response. Where is Zelka?

Sending another stream of clicks into the dark rift below him, Keet feels the shapes and curves of the crevasse run along his lower jaw before it stretches beyond even his ability to see with sound. He listens, then sends out a last series of staccato clicks before he surfaces to breathe. In return, he feels a ripple, a faint echo of the outline of a structure.

As he rises, pushing to the surface to take a breath, he wonders where the ticking noise is coming from. And who, or what, is making it.

He lets the ocean buoy him along its crests and troughs until he sees Zelka in his mind's eye. Diving to greet her, he sings her name and touches her with his pectorals. They surface together and exhale, and Zelka conveys clearer pictures of the house in the crevasse. Then she flips her white belly to the sky and he spirals after her, one note hanging in his head: a picture of Osprey Bay and their two houses. Home.

TWENTY-FIVE

When I'm not working, Sylvie and I take turns making meals. She's quieter than Keet, but I'm comfortable with that. A pat on the arm or a smile carries more meaning when words aren't coming at me all the time.

A week goes by before, to my great relief, I see Keet and Zelka on the dock. As do the dogs; they come with me to welcome them back. Wallace, who sat on the dock each evening after they left, joins Fae in dancing around them, then focuses on Zelka. When she sits, he flattens her, licking her face as she laughs. Forcing myself to withhold my questions, I hand out towels and robes. Keet, damp even after drying off, kisses me, then holds me close. "It's good to be home."

Emotion has stolen my words, so I squeeze him closer, smelling the sea that still lingers on his skin.

Once Zee has untangled herself from Wallace, I tell her how happy I am that she's back. She gives me a slow smile, takes my hand, and lays it against her cheek. Considering how cold the water is, her skin feels remarkably warm.

"No salmon tonight," she says.

"How about pasta?" I ask.

Saying "I'll race you back, dogs," Keet, still barefoot, runs across the rocky beach and into the house, clutching the towel around his hips with one hand. Fae beats him, and Zelka and Wallace jog behind.

Breaking away, Zee waves and takes the trail to the cabin. "I'll be back with Grandmother in a few minutes."

While Keet takes a shower, I put water on to boil and grab a box of angel hair pasta from the pantry. When he walks into the kitchen and pulls me to him and we kiss, I forget about food. "No salmon out there?" I ask.

"Enough to feed my pod, but I didn't want to take one from them. Especially Nana. She needs all the food she can get."

An icy feeling squeezes my chest. "Is she alright?"

"She is. Just older and slower. I enjoy hunting for her, and she can still surprise me with her knowledge of salmon hiding places. She's very affectionate—even for a matriarch orca."

Having once been in the water with his pod, I can recall how gently they caressed my arms and legs with their flukes and pectoral fins. Affection is a way of life for orcas, something I feel drawn to emulating.

"The salmon aren't in their usual spots, so we're having to swim farther in order to eat."

"Keet, given how vocal orcas are, how do they catch salmon? Don't the salmon hear them?"

"Nope. We communicate in a range they don't have access to."

"You once explained sonar as being like using a flashlight in a dark room. The more flashlights—calls—the brighter the light and the easier to see the space."

"Yes. When we're looking for fish, each member of the pod is in a different position, using their own 'flashlight.' Working together, we can locate the school, herd the fish together, then eat."

Noticing that the water's boiling, I add salt, put the pasta in and give it a stir, then turn down the heat. Meanwhile, Keet rummages through the refrigerator and gets out tomatoes, herbs, garlic, and onions, settling himself at the counter with one of the knives I gave him and starts chopping.

"Here's another analogy, but this one is more about how we receive sound and what it does for us."

At that moment, Fae trots into the kitchen, ears up. I look at the clock. "You're right, girlie. It's dinner time. Hold that thought, Keet."

After feeding the dogs, I sit at the table. "You were saying something about another analogy?"

Giving the wooden spoon a tap on the edge of the skillet where tomatoes are simmering, he turns toward me.

"You're listening to a symphony, say Mozart's *Sinfonia Concertante…*" he catches me grinning. "Or any classical music."

"Why not popular music?"

"Because it's easier to explain with music that doesn't have words." Abandoning the bubbling marinara sauce for a moment, he puts on a CD. The house fills with the robust richness of strings and woodwinds. They trade voices, then join in a harmonious whole.

Stirring the sauce, Keet continues. "As the audience, we hear the music, Mozart's artistry, and the musicians' mastery of their instruments. Basically, we take in the music as a total composition. But if we experienced music the way orcas, and most cetaceans, experience sound, we'd also hear every element of that composition."

"Like looking at a painting close up and seeing the brush strokes?"

"Yes. We'd see Mozart's ink-stained fingers as he wrote the music, the violinist's bow and the rosin left behind as it glides across the strings. We'd feel, in our own hands, the sensation of holding the string to create a note and the bow that draws out that note. For an orca, an experience that affects only a human's ears and hearts is also a window into a time that isn't past, because it's unspooling before our eyes, always present."

A solo violin reaches for the high notes, then the orchestra joins in again.

"For an orca, each note is a singular entity that carries layers of visual information. But it's not just a mental vision—we're part of all the sounds, a living symphony."

As Keet turns back to the stove, I close my eyes, listening to the melody, straining to feel an inkling of what Keet says is commonplace for orca.

"Nolee?"

I open my eyes and look at Keet.

"Yeah. I need to sit with that one."

He flashes a smile. "I've made a Burnett speechless!"

The light seeps away as we finish eating, the shared meal filled with the lightness of laughter and the joy of being together again.

Relaxing in the living room, head on Keet's shoulder, eyes heavy, I perk up when Sylvie asks Zee and Keet about their trip.

"The first thing we figured out is that if Keet and I touch while we're orca, we can communicate without sound."

I sit up. "That's wonderful! But Zee, didn't you have this with your mother?"

Her gaze turns inward at the thought of her mother, but then she gives herself a small shake. "I suspected it, but if she knew, she didn't say anything. And I didn't know she couldn't find me when I wasn't near her. I think that's another reason she was so frantic when I started swimming away."

Keet takes my hand. "It took us longer than we'd planned to get out there. The water was rough every day, and it made swimming and hunting more challenging."

"What did you find, Grandson?" Sylvie leans forward now, elbows braced on her knees. Though she's regained some weight, her face is still planes and sharp angles.

"A huge underwater canyon with a house on the edge." Closing my eyes, I see a shadowy picture, the outline of a structure that seems to be all corners. I sense a pressure, as though I can't fill my lungs. I open my eyes. "It must have been far down?"

Keet nods. "Is that what you saw?"

"Saw and felt."

"Zelka didn't have any trouble getting to it. I had to stay above, watching through her sounds."

Zelka moves away from the fireplace and sits next to me on the sofa. "The clicking is still there, Nolee. The story of the water clock is the same. I'm sure someone inside is making the sound on purpose. We need to return the clock to where she belongs."

Bringing in an armful of wood, Keet piles it on the stack, then throws a log on the fire. As he rubs his sap-sticky fingers together, he listens to his family talk about options for returning the water clock. Everyone has a different plan, and no one likes any of them.

"I'll be the one to return it, Grandmother. I'm the only one who can swim that far." Zelka says.

"That may be true, but you need us. We don't know who is down there. And I *am* still the guardian of the water clock."

"You are, but it was stolen a long time ago. It's not ours. I don't have any ties to it."

"Exactly." Sylvie shifts her gaze to the popping fire.

Keet settles next to Nolee and nudges her arm. "As much as I like the idea of chartering a boat and dropping us close to the crevasse," he pauses, including his sister and grandmother with his eyes, "who's going to bring it back? Could you even sail it back to the marina at Neah Bay? What happens when bad weather rolls in?"

Nolee nods, giving him a small grin. "You're right. I feel great about kayaking, but a boat isn't a kayak."

"Right. Besides, once we get down there, even with the water clock, can we get in? If we do, are these distant cousins of ours friendly?"

"We could swim from here, Keet." He looks over at Zelka, her hands clasped together between her knees. He nods, considering the idea.

"We could. Although I think two orcas swimming with wooden bowls would attract attention. That's the last thing we want."

"Could we take your boat and drop the water clock into the ocean above the crevasse?"

Sylvie grunts. "No. We don't know if they would receive it. It is disrespectful to both the clock and the people it belongs to."

Nolee gets up to add another log to the fire, then returns to her place next to Keet. "I think we're making this too complicated. We drive to Neah Bay, find someplace to stay that takes dogs ..." she looks at Fae and Wallace, who both wag their tails "... and you and Zelka swim from there. Sylvie and I can return to Camas and wait for you here."

For the first time since dinner, everyone is silent. Nolee yawns, covering her mouth and stretching her back. "Whatever we do, right now, it's my bedtime."

"Grandmother? Zelka? Any other ideas?"

Zelka shakes her head, then yawns so wide, Keet can see her molars.

"When do we leave?" Sylvie asks.

TWENTY-SIX

The bright morning light wakes me. I lay for a moment, listening to the silent house, then roll over and see that Keet's already up. Brushing the hair out of my eyes, I stand, reaching up until I hear my back crackle, then find my robe and slippers. In the kitchen, I see a mug with a tea bag in it. After turning on the heat under the kettle, I go looking for Keet.

He's in the garage, wedged between the wall and Sylvie's truck. "Good morning, Lia."

"Good morning, honey. What are you doing?"

"I woke up thinking about how two orcas could get wooden bowls into an underwater canyon."

"Right. It's not as though you have hands and arms."

"True, but what I *do* have is miles of marine line. I'm sure I can make a harness of sorts. Zee and I can take turns carrying it."

The kettle whistles, reminding me. "Do you want tea, Keet?"

"That'd be great." He keeps his eyes on the lines, which are different colors and thicknesses.

Back in the house, I see I've missed a call from Chena. After petting the dogs and watching the morning sea roll in, I return it.

"Hi, Chena. I saw you called?"

"Yeah, sorry if it's too early?"

"I've been up for a bit. Everything okay?"

"It is and isn't."

"Uh-oh. What's going on?"

"Mike and I need to move back to Alaska. My parents aren't doing too well up there on their own."

"I'm sorry to hear that. How can I help?"

"Well," she sighs. "Ava and I've been talking about what to do with the pet store. She has this idea that the two of you could be business partners. Would that interest you?"

"Wow. I don't know what to say, Chena. Let me chat with Ava, and I'll get back to you."

"Thanks, Nolee. If I must, I'll close the store, but I'd rather it stayed open. I'm still attached to the place."

"I appreciate you and Ava asking. I'll be in touch."

Keet, who had come in while I was on the phone, notices my expression and sits down next to me, waiting for more information.

"That was Chena. She's moving back to Alaska and wants to sell the store to me and Ava."

"How do you feel about that?"

Suffused with a rush of enthusiasm, I answer. "I want to do it!" I pick up my phone and dial Ava's number.

As I talk with her, I watch Keet set down two plates of eggs with veggies and another plate with tortillas. I pace the length of the living room, unable to sit still and talk about this opportunity.

Ending the call, I slip my arms around Keet's waist. "Ava and I are going to be business partners!"

Keet twirls me, then puts me down. "Ava has a friend at a bank in Seattle. She's going to contact her about getting the loan process started. Chena's price is good, and I have enough in savings to go in half."

We sit down and begin eating. I'm buzzing with so much excitement that my fork shakes. "Oh." Keet looks over at me. "What is it?"

"I need to talk with Andi. I might need to quit my job at the shelter."

"Let's take it step by step." Keet reaches for my hand and holds it to his cheek before going back to eating.

"Ava and I will rename the store. I'll pull together my bank statements from the last year and make copies for her, then we'll go to Seattle as soon as she can get an appointment …" I take a breath, then laugh.

"It's good to see you this happy, Lia."

"It feels pretty good. After breakfast, let's go over and share the news with Sylvie and Zee."

Fog is running its fingers through the trees when we set off for Neah Bay after shopping at a co-op in Port Angeles. It's been drizzling most of the trip. Out of the corner of my eye, I catch a white sign with hand-painted black lettering buried in the grass and slow down to read it. "When the power of love overcomes the love of power, there will be peace." Nailed to the tree stump next to it are two more signs. "No Trespassing," and "Beware of Dog." I flick the windshield wipers on full blast as another spate of driving rain pours over the car, drowning out the music.

After trying to fit two dogs, four adults, suitcases, food, and dog beds and dishes into Keet's 4Runner, we decide to take both cars. Fae and Wallace are riding with me in the Honda, as are their supplies, food, and several jackets, hats, and gloves. I hear my phone ping from somewhere in the depths of the supplies and ignore it.

We stop for lunch, then continue driving. Used to the long flat stretches of western Texas, this landscape reminds me of the forests I used to read about in fairy tales; if I took a couple steps into their green and fog laden midst, would I see unicorns? Hobbits? Ahead of me, I see Keet signaling and turn right by a sign that says Hoko River Resort and Cabins. We park and get out of our cars to stretch, then Keet wrap his arms around me and buries his face in my neck.

"I haven't driven this much in ages," he says, taking my hand as we walk to the office to check in.

The lobby smells of day-old coffee. On a folding table in front of us are a coffee maker, a tray of fruit, and a clear plastic container with four doughnuts. Letting go of my hand, Keet makes a beeline for the doughnuts.

"You're hungry, aren't you?" I laugh when Keet nods.

An Asian man smiles at us from behind the check-in desk. "Those are from this morning. Please, take them off my hands before I eat them." He pats the sweatshirt pulled snugly over his belly. Keet doesn't hesitate.

"I'll take Grandmother and Zelka a doughnut too. Which one do you want, Nolee?"

"The one with the chocolate glaze, please." Turning back to the paperwork in front of me, I pick up a pen.

"Leftie, huh?"

"Yes, sir. We're the only ones in our right mind."

Laughing, he offers me his hand.

"Alvin Tanaka, owner of this place."

"Hi, Alvin. Nolee Burnett, transplanted Texan."

"Traveling with the family?"

"I am. Glad the dog-friendly cabin was available."

"Most things are this time of year." The view though the office window is heavy with dark clouds. More rain is on the way.

The chimes on the door sound, and Keet is beside me.

"Doughnuts gone?"

"Demolished and loved by all." He smiles at Alvin, holds out his hand. "Keet Noland."

I sign the last page. "Keet, this is the owner, Alvin Tanaka."

"If you want more, I have them in the fridge." He steps away from the desk, motioning to the door behind him.

Keet raises his hands in front of him. "Don't tempt me."

I hand the paperwork and our credit card to Alvin. "I think we'll be here three nights, but if we need another couple of nights, will that be a problem?"

"Not at all. Stay as long as you want. We've got room until next April." He gives me the receipt and a set of keys with a plastic fob in the shape of a husky. "You're in cabin five. Drive between the first set of cabins, make a right, and it's at the end of that driveway. Let me know if you need anything." Smiling at me, he shakes my hand, then Keet's.

Outside, Keet suggests that we get settled in the cabin and have an early dinner, which sounds perfect to me. Back in the car, to the accompaniment of the dogs' excited panting, my own doubts resurface.

We're one step closer to Keet and Zelka attempting to return the water clock. One step closer to Keet putting himself in danger. One step closer to me and the dogs wandering around that big house, hoping he'll swim home. I shake my head, trying to clear my mind; the clouds seem to have found their way from the sea into my thoughts.

I put the car in gear and follow Keet's taillights.

After bringing in the last of the groceries, Keet reaches into the bag of tortilla chips and takes a handful. As he crunches on the chips, he checks out the kitchen, pulling open each drawer, looking in the oven, and turning each burner on and then off. Sylvie walks into the kitchen, gets a glass of water, and goes back to her room. Brushing his hands together, Keet has his eye on the chips, but Nolee gets there first.

"Abbie wants to come visit next summer," she says before popping a chip into her mouth and handing her phone to him so he can read the text.

Hi Momma! Since I can't get you back to Texas, I thought I'd come to you. Next summer? Bonus: I could borrow Dad's truck with the camper shell and bring your books. Road trip!! Love you xoxo

"This is good, right?"

"Any time I get to see my daughter is *very* good. I can't wait for you to meet her, Keet."

Finishing up the chips, he nods, then wipes his mouth with the back of his hand. "I'm looking forward to meeting her, too."

Hearing a bark, they go outside to watch Zelka and the dogs playing on the beach. After pitching a ball for Fae, she throws another in the opposite direction for Wallace. "That beach is huge! The dogs should wear out more quickly than they do at home," Nolee comments as they go back inside.

She turns to him, and he sees a flicker of worry in her eyes. Closing the refrigerator door, he takes her in his arms. "What's going on, Lia?"

"The usual. I'm worried about the two of you returning the water clock."

Resting his cheek against her head, he holds her closer. "Do you want us to change our plans?"

"No." She moves away from him. "It's not that. Well, I mean, yes, your potential drowning worries me—" She exhales. "I wish I knew how to stop myself from worrying about y'all."

"I'm worried too. But it would take a lot for me to drown." An image of his mother's body floating into the black water, sinking away from him, drifts through his mind and heart. "If I can't swim that deep, I won't. I'm not looking to endanger myself, not to mention everything you and I have."

He closes his eyes, feeling her heartbeat slow, feeling her breathing sync with his. She holds him tight against her own body. "Let's get dinner started."

While Keet spoons the leftover butternut squash stew into a container, I toss a log in the woodstove, the heat like a warm hand against my face. Wallace dream-barks, white feet twitching.

"I bet he's chasing a ball," Zelka says, sitting cross-legged beside me, watching the flames dance through the woodstove's glass doors. I rest my head on her shoulder.

"You didn't eat much, Nolee."

"I can't eat when I'm worried. Besides, the three of you emptied your bowls so quick I thought you might eat them, too."

Zelka laughs. "Grandmother says that Keykwin are known for their healthy appetites."

"I've noticed the same thing."

Sylvie looks outside at the dimming light. "When will we find a place for Keet and Zelka to leave from?"

"Soon. We need enough light to see, but not so much that we can easily be seen."

Keet, who joins us by the fire, looks outside as well. "I think 'soon' has arrived. Let's go check out some options."

We drive into the town, then through it. On our right is a small marina; at the end of the marina is a wooden pier. I point. "Keet, do you want to check it out?"

Finding a wide spot in the road, he parks the 4Runner and we walk back to the pier. At the end of it, a staircase leads to a dock. We make our way down, taking care with each step. The dock sways with the tide and through holes in its water-softened surface, I can see water roiling.

"Is this going to be sturdy enough?"

Keet and Zelka, standing at the end, turn to me. "It'll work great. We're hidden by the pier, and it's too cold for anyone to be out on it. At least, we hope there's no one out on it," Keet says.

We stand in a cluster at the end of the dock. Sylvie has the water clock pressed against her body, looking at it. I step closer and rest my arm against hers. "This is the test dive. They won't swim to the canyon tonight."

"That's the idea, right, Zee?" Keet replies.

She nods, then takes my hand. "Test dive only."

"I can't dive as fast as you," Keet says, looking at Zelka. "I don't know if I'll even be able to reach that house in the canyon, and we're unlikely to be able to touch once we go below a certain depth."

"You can do it, Keet. I want you there with me when we return the water clock."

Keet touches his sister's shoulder. "I need a constant stream of information from you. Can you do that?"

She nods.

Sylvie, the water clock still clutched against her chest, whispers. "They passed the water clock to me. I should be the one who returns it, who makes the apology and seeks amends and peace with our cousins."

Zelka and I look at Keet. He steps forward and takes his grandmother's hand. "It's a tough swim, Grandmother. I'm not sure I can make it. I don't want to risk your life."

Sylvie juts her chin out. "It is not your decision to make, Keet. Besides, there's nothing wrong with me."

"I'm not saying there is. But it's a hard swim and there are too many unknowns. If I'm worried about you, I can't do what I need to do."

Sylvie sighs. Her upright stance deflates as the air evaporates from her idea. Finally, she nods.

Zelka puts her arm around her grandmother's waist. "If it's our cousins down there, they can meet you another time."

"Maybe." Sylvie's voice is flat.

She continues to clutch the water clock, which Keet had secured in a web of brightly colored marine lines. Touching Zelka's shoulder, I motion with my head that we should move away from her.

Sylvie closes her eyes and presses the water clock against her forehead. After a moment, she opens her eyes again and looks at each of us before handing the water clock to Zelka. I step closer to Sylvie. "We'll meet you back here at moonrise?"

Keet and Zelka nod. "We're doing a test dive. Nothing more. I want to find out how far I can dive, and if Zee's able to carry those bowls."

Zelka hands the water clock back to Sylvie, who holds it away from her body while Keet sheds his clothes and dives into the black water. When he surfaces, he's a giant orca with a dorsal fin blacker than the sky. Zelka loosens her hair from its ponytail, sweeps her cotton dress over her head, and dives into the water. I pick up their clothes, still warm in my hands.

A second, smaller dorsal fin pops up beside the larger one, then both head toward us. Wrapping her hands around the rope handle, Sylvie kneels at the edge of the dock and whispers as she places the handle in Zelka's mouth. Once upright, she presses her hands over her eyes. I turn toward the dark water, watching as two dorsal fins cut into the waves.

Sylvie turns to me. "Now we wait."

"Can we wait back at the cabin? I'm freezing."

The dogs sit at my feet, grinning and wagging their tails, as I add warm water to their food. Sylvie's resting in one of the mismatched chairs that circle the dented kitchen table like uneven teeth. "What was it you were saying to the water clock as you gave it to Zelka?"

"It was a blessing my grandmother taught me. I was asking the waves to protect it from harm. To protect my grandchildren."

Setting a cup of steaming coffee in front of her, I join her at the table with my mug of tea. When I tap my phone's screen, I see that only an hour has passed since we watched Keet and Zelka swim away with the water clock. According to the weather app, moonrise is two hours from now. An edginess courses through me, and I wonder if chamomile would've been a better choice.

Sylvie looks out the window, then rises to pull the curtains closed. "I'm going to nap before we go back out."

"I'll take the dogs for a walk."

Bundled in several layers, I wend my way along the beach, Fae and Wallace nearby. Their jingling tags and the low thrum of the waves are the only sounds keeping me company. Looking up at the stars through a hole in the clouds, I wish I could coax them to tell me the future, to tell me what will happen, to tell me that the people I love are safe.

TWENTY-SEVEN

In the frosty night breeze, Keet and Zelka tread water, their breath hovering around them in a fine mist. Moonlight shines on the waves and catches in Zelka's slick, wet hair. Keet holds onto the water clock's rope harness, hoping Nolee and his grandmother come back soon; his hands are starting to chill.

"There they are!" As Zelka swims back to the dock with efficient strokes, Keet rolls over on his back, holding the water clock against his belly and kicking hard to propel himself.

Once on the dock, Zelka hands the water clock to her grandmother, who's quiet until she and Keet have dried off and dressed. Then she can restrain herself no longer. "What happened?"

Keet looks at his sister, who's winding her hair in a towel and gazing out at the water.

"Neither of us could get deep enough. The water clock seemed to pull us back to the surface."

"Keet, I think we need to separate the water clock, and each take a bowl instead of trying to carry her in one piece." She fumbles with the ropes binding the water clock, then Keet takes over and undoes the knots with ease.

"That might work. But right now, I'm starving and I'm tired. Let's try again tomorrow night."

Nolee wraps an arm around his waist. "You're in luck, mister. We have plenty of leftovers waiting for us back at the cabin."

The next night, we return to the dock. I look at the moon shining through a translucent curtain of clouds, its light diluted and milky. I stand beside Sylvie holding the small bowl in my gloved hands. Despite the down jacket and the hat snugged down past my eyebrows, I'm shivering, and my breath leaves me in small, smoky puffs. Sylvie, hands bare, holds the large bowl, whispering to it, running her hands along its smooth surface. Her breath is a long tendril lifted by the breeze.

We spent our day walking the dogs on the beach, familiarizing ourselves with our surroundings and the habits of the people who live here. This time of year, most are indoors; few are hiking or camping. This helps us; we need secrecy on this second night, even more than on the first.

Over a late dinner, we discussed how to get the water clock down to the canyon house. In the end, we decided that Keet would take the small bowl, and Zelka—a stronger swimmer in deep water—would take the large one.

Zelka, who's clearly been giving this some thought, has a suggestion. "How about not using the marine lines and instead turning the bowls so our rostrums fit inside them. I'm pretty sure that as we dive, the force of the water will keep them there."

As he thinks about Zelka's plan, Keet runs a hand across his forehead, then says, "I want to test this theory before I try swimming into the canyon. We'll change to orca. Nolee and Grandmother will set the bowls on our rostrums, and we'll dive. I need to feel if they're stable or if I'm going to have to carry it in my mouth."

Zelka's bright expression matches the enthusiasm of her words. "This night, it will work, Keet. I can feel the water clock; she wants to return to her people. She'll help us."

Keet flashes his sister a quick smile. "I hope so."

In the moment between Keet and Zelka's dive into the black water as humans and their transformation to orca, I watch the moon again. I'm reminded of the recurring dream that started not long after I met Keet more than a year ago. In it, his body lit by the moon, he stood wearing the sea as a hooded cloak. My life with him is so much bigger, and the full moon echoes how I now feel in my skin. My breath swirls in the cold air, merging with Sylvie's whispered prayers and carried by the breeze out to where water knows nothing of land.

Two sharp exhales bring my gaze back to the end of the dock, and I see Keet and Zelka floating there. Removing my gloves, I touch Keet and close my eyes, surrendering to the flood of emotion that flows between us; at its heart is the solid ground of trust. Then I fit the small bowl on Keet's rostrum. I watch as he balances it, bobbing on the tide like a large black-and-white cork, then fills his lungs with a loud in-rush of air.

Sylvie has one hand on the upside-down bowl on Zelka's rostrum and the other on Zelka. "Go in peace, Granddaughter. Go in peace, Grandson." She stands and loops an arm through mine, and I lean into her warmth.

We watch as they swim away from the dock, bowls balanced on their uptilted heads. Then, pushing out of the water, rising past their flukes, they curve their bodies and dive.

Keet is the first to resurface. Human again, he holds the bowl in one hand as he swims back to the dock. Zelka, still in orca form, continues to balance the bowl on her rostrum.

Handing the bowl up to me, he seems confident. "Lia, this will be easy—we can do this. Zelka and I will go to the water-canyon house now."

Eyes open, shining with moonlight and tears, I place my lips against his. "See you at home, Keet Noland."

His answering smile is electric. "Count on it."

He swims from the dock, changes, and then comes back so I can once again put the bowl on his warm rostrum. He and Zelka swim out, then, taking giant inhales, they dive. The glowing white undersides of their disappearing flukes are the last thing I see.

Bobbing on the surface, the orcas breathe, watching the night dance across the waves, admiring the moon. Keet spins toward the dock, where Nolee and his grandmother, their arms around each other, stand looking toward them.

He closes his eyes. Concentrating on his breathing and the bowl cupping his rostrum, Keet fills his lungs, feeling them stretch. Zelka, floating nearby, touches him with her pectoral fin and he feels her need to dive, to deliver the water clock, to discover their cousins in the Water Canyon.

Together, they take one more breath, then dive. In the distance, he hears the ocean's deep bass and a series of long, low notes bouncing from the seafloor far below. He pushes through the water at a steady pace, neither too slow nor too fast. His sister's clicks show him that his lungs are full and bright with oxygen.

Zelka swims ahead, bowl balanced on her rostrum, then slows and touches him with a pectoral fin. He receives a picture of the canyon far below them, and the excitement that courses through her feels like it's his own. He nudges her and she breaks away to race ahead, angling her body down. Following her faint clicks and whistles, he dives deeper. With each fathom they descend, the ticking sound becomes clearer, more distinct. He wonders if another water clock is housed in the canyon.

Pausing in his dive, he makes a series of rapid clicks and sees the picture they return. The many-cornered house is the same; the surrounding houses are still in ruins. Although the house is made up of multiple angles, its closed door is large and round, a wavering patch of hazy darkness. His sister floats next to it, and he can hear her singing, asking for entry. She sings of the water clock, and of her brother, and of their desire to return the clock to atone for Janadsila's mistake.

Keet, swimming deeper than he ever has in his life, ignores his discomfort as the water around him changes with each push of his flukes—currents below currents below more currents. Whale song in the distance ripples along his body and gives him a picture of the leviathan who's singing it. Changing his focus, he searches for the surface, knowing that he no longer has enough air to get there, not with the instability of the water clock's bowl pressed against his rostrum.

Zelka's steady stream of sound shows him that the house's door is still closed. Resolved, he pushes forward and is almost immediately engulfed by a squeezing force that concentrates in his head.

Zelka's clicks fade; the last image she sends is of the location of the shadowy door. The steady ticking sound surrounds him. Saving the air he has left, he angles his body downward again, pushing toward the wavering shadow, following the memory of her voice. His oxygen-deprived brain is foggy, then goes black.

A loud bang startles Keet's eyes open. The pressure is gone. Taking a gasping breath, he realizes he's once again human. He's on his hands and knees on a smooth wood floor, his dripping hair leaving small puddles; the bowl lies upturned in front of him. Slowly, he repositions himself to sit cross-legged, and someone drapes a blanket around him. He uses a corner to wipe his face.

Once his vision clears, he sees groups of people. Their skin is darker than his, and their eyes are large and round. Most are middle-aged or older, though he does see a few children peeking out from behind the adults. All of them wear clothing of the same material as the blanket around his shoulders.

Nearby, men and women with mallets in their hands had been chipping away at stones; the shards on the floor in front of them glitter in the light of a fire that is placed in a round pit. Multiple small fires light the large space. Around each are people, staring at him, protecting their loved ones, some with their bodies, some with short stone knives. On the other side of the room, an older woman sits next to another brightly blazing fire. Her hair is white, and in her hands are two long stones crafted to fit into her hands. Eyes closed, she strikes the stones together, and Keet feels the small bowl in his lap grow warmer.

A young woman sits next to the old one. Her eyes flicker between the two intruders, then settle on Keet. Taking the bowl in his hands, he turns to Zelka, who kneels beside him, the large bowl in her lap. Both bowls are now a deep, warm red. They remind him of the cabernet sauvignon one of his regular customers would bring him from a Napa Valley winery.

He wishes he had Nolee's ability to talk to Zelka without words. The silence, the clicking/ticking of the rocks, the oppressive sensation of being strangers amongst people who keep themselves secret: the atmosphere of this house in the water canyon feels like it's simmering with the potential for chaos.

But they wouldn't have allowed them in only to harm them, would they? Keet shifts closer to his sister, and they wait through many clicks of the stones for someone to speak. Their steamy breath hovers around their faces. It's chilly away from the fires, and he pulls the blanket tighter against his body, unused to feeling cold.

Then the old woman speaks. "Bring the water clock together, cousins." Hands still, rocks on the floor together by her side, she looks at them for the first time. Her dark eyes have a thin lavender ring around the iris.

He hears Zelka's quick intake of breath, then she holds out her hand for the small bowl, which he gives her. When she settles it inside the larger one, the set glows into a deeper and brighter red until Keet can see the faint outlines of the long bones in Zelka's fingers. The old woman says, "She knows she is home again, and she brings her warmth back to us."

Holding the water clock, Zelka rises. "May I return her to your people?"

The woman nods, and, with the help of the younger woman, stands. As the distance between Zelka and the old woman closes, a ringing fills the room. It reminds Keet of a bell on clear morning air.

"Our water clock sings for us," the old woman says. "The heart of our people returns, and she beats with strength once more."

TWENTY-EIGHT

Kneeling in front of the old woman, Zelka raises the water clock above her head. "We offer our apology for Janadsila's theft of your water clock. We are sorry and ask your forgiveness for a crime that's too long brought you suffering."

The air thickens, warms. It stretches with tension as Keet watches the people close in, tightening the circle around Zelka and the old woman. He moves through the crowd until he stands beside his sister, watching as she hands the water clock to the old woman.

Taking the water clock in her hands, the old woman presses it against her forehead, then looks at Keet and Zelka. "For many generations since Janadsila's theft, we have played the stones against each other, calling our water clock home, back to sing in her rightful place, with us."

Zelka repeats her apology. "We ask you to forgive the length of time it has taken to right the wrong done to you and your people."

The old woman acknowledges Zelka with a nod. She sits, settling herself near the fire, the water clock in her lap. The younger woman sits next to her, unable to look away from Keet. Keet draws the blanket closer around his body, even though the air has begun to warm. Her gaze feels colder than the room when they first entered. "We accept your apology." A tall young man with his hair in a shiny black bun on top of his head comes to stand beside the old woman. In his hands is a pitcher of water; firelight reflects off the pitcher in quick silvery bursts. When she nods at him, he fills the basin until the small bowl floats to the top.

"What is your name, cousin?" Zelka asks.

"I might ask for your name first."

"Zelka William Eils Noland."

Whispers run around the circle surrounding them.

The old woman removes her hands from the water clock and gestures at the circle. "We are the Water Canyon People. I am Byree, Stone Singer. This," nodding toward the woman on her left, "is my daughter, Yiskal, Cloth Weaver. You are from the Nations on the land."

Keet notices that, like Zelka's, the ankles of each member of the group are encircled with black wavy lines.

"What is your name?" she says, looking at Keet.

"Keet Noland. I'm Zelka's brother."

"We don't know either of you, yet you," she nods to Zelka, "have our markings around your ankles. You have the same eyes. You will tell us how."

Zelka repeats the birth story her mother told her. The house continues to grow warmer. In one corner, children are drifting to sleep in their mothers' arms. Everyone else leans toward Zelka as she speaks of hearing the clicking of the stones, of her mother hearing the story of Janadsila in the ticking, of her mother's storm, ending with how she, Zelka, found her brother. Looking at Keet, she gives him a calm smile.

By the time Zelka has finished her story, Byree has emptied the small bowl and set it on top of the water four times. Now Keet watches as the young man, his eyes lowered, offers Byree a cup of water. She drinks, asks for a refill, then passes the cup to Keet. The water glides down his throat with refreshing coolness.

Byree speaks again. "When Keykwin visited each other on land and under the waves, we knew each other by signs. Those of us under the water have these marks." She touches first the wavy lines around her ankles, then her face. "And these eyes. The land Keykwin did not. Your story of your mother, and her choices, interests me."

Zelka and Keet remain silent.

"I was taught that Keykwin of the land could only have land children, just as we could only have children from under the waves. Our children, through tradition, are created just as your mother unknowingly created you."

"What do you mean?" Zelka leans toward her.

"When a woman of the Water Canyon knew she was pregnant, she swam to our land cousins' dwellings, staying there until the moon changed six times. Then, she would swim away and return to her village under the waves. When the child was born, the child had these circles around their ankles. Our eyes have different circles of color. We're different from other

Blackfish. Others can hear us through sound, but people of the Water Canyon can only share our inner world through touch."

Zelka asks, "Can we also swim fast and dive deep? And we have no markings on our backs?"

Byree nods.

Keet looks at Zelka, and then at Byree. "This is why when I first met my sister, I thought perhaps she was only a distant cousin. I wasn't convinced she was my sister until my mother arrived and confirmed it."

"Yes," says Byree. "This is confusing for us as well. The traits we thought separate us seem to be traditions of our own choosing."

Keet sees that the small bowl has sunk once more. Byree reaches into the water and removes the bowl, drying it with care on her robes. After handing it her daughter, she lifts the larger bowl to her mouth and drinks from it, then passes it around to each member of her family, then Zelka, then Keet. Leaving a bit of water in the bottom, he hands the bowl back to Byree, who tips it above her mouth and swallows the last of the water.

After placing the large bowl in her daughter's hands, she says, "Thank you for returning our water clock. Please, stay with us so we can get to know our land cousins."

The people disperse, each going to a fire and pulling a tray from the ashes. Once the ashes are swept away, Keet sees the tray has a lid. Under it is a large, filleted fish; its aroma makes Keet's mouth water.

Dinner is served on plates made of flattened stones. The young man with the topknot sits across from Zelka; Keet hears him say that his name is Arogem, Stone Carver. Between bites of fish, he eyes this man who's absorbing Zelka's attention. Everything about him is square: square jaw, square shoulders, blocky torso, sturdy legs. His dark eyes, rimmed in that otherworldly lavender, stare into Zelka's. Laughing with him, she accepts the plate he refilled for her.

Byree's daughter, Yiskal, moves from her mother's side to sit across from Keet. When she asks him if he'd like more to eat, he nods and smiles his thanks. Curiosity shows on her round face as her eyes rove over him. She leans forward as if to touch him, but when Keet leans away, she smiles.

Warmed by the water clock and the fires in pits along the length of the house, the interior is now comfortable. Musicians play wild music, people dance, and stories are told. Keet loses track of time, but never of his sister. He stands by her side or watches as she dances with young men and women; he notices that she most frequently returns to Arogem. Keet joins in, feeling in the dance the same spinning sensation of becoming orca. Yiskal keeps herself in his sightline, beside or in front of him, holding his eyes with her bold stare.

When he can't dance anymore, he asks for a place to rest. Zelka, overhearing him, breaks away from Arogem and asks for a place close to her brother. Shown to a corner with a small fire near it, they lay down on blanket-covered raised platforms and fall into the dark reaches of a dreamless sleep.

When he wakes, Yiskal brings him another meal. Hearing movement, Keet looks around and sees groups of women, men, and adolescents disappear through the door he and Zelka came through. He brings his gaze back to Yiskal, who kneels in front of him. "They are the Hunters. They keep us fed. I am a Cloth Weaver and the next Keeper of the Water Clock."

She holds a belt as black as his body when he's orca, made of the same cloth as the blanket wrapped around him. "I made this," she says, giving it to him. As he starts to tie it around his waist, she moves his hands and finishes tying the belt herself. Thanking her, he stands, taking his plate and walking to the main fire to join Zelka. Arogem, sitting beside her, is touching the lines on her ankle. As she looks up at Keet, Arogem withdraws his hand from Zelka's skin and resumes eating.

"Keet."

"Arogem. Zee."

Arogem stands, moving away from Zelka. Keet hears her let out a quick breath. "I'm so glad you're here."

Keet leans close and whispers into her ear. "Had to escape from Yiskal." Zelka laughs. When Keet looks around the fire, he notices that the many dark eyes on them quickly dart back to their plates. Arogem returns with two plates, setting one down in front of Zelka. "I made the plates." Keet compliments him on the workmanship, but Zelka concentrates on her food, avoiding both Keet and Arogem's gaze.

Keet startles when he feels a warm caress on the back of his neck. He turns to see Yiskal smiling at him. She gestures to his empty plate. "Would you like more, Keet?" He does—the sharp edge of his appetite has yet to be dulled—but decides it would be better to decline. "No, thank you, Yiskal." Moving away from her touch, he puts his plate on the floor beside him.

She takes his hand. "Come with me." Keet looks around the fire. All eyes are on him, the faces unsmiling, the talking silenced. He removes his hand from hers. "Come with you where?"

She laughs, a throaty sound, and tilts her head. "To another part of the house."

As he motions for her to lead the way, he notices that she's only a little shorter than he is, and that she's restyled the cloth covering her body to show a long stretch of thigh and a bare shoulder. Keeping his gaze forward, he sighs.

At a far corner of the house where there aren't as many fires and the light is dim, Yiskal hugs the child tending a fire, kisses him on the head, and asks him to leave them.

"How many corners does this house have?" Keet asks as he sits down.

"As many as we need." She sits behind him and starts working the muscles in his shoulders.

Keet turns toward her, then stands up. "Whatever you think is going to happen between you and me, Yiskal, it's not."

Her laugh is a low, mirthless rumble, a laugh that says she knows she'll get what she wants.

"I already have a partner, a woman who isn't Keykwin."

"This is important why?"

"Because she's important to me."

"I can be important to you too, Keet." She pats the ground in front of her. "Sit down. I won't touch you again unless you ask me to. When you ask me to."

Keet sits, his back against a wall, and she does the same. He moves away.

"Where I'm from, Yiskal, most people fall in love with one person. I've fallen in love with Nolee, and she feels the same about me."

"Love is bigger than one person can satisfy, Keet. It makes little sense to limit love to only two people."

Keet stands. Looking down at her, one bronze shoulder bare, skin glowing in the firelight, he says. "It may not make sense to you, Yiskal, but it makes sense to me."

Through the next two sleeping cycles, Zelka watches Keet circulate among different groups of people; none include Yiskal. But Yiskal is patient. Instead of following him, she positions herself where she can keep Keet in her line of sight and arranges to be the one who brings him food at mealtime. The fabric she wears covers less of her body with each plate she gives him.

Arogem brings Zelka her meals. Quiet and thoughtful, he listens to her stories of the world above the waves and asks questions. "How many people live up there?" and "What are the things I see crossing the sky, like shiny birds that don't flap their wings?" As she grows easy in his company, she sits closer to him, enjoying looking into eyes that are the same shape and color as her own.

One evening, as they stand near her sleeping corner, Arogem steps close and looks into her eyes. She puts her hand on his shoulder and leans toward him. Heart racing, she presses her lips to his. Bringing his hands up to her face, he gently cradles it and returns the kiss.

Drawing away, she feels her skin flush. "Goodnight, Arogem."

"Goodnight, Zelka."

Smiling, she turns, fingertips against her lips, and lies down. She's still smiling as she falls asleep.

On his back, his head turned away from the light of the morning fire, Keet feels a weight pressing against him through the soft blankets, and a heated breath against his cheek. Half asleep, he wraps his arms around Nolee, bringing her closer. Then he hears a soft humming, but it's deep, not Nolee's light tones. He jerks awake to the sight of a naked woman with dark eyes pressed against him. Rolling, he pushes her away, then blinks to clear his vision. "What are you doing, Yiskal?"

She doesn't get up. Rather, she stretches her long curves and rearranges her long hair. Eyes half-closed, she gives him a smile meant to tempt, but he only feels repelled.

"Yiskal, my heart belongs to one woman."

"I don't need your heart, Keet. Aren't you curious about what it would be like to lie with me? To make a child that's part of each of us? Women of the Water Canyon People have babies until our hair goes white. I want to make a baby. With you, Keet."

Keet puts his hands up in front of him. "No, Yiskal."

Furious, Yiskal gathers her blanket around her. Keet walks away, looking for Zelka. When he finds her, he steers her away from the main fire.

"I need to leave, Zee."

Her smile falters when she sees Keet's expression. "What happened?"

"Short story? Yiskal wants to make babies with me."

Although she covers her mouth with her hand, Zelka's laughter escapes between her fingers.

"It's not funny!"

She tries to shove down the mirth, but a grin escapes. "If you need to go, you should do that. But I'm staying."

"How do you plan to fend off Arogem? Does he want to make babies with you?"

She wraps her arms around herself, smiling. "I don't know, he hasn't said. Besides, no 'fending off' is required. Here, the women decide who they lie with."

"That's a relief."

"And it makes me happy to be with people like me. I want to learn about them."

"You'll come home eventually, won't you?"

She nods. "I will. I love you and Nolee and Grandmother. You three are the most family I've ever had, but now my family's grown, even if they are distant cousins."

Keet hugs her. "I'm going to ask the Hunters how to leave. Are you sure about staying here?"

"Yes. Don't worry, Keet."

As Zelka joins the group near the community fire, Keet looks for Byree. He sees she's talking to Yiskal, who's clearly still furious. When she sees Keet heading toward them, Yiskal turns and leaves.

Keet takes Byree's hand in his. "Cousin, I'm grateful for your welcome, but I need to go home. I'd like your blessing to leave."

"Of course. You are always welcome in our house, Keet Noland." She touches his face, then turns away. He waits, hoping she will offer advice on how to leave, but she rejoins her daughter and the conversation he had interrupted.

Now Keet looks for Arogem. "How do I leave?"

Arogem nods toward the door. "Through there."

"I don't know if my human lungs will hold enough air for me to make it to the surface. As orca, I barely got here alive."

Arogem shrugs and walks away, but Keet notices that others have gathered around him and are moving him toward the dark circle of the door. When he asks again if he'll be able to reach the surface, they laugh and thump his back. "You'll find out."

"What do I do?"

"Walk to that door," they motion with their heads, "take a breath, and step through it."

"That's it?"

They laugh and give him a playful shove.

Keet looks back to see his sister standing nearby. "I'll be home soon, Keet. You know where to find me if I'm not."

Reluctant to return to Camas without Zelka, Keet wavers, then gives her a hug. She kisses his cheek, and with a playful push, moves him toward the door. With that push and Zelka's permission, Keet realizes that the longing for his home with Nolee is stronger than his desire to stay, stronger even than his fears for his own survival in getting there.

Ignoring Yiskal's icy gaze, he looks at his sister once more with love, then turns from the Water Canyon People. Letting his blanket fall to the ground, Keet takes a deep breath and steps through the door.

ACKNOWLEDGMENTS

Thank you to my husband Mark, whose consistent and loving support allows me to flourish, not only as a writer but also as a person. Thanks to my mom for her editing expertise; I count myself lucky to have benefited from her editorial eye since I was in high school. Thank you to Kristin for her kind heart and astute insights in helping me develop this book more fully. Gratitude to Dianne Adel: our magical writing group of two was the birth point of many of these passages, and our laughter and tears are woven into this book. Gratitude as well to Maryann Flett, sensitivity reader extraordinaire, for her kindness and professionalism in guiding me through the ways of respecting Indigenous peoples and their culture. Another big shoutout to Stefan Freelan for his masterful guidance about all things sailing in the Salish Sea. For helping me polish the final versions of this book, I have boundless gratitude to dear friends Sarah Barnes and Hunter Purdy for their sharp eyes and kind suggestions. Jane Dixon is a miracle worker when it comes to graphic design, and Carissa Sorensen is an artist who intuitively captures in the cover art the spirit of each book. I couldn't ask for a more amazing group of people.

And a very large thank-you to everyone who supported and loved *North to Home*. When I began that book, I didn't realize there would be a sequel. When I got to the end of this one, I was overjoyed to discover a third Keet and Nolee book waiting in the wings. As of this writing, it's only a few hundred words, but I promise not to keep those waiting to find out what happens next hanging out by the Water Canyon House's door indefinitely.

Clearly, *The Clock in the Water* is entirely fictional. However, I need to acknowledge my debt once again to the Indigenous cultures of the Pacific Northwest, their Oral Traditions, and Traditional Knowledge of animals, including the Blackfish. I honor and respect their cultural rights as the primary guardians of their unique Traditional Stories.

Find updates on the third book in the "North to Home" series at crissimcdonald.com, or on Reedsy, BookSirens, and GoodReads.